Lincolnshire

COUNTY COUNCIL
discover libraries

This book should be returned on or before the due date.

To renew or order library books please telephone 01522 782010
or visit https://lincolnshire.spydus.co.uk
You will require a Personal Identification Number.
Ask any member of staff for this.

The above does not apply to Reader's Group

D1420375

05088967

FATAL
PURSUIT

Also by Martin Walker

Death in the Dordogne
(originally published as *Bruno, Chief of Police*)
The Dark Vineyard
Black Diamond
The Crowded Grave
The Devil's Cave
The Resistance Man
Children of War
The Dying Season

FATAL
PURSUIT

A Bruno, Chief *of* Police Novel

MARTIN WALKER

Quercus

First published in Great Britain in 2016 by

Quercus Editions Ltd
Carmelite House
50 Victoria Embankment
London EC4Y 0DZ

An Hachette UK company

A CIP catalogue record for this book is available
from the British Library

HB ISBN 978 1 78429 457 1
TPB ISBN 978 1 78429 458 8
EBOOK ISBN 978 1 78429 460 1

10 9 8 7 6 5 4 3 2 1

Typeset by CC Book Production

Printed and bound in Great Britain by Clays Ltd, St Ives plc

To my fellow Grand Consuls of the Consulat
de la Vinée de Bergerac, a body established in 1254
by King Henry III of England to ensure and uphold the
quality of the wines of Bergerac, and later ratified
under French law by King Charles IV in 1822, and by
the Assemblée of the French Republic in 1954.

Retirement Home

to St Alvère

Lespinasse Garage

Rue de la Republique

Tourist Office

Father Sentout

Church

Gendarmes

Rue de Paris

e Royal

Photo Shop

Rue Gambetta

Bar

to Périgueux & to Bruno's house

Ivan's

Mairie

quet's

e la Liberation

St Denis

to Les Eyzies

1

The lunar calendar said that the new moon made this a good day to plant broad beans, rocket and spinach, just as the previous days of a waning crescent moon had been the time to weed and to start a new compost heap. As Bruno Courrèges sowed the seeds he'd brought from his greenhouse, he wondered if this was some old wives' tale. Other gardeners Bruno knew and trusted, prime among them the Mayor of St Denis, the small French town where Bruno served as Chef de Police, swore that the traditional ways of the lunar calendar worked for them. Certainly there was no arguing with the quality of the crops they harvested. So when the Mayor had given him a copy of the lunar almanac and advised him to follow its advice, Bruno thought he'd try. At the far side of his vegetable patch, his basset hound, Balzac, gazed at Bruno curiously, probably wondering why he was not allowed to play in this part of the garden.

'There's some science behind it,' the Mayor had insisted. 'It's like the tides of the sea. The moon's gravity draws up the mois-ture in the soil when it's waxing and lets it down again when it's waning. So plant your above-ground vegetables when it's a waxing moon and your below-ground ones when it's waning. It works for me.'

The last of the seeds sowed, Bruno used his watering can to sprinkle the ground and then stretched to ease his back, turning his face to the early morning sun. He'd picked the last of his vegetables when the moon had said the time was ripe, and some of them were already in the big stockpot he kept atop his wood-burning stove. Cooking a couple of quartered chickens with carrots, onions and potatoes had made a plain but filling meal for his friends the previous evening. Now with some more vegetables and garlic and a pack of green lentils added it would provide him and his dog with a hearty stew throughout the week.

Back in the house, Bruno heard his guests moving around upstairs in the new bedroom he'd built under the roof. He added some logs from his woodpile to the stove, closed the damper and then reopened it a notch. It would keep the place warm all day and let the stockpot cook slowly, the way he liked it. He poured the last of the previous evening's wine into the stew and added some hot water.

He wanted to clean his Land Rover and get to the tennis club early for the meeting and subsequent parade of classic cars, a new event in the calendar of St Denis. His house guests would get there on their own. Despite the work he had put into organizing the event, Bruno had never thought of himself as a car enthusiast. He didn't read car magazines and he seldom recognized the make of a new car until he saw its insignia. He put fuel in one end of his own vehicles and water in the other and expected them to function – they were merely tools to take people or goods from one place to another. He entrusted their repair and maintenance to experts. He had driven many different vehicles, military and civilian. These days he mostly drove the utility police vans supplied to him by his employer, the Mayor and council of St Denis, or the elderly Land Rover he had inherited from a hunting friend.

The Land Rover had inspired a surprising affection. It was not a comfortable vehicle to drive, built before the modern conveniences of adjustable seats, power steering and anti-lock brakes. Indeed, it was nearly twenty years older than Bruno. He had been surprised to learn this qualified it as a classic car. But it could go just about anywhere – cross rivers, climb the steepest and muddiest slopes, and negotiate the rock-strewn trails through the woods where he hunted the region's abundant game. And it had never let him down. This was more than he could say for some of the fancy cars his friends drove, which seemed to require the skills of a computer expert as much as a traditional car mechanic. In his days in the French army, Bruno had driven jeeps, trucks, motorbikes and even the occasional armoured car. He had a painful memory of the deafening and bone-shaking experience of driving an AMX-30, France's main battle tank, on the testing grounds at Saumur and had vowed never to repeat it. Forty tons was more than Bruno felt he could handle, particularly when the instructor had closed the driver's hatch so that his vision was limited to two narrow slits and a blurry periscope. Driving had held little appeal for him ever since.

Nor did Bruno consider himself to be a particularly good driver. He took little pleasure in driving fast and had been called to the scene of too many road accidents to want to push his limited skills. He had once been taken frighteningly fast around a course by a skilled rally driver, his friend Annette, a magistrate in Sarlat. She had skidded around bends, missed trees by inches and accelerated over the crests of hills with a force that slammed Bruno's head against the roof of her specially equipped Peugeot. He thought he had been saved from unconsciousness only by the helmet she had supplied. Such driving was not for him. Bruno's sole ambitions as a driver were to be competent and safe.

Bruno decided to skip his usual morning run so that he could wash and polish the Land Rover. He scrubbed the mud from the wheel wells and used a touch-up pen to cover the deeper scratches in the faded green paint. He wiped clean the canvas-covered seats and washed the windows, inside and out, and swept away the dust and gravel from the interior. He tidied up the rear, putting his tennis gear in one bag, his rugby boots and tracksuit in another, and his all-weather garments and hunting clothes in a third.

A freshly washed dog blanket now nestled between the bags, where Balzac could rest while waiting for his master. A bowl and water bottle stood ready for Balzac's refreshment. When Bruno drove, Balzac preferred to ride on the passenger seat where he could watch the road and landscape and, in the absence of a car radio, listen to Bruno sing. Other than his occasional attendance at church or on convivial evenings at the rugby club, Bruno reserved his singing for his Land Rover and his shower.

As Bruno drove into town, Balzac seemed to appreciate his owner's version of 'Que reste-t-il de nos amours?' Bruno tried to catch the breathy, almost playful tones of the Charles Trenet 1943 original. For Bruno, no other version would do, although most French singers had made their own recordings, singing it too slowly or making it too sad. His own mood when he thought of his past love affairs was of fond nostalgia rather than tragic loss. The memories made him grateful, so when Bruno pulled his gleaming car into the parking lot by the tennis club, he was pleased to see a familiar ancient Citroën *deux-chevaux*.

Pamela, its owner and his former lover, was standing nearby and admiring the Baron's venerable 1958 Citroën DS, which still looked more modern than most of the vehicles on the road. Its owner was leaning with one elbow on the car's roof as he chatted to her and gestured proudly at his second car, the old French military jeep that he used for hunting. It was being driven today by Sergeant Jules from the Gendarmerie. Pamela waved and beckoned Bruno to join them. He let Balzac jump out of the car and scamper across to her. He waved back but went to greet his two house guests, who had followed in their own car, before leading them across the parking lot to meet his friends.

It was a fine turnout for the classic car meeting, thought Bruno proudly, as well as a very international gathering. Bruno's English friend Jack Crimson was at the wheel of his Jaguar Mark 2, his daughter Miranda beside him. Horst, a German archaeologist, was dressed for the part, wearing white gloves and a flat cap as he helped Clothilde, curator of the local museum of prehistory, from the seat of her Porsche Speedster. A retired Dutch architect had brought his boxy DAF Variomatic and someone else had an elderly Saab. Lespinasse from the garage was flicking a duster over his perfectly restored Citroën *traction-avant* from 1938 – the oldest car at the gathering. To Bruno's eye the most striking vehicle was a white Jaguar E-type. From its passenger

5

seat Annette was waving at him; at the wheel beside her sat a good-looking and fair-haired stranger.

'Meet George Young, a friend from London,' Annette said to Bruno as he approached, her hand on the young man's arm. 'He runs a company bringing British drivers over to take part in French rallies and races. I met him at the Rallye des Remparts in Angoulême and persuaded him to bring his Jaguar to St Denis for our parade. He's going to navigate for me at the race tomorrow.'

Her voice was animated, Bruno noted, almost giddy. The two men shook hands and then Bruno introduced his two guests from Alsace. It was about time Annette found herself a boy-friend, thought Bruno, and the Englishman looked suitable enough. He was about Bruno's height, slim but with powerful shoulders and a friendly smile. His French was fluent as he chatted to the couple from Alsace about his visit – he called it a pilgrimage – to the Bugatti collection at the Musée Nationale de l'Automobile in Mulhouse, near their home.

From the corner of his eye, Bruno saw movement in the woods behind the tennis club and recognized Félix lurking in the trees. Félix was an undersized, sullen teenager who shunned the tennis and rugby lessons Bruno offered to the other students in the town's collège. He was the youngest child of two parents now well into in their fifties. Félix's older siblings had long since left home and the father had been unemployed for years. His mother, from a French island in the Caribbean, worked as a cleaner at the school. She had bequeathed to her son a skin just a shade or two darker than café au lait, which meant some fellow pupils sneered at him as a *métis*, a half-caste. Félix had suffered a number of brushes with the law for shoplifting, petty vandalism and one case of joyriding in a stolen car. Bruno reminded himself to check on the boy's age; once past sixteen, his next offence could mean juvenile detention. Bruno felt disappointed that he'd never been able to straighten the boy out; he thought of Félix as one of his failures.

'Him again,' said Yveline, commandant of the small Gendarmerie in St Denis, who had suddenly appeared at Bruno's side. She was in uniform. 'You know we're going to have a lot of trouble with that kid.'

'We already have,' said Bruno, and gave Félix a stern stare before leading his friends to join a group congregating at a long trestle table set up in front of the club. One of the waitresses from Fauquet's café was serving croissants and pains au chocolat and dispensing coffee from two large thermos flasks.

Bruno had chosen this spot for the cars to assemble, away from the main road and out of sight of the crowds who were expected for the parade. He had almost finished his coffee when two strikingly modern cars arrived. Fabiola was at the wheel of her new Renault ZOE electric car, and behind her came Alphonse, the town's only councillor from the Green Party, in his electric Kango van. Alphonse had persuaded the Mayor to make a nod to the environment by welcoming electric cars into St Denis's first Concours d'Elégance. That was the title Annette had dreamed up for what Bruno thought of simply as a vintage car parade, one of the events marking the name day of St Denis.

The idea had come from the Baron over a rugby club dinner the previous year when the Mayor had been looking for ways to extend the tourist season beyond the summer months. The first idea had been a visitors' day at the town vineyard, then Stéphane had suggested a special rugby match and Lespinasse had proposed a sports-car rally. Ah said the Baron, always keen to show off his splendid Citroën, that could be combined with a vintage car parade. Bruno had remained silent, knowing that whatever plans were made he'd be the one the Mayor assigned to make them work.

At that point Xavier, the efficient deputy Mayor, had opened his diary and reminded his companions that the date fell on the weekend when the delegation from St Denis's twin town in Alsace came for their annual visit. They came each year to commemorate the welcome the refugees from Alsace had been given in 1939 and 1940. The first wave had come just after war was declared in September 1939, when the French government evacuated to the Périgord the civilians from the regions near the German frontier. The following year, after the French surrender and the German reoccupation of Alsace and Lorraine, Alsatians of French stock had been deported to make room for German settlers. Most of the deportees came to the Périgord. Inevitably, in the four years before D-Day and France's liberation, friendships were forged between the refugees and their hosts, marriages took place, and after the war towns throughout Alsace twinned with those where they had been welcomed.

So the weekend of the town's name day now included a special market with stalls and vendors from Alsace, a rugby match with a team from Marckolsheim and a visitors' day at the vineyard followed by a feast. Lespinasse had arranged that St Denis would at the same time host the regional heats for the French rally drivers' championship. Father Sentout, St Denis's priest, had arranged a choral service for two choirs with his counterpart from Alsace and Antoine the boatman had organized a fishing competition. Bruno had been assigned to coordinate it all, and to arrange a fireworks display to round off the celebration. It was not what he had been trained to do in his course at the police academy, but this role as impresario of civic events gave Bruno great pleasure. It also meant that he had established a firm friendship with his Alsatian counterpart, Thomas, who with his wife was staying at Bruno's home for the weekend. Bruno had been their guest during his visits to Alsace for the twin town reunions.

'I don't see Sylvestre,' said Thomas, a worried look on his weather-beaten face. 'He's a friend from Marckolsheim and we're counting on him to bring something very special for the parade. I hope he hasn't lost his way.'

Thomas and his wife were devoted hikers, striding across the Vosges near their home most weekends and spending their summer vacations walking in the Alps. Bruno recalled with respect the pace they had set on a long day's hike from Colmar to Mulhouse on his last visit to Alsace. A few years older than Bruno and a little taller, Thomas was trim and fit. His wife Ingrid looked equally healthy, despite the bottles of Alsace wine they had brought and downed at Bruno's dinner table the previous evening.

'I'd better give the drivers their briefing,' said Bruno, looking at his watch. 'It's almost time to begin.'

Thomas pulled out his mobile phone to call Sylvestre as Ingrid greeted Fabiola and Pamela, whom she had met over dinner at Bruno's house the previous evening. Bruno took from his shoulder bag, and began handing out, a sheaf of photocopies he'd made of the route the drivers would take through St Denis. Each photocopy carried a number, indicating the order in which the cars would start.

'If I could have your attention,' he began, using his parade-ground voice. 'The route of our motorcade is clearly marked on your maps. We'll go through the main streets before turning onto the quayside, where we'll park on the long stretch before the bridge. Please park as I do, facing the stone wall and with your back to the river. Leave enough space for people to walk all around the cars, and keep an eye on your vehicles in case kids try to climb in. I'll lead the way, so nobody should get lost. The Baron will bring up the rear in the Citroën DS. And please keep at least two car lengths' distance from the vehicle ahead. Thank you.'

As he finished, what looked like a furniture truck turned the corner, sounded its horn and pulled up on the street, too big to fit into the already crowded parking lot. Two men in white overalls, white caps and goggles jumped from the driving compartment, waved at the crowd and went to the rear of the truck. One opened the wide double doors while the other pulled out a long ramp, lowered it to the ground and then clambered inside. Bruno heard the sound of a powerful engine being started, dying with a ragged cough and then starting again. A cloud of exhaust fumes surged from the rear of the truck and then a bright blue open-topped racing car from another era began to back slowly down the ramp.

The windscreen was no more than ten centimetres in height and the hood took up two-thirds of the car's length. The front wheels and axle were at the very front of the vehicle, ahead of the curved flat radiator. Leading back from the driver's seat the sides of the car curved in to form a pointed rear that looked as sharp as an axe blade. There were no mudguards above the wheels and a spare tyre was attached to the car's side with thick leather straps. The driver revved the engine and unleashed the harsh, potent roar of a thoroughbred before turning and driving slowly to face the suddenly silent crowd. Bruno could read the red badge on the arch-shaped radiator: Bugatti.

'Sylvestre always likes to make an entrance,' said Ingrid drily, once the throaty growl of the engine note had quietened. 'That's the one he bought last year. He paid seven hundred thousand euros and he says it's worth a lot more now.'

'A Type 35 from 1928, the car that made Bugatti's name,' said Thomas, something close to reverence in his voice. 'It was the only car of its day that could be driven both on the road and in Grand Prix races. Despite the Italian name, it's a French car, designed and built in Alsace.'

'It won every race going,' said Young, Annette's friend, in worshipful tones. 'It took the world championship in 1926 and the Targa Florio five years in a row.' He moved forward to help the driver from the cockpit and, as if suddenly released from bondage, the rest of the crowd surged forward to cluster around the Bugatti.

'Welcome,' said Bruno, introducing himself and handing the driver his photocopied map. 'We're honoured to have your car here. You're number nineteen, next to last in the parade. You'll follow the *traction-avant* and be just ahead of the DS.'

'Thank you, and please call me Sylvestre,' said the man in

11

white, pushing his goggles back onto his brow. He looked to be in his thirties. He had bright blue eyes, a prominent nose and a firm jaw. The grip of his handshake was unnecessarily strong but his smile was affable.

'This is my friend Freddy, he's from India,' Sylvestre said, beckoning forward his companion. 'We're both glad to be here. My grandmother told me a lot about this place. She was born just outside St Denis and I thought this was a good opportunity to take a look at some property she left me.' His expression was arrogant, almost haughty as he gazed around at the crowd, before raising his voice to ask, 'And which of these charming ladies would like to ride in the Bugatti with me?'

Sylvestre's eyes settled briefly on Fabiola, standing alone. 'How about you, Mademoiselle?'

'Thanks, but I'm driving my own car, the new Renault,' she replied coolly. 'We have electric cars in the parade.'

'Excellent,' said Sylvestre, and looked at Bruno. 'In that case, would you have room for one more? I've got a Tesla in the back of the truck and Freddy can drive it.'

Suddenly he seemed aware of Félix, who had somehow pushed himself forward to stand at the side of the Bugatti and gaze reverently into the driving compartment.

'What about you, young man. Would you like to take a spin?' Sylvestre asked. And with what Bruno thought was an understandable glance of triumph at him, Félix clambered inside and seemed to glow with pride. As he took his seat, Félix looked up at Sylvestre in awe.

Bruno had heard of the Tesla, an American-made electric sports car that ran on some revolutionary new battery, but he'd never seen one. Freddy clambered into the back of the big truck and backed out a sleek grey car. When Sylvestre turned off the Bugatti's engine, Bruno realized that the Tesla was utterly, eerily silent.

2

Shortly after the motorcade had ended and the cars had parked along the quayside, Bruno felt his phone vibrate. What with the noise from the crowds clattering down the stone steps to the riverbank to inspect the cars, he could barely make out that Dr Gelletreau was reporting a death. Bruno walked away to get clear of the clamour.

The doctor told him that an elderly man had been found dead by his wife in Savignac-le-Miremont when she returned from visiting her sister. She'd called him at once. The doctor said the cause of death looked like a heart attack. The town wasn't in the commune of St Denis, but as a courtesy, Bruno took care of the births and deaths registration for the small neighbouring communes, hence the call. He went in search of the Mayor to explain why he had to leave and found him admiring the Bugatti with the wide-eyed look of a little boy. Bruno entrusted his dog to Thomas and Ingrid and headed for the Gendarmerie where he had parked his official police van.

The commune of Savignac was composed mostly of farms, woods and heathland, its village tiny. Barely a hundred people lived in the whole commune. Henri-Pierre Hugon, the dead man, had been serving his third term as a member of the local council. Bruno found his house easily. In rural areas, friends and neighbours erect a pole at the home of each new council member, bedecked with a French flag and laurel wreaths and a sign saying 'Honour to Those We Elect'. Bruno followed Dr Gelletreau's directions until he saw the pole, its flags now somewhat faded, and turned in to see the doctor's elderly Citroën. The plump old man came to the door as Bruno pulled in.

'How goes the vintage car parade?' Gelletreau asked, shaking hands. 'I'm hoping I'll get there in time to see them all. This shouldn't take long. Madame Hugon is bearing up well. In fact she's making us some coffee. As soon as you've finished I'll call the undertakers.'

'Has he been dead long?' Bruno asked.

'He died in his study and the light was on so I think it was sometime yesterday evening. The central heating was on, which means the body temperature doesn't tell us much. I've been treating him for heart trouble for several years, since he was working in Périgueux. I've had him on beta-blockers and he'd been overweight as long as I've known him, even more than me. You knew him, didn't you?'

'Only to say hello to, mainly through SHAP, and I have a copy of his book at home,' Bruno said. 'He made his living as a researcher. I don't think I know his wife.'

SHAP was the Society for the History and Archaeology of the Périgord, a body of local enthusiasts and scholars who held monthly meetings and organized lectures in a splendid sixteenth-century townhouse in the heart of Périgueux. The Mayor had been a member for years and had encouraged Bruno to join, for which he was grateful. He tried never to miss the sessions and remembered with pleasure lectures he'd heard on the diet of the prehistoric peoples of the region, the development of medieval castle design and on the brief period in the sixteenth century when Bergerac had been the capital of France, or at least of the Protestants rallying to King Henri IV. He'd also heard the dead man give a memorably dry lecture on Périgueux during the Second World War, during which few in the audience managed to stay awake. SHAP had helped Hugon publish his book, an encyclopedia of the members of the Resistance in the Périgord. Hugon had spent his life working as an archivist for the *département* and since his retirement had continued to visit them regularly in his new role as freelance historian and researcher. He was invariably neatly dressed and Bruno had heard he was a meticulous worker with a good reputation among local lawyers and notaries.

'How old was he?' Bruno asked.

'He'd have been seventy-five next month. But he never exercised, always down in those gloomy archives. He lived a very sedentary life and he was a smoker.'

Once indoors, Bruno gave his condolences to Madame Hugon, accepted a cup of coffee and asked when she had found her husband.

'About an hour ago, when I got back, maybe it was a bit more than that,' she said. Madame Hugon was dry-eyed and composed, with no sign of shock or grief. Her hair was white and she looked to be about the same age as her husband but in much better health. Short and slim, she wore lace-up flat shoes, a dark skirt and a light-blue blouse.

'I'd been at my sister's in Sarlat for a few days. She has a new grandchild. My nephew drove me back because he wanted to see the old car parade and Henri was using the car while I was away. He was working on a big research job and needed to go back and forth to Périgueux and Bordeaux. I'd left meals in the freezer for him.'

Her nephew had dropped her at the house, and she'd let herself in. The front door had not been locked. She'd called for her husband, got no reply and found him dead on the floor beside the desk in his study. She had touched his cheek, found it cold and called Dr Gelletreau.

'You didn't call the *urgences*?' Bruno asked. The *pompiers* of the St Denis fire brigade provided the local emergency service.

'There was no point. He'd obviously been dead for hours. The doctor kept warning him this might happen but Henri would never listen.' She shrugged and then looked at Dr Gelletreau. 'He hadn't touched those meals I'd left for him, and from the dishes he'd left in the sink it looks like he'd lived on steaks and fried potatoes, all those things you'd told him not to eat.'

'I'm sorry for your loss,' Bruno said. 'I'd better take a look in the study. What was this big research job he was doing?'

'He'd been at it for a couple of months, five days a week. Never told me what it was, just something about the war and the Resistance, but he said he'd make enough from it for us to have a nice holiday in the sun this winter. He used to get a hundred and fifty euros a day for his research work. I'd always wanted to see Morocco and I was looking forward to it.'

'Do you know who hired him?' Bruno asked. She shook her head and Bruno did the maths as Gelletreau led the way into the study, where the desk lamp was still lit. If Hugon had been working on a research project for two months he'd have earned six thousand euros, a tidy sum.

The chair had been overturned and Hugon's plump body lay sprawled beside it, one leg partly under the desk. His right hand was clutching at his shirt front and his face looked as though he'd died in pain, his lips drawn back from his teeth. On his desk was the lamp, an old-fashioned telephone, a blank message pad and pencil lined up neatly beside it, and a closed laptop computer. The printer was on a small side table, switched off, and with no printouts in the tray.

There was no sign of a diary or notebook that might provide a clue to his researches. The drawers of two filing cabinets against the wall were closed. Bruno pulled on a set of evidence gloves and opened each drawer in turn. Most of the files were organized alphabetically and seemed to reflect the names of the people to be included in his encyclopedia. One file marked 'Current Projects' was empty. His bank statements showed no unusual activity, just his pension payments, reimbursements from medical insurance and some modest bank transfers from lawyers, presumably research fees. There was no sign of the six thousand euros. Bruno wondered where was the account book he would have to keep for tax records?

In the bookcase, filled with well-thumbed works of reference, were two shelves filled with hardbacked notebooks, covered in black leather and much too big to fit into a pocket. Bruno leafed through them. Hugon's handwriting was neat and precise and every entry was dated. They were filed in order. The last one on the bookshelf ended with an entry for 30 July of that year. There was no sign of any current notebook, just two virgin notebooks, ready for use.

The only item in the waste paper basket was an empty envelope from France Télécom. It was postmarked two days earlier, so it had probably been delivered the previous day. Bruno found a file for phone bills. In the past two months there had been far more calls than usual, including daily calls to and from a mobile number that did not feature in earlier bills. Bruno took out his own phone and dialled the number but an automated reply said the number was no longer available. That was odd. He called the security line for France Télécom and was told the number belonged to an unregistered pay-as-you-go phone.

Bruno went back to Madame Hugon to ask if she knew the password for the laptop, but she shook her head; and nor did she recognize the phone number. She added that her husband had kept his diary and account books in his desk, unless he was going to the archives, when they'd be in his briefcase.

'They aren't there now,' said Bruno. 'And there's no sign of the briefcase.'

'Maybe he left them in the car,' she said with a shrug, not seeming much concerned.

The briefcase was in the car but it contained only blank notepads, pens, a copy of the previous day's *Sud Ouest* and a half-empty pack of Royale cigarettes. Bruno went back to the body and found a wallet in the hip pocket. Inside were the usual identity, health and credit cards, along with five crisp new 200-euro banknotes. Bruno asked where Hugon had kept his clothes and was shown to a wardrobe in the marital bedroom.

He checked the pockets of the jackets and the bedside tables but found nothing.

'Was there any sign that anybody else might have been in the house while you were away?' Bruno asked Madame Hugon.

She thought for a moment, then: 'Not that I noticed. We never had many visitors, except for my sister.'

'Did you have any unusual visitors in recent days?' She shook her head. 'Did he seem worried by anything?'

'Far from it. He was pleased to have this new research project. Henri liked it when he was busy. He was never one to hang around the house, and he didn't watch much television. There was nothing he liked more than poking around old archives, and getting paid for it was even better.'

'Was he working very hard?' Gelletreau asked.

'More than usual. He was in his study until all hours, night after night. But that wasn't so unusual when he had his teeth into something. It was like when he was writing that book. But it didn't seem to be a strain. It was work, but the kind of work he loved. It always cheered him up to be on the trail of something.'

'Did he always work on the laptop or did he work with documents?'

'Both. He had a big file of papers he'd collected but he always had one of those black notebooks going as well.'

'There's a file marked "Current Projects" in the filing cabinet but it's empty and the last entry in the latest black notebook was for some time in July. So where's the one for August and September?'

'I don't know. Maybe he left it at the archives in Périgueux.

He used to be in charge of the place, so they'd always let him leave stuff in his desk.'

Bruno went into the kitchen and looked at the dirty dishes in the sink and piled up on the draining board, as if Hugon planned to leave them for his wife to wash on her return. There were four or five dinner plates, smeared with grease, some wine glasses, and bowls that might have held soup or breakfast cereal.

'He used the good coffee cups, that's not like him,' she said, sounding surprised for the first time since Bruno's arrival. There were three dirty coffee cups beside the sink, all piled together as if they had been used at the same time.

'Did he drink much?' Bruno asked, eyeing three empty bottles of Bergerac red wine, an undistinguished brand that Bruno recognized from the local supermarket.

'He liked his glass of Ricard before dinner and red wine with his meals, just a glass or two. Doctor Gelletreau had told him to cut back on his drinking.'

'How long were you away?' Bruno asked.

'Just the three nights.'

'So he got through three bottles in three days. That seems like quite a lot for a man on his own.'

She frowned, something like distaste in her expression. 'I think he usually drank more when I wasn't here, just like he'd go back to his steaks rather than defrost those nice meals I made.'

Gelletreau nodded sagely. 'He was never what I'd call a good patient. You can give them all the advice in the world but if they don't want to take it . . .'

Bruno thanked Madame Hugon and asked her if she wanted

him to call anybody, perhaps her sister or a priest? She shook her head, saying she'd already called her sister in Sarlat to tell her of the death and her husband had never been a churchgoer. Once the undertaker had taken the body to the funeral home she'd drive back to Sarlat and stay there.

'I might put the house on the market,' she added.

In the garden, Bruno asked Dr Gelletreau if he'd signed the death certificate yet.

'No, I was waiting for you to arrive,' the doctor said, a little stiffly. On an earlier occasion, he'd been embarrassed after putting down natural causes on a death certificate when Bruno had later discovered that the victim had been murdered.

'I don't like this,' Bruno said. 'All that cash in his wallet, the disappearance of his diary and account book, those phone calls . . .'

'And the three coffee cups,' said Gelletreau. 'Still, I'm pretty sure it was a heart attack. You saw the way he was clutching his chest. It doesn't look much like a murder to me. Hugon was a heart attack waiting to happen. And he certainly died yesterday.'

'So if his wife has an alibi from her family in Sarlat . . .' said Bruno, thinking aloud.

'If that's the case you've got a real mystery on your hands, unless you've got another one of your hunches.'

Bruno looked back at the house, pulled out his phone and called his friend Jean-Jacques, the chief detective for the *département*, to explain his suspicions.

'What does the doc say?' J-J replied.

'Heart attack, looks natural enough.'

'And the wife? Does she think it was a natural death?'

'Yes. She found the body after staying with family in Sarlat for a few days and she doesn't seem concerned. It's just me who thinks there's more to this than meets the eye.'

'*Merde*, there's no sign of any struggle, the doctor and the widow aren't worried and you know the state of my budget and what we have to pay to get an autopsy done. If it wasn't you saying this, Bruno . . .' J-J's voice trailed off. 'Who's the doctor present? Is it Fabiola?'

'Doctor Gelletreau seems ready to sign the death certificate, citing cardiac arrest.'

J-J grunted. 'Well, we can always ask for a second opinion. See if you can persuade Fabiola to take a look at the body when the undertaker comes for it. If she thinks it's worth having an autopsy I'll go along. By the way, have you heard anything from Isabelle?'

'Not lately,' Bruno replied cautiously. In his own paternal way, J-J was almost as devoted as Bruno to Isabelle and claimed she was the best detective he'd ever trained. He liked to hope that she might one day give up her meteoric career, first in Paris and then with Eurojust in The Hague, and return to the Périgord to be his successor as chief detective. Bruno, who still dreamed of her and could never forget their passionate summer together, thought of Isabelle as the lost love of his life. But he cherished no such illusions of her possible return to the tranquil charms of the Périgord.

'Word from Paris is that she's had a bit of trouble in some big operation in Luxembourg, ruffling some diplomatic feathers.'

'That's news to me,' said Bruno, making an effort to keep his voice neutral. He knew he would never stop caring about her.

'But you know Isabelle, she'll find some way to turn it to her advantage.'

'I thought maybe the Brigadier might have said something,' J-J said. 'I know he's more in touch with you than with me, for which on the whole I'm quite grateful. It always means trouble when he's around.'

'I haven't heard from him for a while.' The Brigadier, a senior figure in the ministry of the interior with wide-ranging responsibilities in security matters, had been Isabelle's boss before she transferred to Eurojust. 'And diplomatic trouble sounds way above my pay grade.'

'Mine, too, I imagine. Still, Isabelle always trusted your hunches and I've learned there's usually something to them,' J-J said. 'So if Fabiola agrees that it's worth taking a closer look, I'll approve the autopsy.'

3

'This event has been a great success,' said the Mayor, leaning back in his chair with a glass of wine and staring contentedly at the crowded tables that filled the St Denis winery. 'Our vintage cars made the TV news, thanks to that old Bugatti, and Fauquet's café was packed all day. And just look at this turnout tonight! We'll have to start doing this every year.'

That means more work for me again next year, thought Bruno, clinking his glass against the Mayor's, but he was pleased that the car show had brought in a crowd. Mauricette had told him her hotel had never before been full so early in the season. She'd devised a special offer for the weekend that had attracted tourists who liked the idea of a winery dinner without the risk of being breathalyzed on a long drive home. And after the local TV and radio publicity for the Concours, a lot more people were expected next day to watch the rally. Bruno had spent most of Friday checking on the safety barriers along the route. Once the race was over he'd have to help the farmers pick up the hay bales they had placed at every corner.

At a sign from Julien, who ran the town vineyard, the Mayor rose to his feet and went to the dais that stood in front of the stacked wine barrels at the end of the winery. There wasn't much space, with the drums, guitars and keyboard for that evening's music and dancing already in place. More barrels stood against the wall and between them ran long rows of tables and chairs, all filled with people who had paid twenty euros a head for the vineyard dinner of soup, pâté, roast duck, cheese with salad and a piece of walnut tart. As much wine as they wanted was included in the price of their meal, all of it from the town vineyard. Most of the diners had also bought tickets for the raffle, five euros for six chances to win. Tapping an empty bottle with a fork, the Mayor called for silence and announced that the draw was about to take place. The first prize was a case of the local wine, the second prize six bottles, and there were three third prizes of two bottles each.

'Would our lovely ladies come forward please to draw the winning tickets?' the Mayor called, and Fabiola, Annette and Florence made their way towards him, Fabiola shaking her head in mock despair at the Mayor's old-fashioned way of introducing them. He identified each woman as they joined him on the dais: Fabiola as one of the town's doctors, Annette as the local magistrate and star rally driver, and Florence as the science teacher at the *collège*.

'We didn't have teachers or doctors or magistrates like these when I was a boy,' the Mayor said. 'But because we all want to wish Annette the best of luck in tomorrow's rally, I'll ask her to wait a little so she can draw the ticket for the first prize. Florence, please draw three tickets for the third prizes. Each winner gets a bottle of our excellent Vézère red and another of our delicious dry white wine. And Fabiola will draw the ticket for the second prize.'

26

The third and second prizes went to strangers, which was as it should be, thought Bruno, hoping that a tourist would also win the first prize. Each winner had been cheered by his and her neighbours at the various tables, but then a silence fell as Annette reached into the bucket to draw out the winning ticket. She read out the number.

'That's me,' called out a male voice, and Bruno saw the Bugatti owner, Sylvestre, rise in his place and clasp his hands above his head in victory. Then he raised his voice to call across the tables to the Mayor.

'Have another draw. I donate my prize back to you.' He paused and grinned around the winery. 'I can't drink, I'm driving.'

He sat down to a round of applause. Annette drew again and this time Bruno cheered when his friend Ingrid rose to claim the prize. The Mayor made a point of saying how pleased he was that the prize went to someone from their twin town in Alsace, adding that the visiting delegation would be at the St Denis market the next morning, offering their wines and crafts and special foodstuffs.

'And then our local restaurants and producers will offer a food market in the main square after the end of the race, just as we do each Tuesday evening in July and August,' the Mayor went on. 'There'll be roast chicken from rotisseries, hams grilled over open fires, snails, *moules frites*, along with salads, pizzas, *tartes aux pommes*, and wine from the town vineyard. So we'll hope to see you again tomorrow. Now it's time for the dancing.'

He stepped down and St Denis's own rock band took their place on the dais. Lespinasse from the garage started with a drum roll. His son Edouard was on bass, Robert the singing

27

architect on rhythm and Patrice from the camera shop played lead guitar. Jean-Paul, the church organist who was also the local piano teacher, climbed up to join them with his accordion around his neck and began with the theme from 'Mon Amant de St Jean'. A classic from the *bal musette* dancehalls of the 1930s and recently revived on one of the best-selling CDs in France, it was a song known to all present. Bruno led Florence to the dance floor and saw Fabiola and her partner Gilles, Thomas and Ingrid, Annette and her Englishman come to join them and suddenly the floor was full. A cheer went up when the Mayor joined them with his friend Jacqueline just as Robert was singing the line about how the girl knew the young man was lying to her but she liked him anyway.

The music went on with the band's usual mix of Edith Piaf, Sixties' classics, Johnny Cash and Francis Cabrel numbers until Florence and Annette said they were thirsty and hauled the two men back to their table for more wine. Annette kept her hand in Young's as they sat and Bruno wondered if Young knew that Annette was the daughter of an extremely rich and controversial financier.

'I'm so glad Sylvestre brought his Bugatti. It was the star of the show,' said Annette, over the sound of the music. She gave Young a fond look. 'How did you persuade him to come?'

'He didn't need much persuading,' Young replied. 'He told me he'd been planning to come down here to see some family property and the chance of winning a Concours d'Elégance was too tempting to pass up. Even if nobody outside the Périgord has heard of the St Denis Concours, he reckons the title will raise the price of the Bugatti when he wants to sell it.'

'If I had a car like that, I'd never let it go,' said Florence, so firmly that Bruno and the others turned to look at her. 'I'm not really a car person and I can't say I think of it as good to look at in a conventional way. It was too brutal, too arrogant in the way it seemed to embody raw power, but it still struck me as extraordinarily beautiful.' She paused, and then tossed her head and laughed, trying to shift the mood that she had suddenly made serious. 'Anyway, I'd be far too terrified even to think about driving some mechanical beast like that. But there was something very seductive about the way it sounded.'

'A mere seven hundred thousand and it's yours,' said Bruno, grinning. 'I heard that was what he paid for it. I had no idea they were worth so much. How about that E-type of yours?' he asked Young. 'What's that worth?'

'I got it years ago as a wreck for the equivalent of eight thousand euros, restored it myself and now it's probably worth a hundred grand,' Young replied. 'I put years of work into it because that's the only way I was able to afford it. The old Porsche that was in the parade will probably be worth about the same. If you cleaned up that Land Rover, you'd get a pretty good price. What year was it built?'

'Nineteen fifty-four,' said Bruno. He remembered Hercule, the friend who had bequeathed it to him, saying that he'd been in the French army, fighting in Indo-China, the year his Land Rover was made. Bruno knew that 1954 was a year of special significance for his friend, the year of the French defeat at Dien Bien Phu. Hercule had bought the vehicle decades later, when he'd taken his pension and settled down in the Périgord to hunt and raise truffles.

'Fully restored, you might get fifty or sixty thousand,' said Young. 'It's a booming market, now that the Arabs and Chinese are starting to invest in classic cars. That's how Sylvestre does so well with his auctions. He's already got a showroom in Dubai and he's planning to open another one in Shanghai. I know he's expecting to get at least a million for his Bugatti and I presume that's how he plans to finance his Chinese operation.'

Florence rolled her eyes and Bruno shook his head, stunned by the figures he was hearing.

'Is that how you got to know Sylvestre, through these classic car sales?' Florence asked Young.

'In a way. I first met him at an auction in England a couple of years ago but we've met since at several rallies. He's a very good driver and unlike me he's got the money to pursue his hobby seriously.'

Young explained that he'd first noticed Sylvestre bidding for a Ferrari Modena Spider. He himself had dropped out when the price reached a hundred thousand pounds, about a hundred and thirty thousand euros. The auction was held at the old Goodwood race track and it had gone down in history because a 1954 Mercedes Formula One racing car went for just under thirty million dollars, still the record for a public auction.

'The real money tends to be restricted to private auctions,' Young added. 'A Ferrari 250 GTO is supposed to have gone for over thirty million at a private auction in Italy, though it may just be rumour. Those private events are by invitation only and I'm not on the list for any of those. Sylvestre gets invited to them, probably because of his Dubai connections.'

'It makes my Land Rover seem cheap,' Bruno said. 'Are these classic car sales the way Sylvestre made his money?'

'No, you have to start with a lot of money to get into the game. His family in Alsace is into property and I gather they're very rich and own shopping malls and office blocks, but I don't know the details. We're quite friendly and usually have a drink or a meal together when we meet up or when Sylvestre comes to London, but I couldn't claim that we're close friends. He's a prickly type, a bit arrogant, but he certainly knows his way around cars.'

'Talking about our neighbour Sylvestre?' came the voice of Bruno's friend Thomas, Ingrid on his arm.

'We were just hearing about Sylvestre's car-sales business,' said Bruno, shifting his chair to give them room to sit down.

'His family was very lucky,' Thomas explained. They had been farmers, with land between Marckolsheim and Strasbourg. Just before war broke out in 1939 the French government bought some of the land to turn it into a military airfield. There was a court case because it was a compulsory purchase and Sylvestre's grandfather had sued because the government offered too little money. After the war the air force still wanted the airbase and offered a deal by which they paid rent and promised that if they ever gave up the airfield Sylvestre's family could buy it back for the original price. In the 1960s, when de Gaulle thought French security would depend on nuclear weapons, France began cutting back on conventional forces. Sylvestre's family got the land back cheaply, complete with a runway, hangars, underground fuel bunkers, offices and barracks.

'Strasbourg was then becoming one of the centres of the new European community and wanted a civilian airport,' Thomas went on. 'Sylvestre's father sold the airfield itself for many times more than he'd paid to buy it back. But he kept the rest of the land, thinking it was bound to increase in value.'

'And it certainly did,' Ingrid chimed in. 'His heirs became one of the wealthiest families in Alsace. That's how Sylvestre can afford to spend seven hundred thousand on that Bugatti of his.'

'That's nothing,' said Young, taking out a smartphone from his shirt pocket. He tapped a few buttons and then held up the screen to show an extraordinary, gleaming black car with the sweeping aerodynamic lines of the 1930s and a hood that seemed to stretch out for ever.

'*Mon Dieu*, it's beautiful,' said Florence.

'This is the most expensive car of all time. What do you think it might be worth?' Young asked.

'Twenty million,' Bruno suggested, plucking a figure from the air. Prices like that were meaningless to him. The only sense of value he could ascribe to them was to think of the prices of châteaux he knew were for sale. A million could buy a charming and habitable seventeenth-century château just a few kilometres away. Ingrid said five million and Annette shook her head, saying she knew the price and their estimates would have to go a lot higher.

'Thirty million,' Florence suggested, laughing.

'More than that even,' said Young. He suddenly looked solemn, as if this were serious business.

'What is it?' Bruno asked.

'It's another Bugatti, a model known as the Atlantic. Its real name is Type 57C, built in 1936. One of these was bought by the Mullin Museum in California for an undisclosed sum. The word is that it went for thirty-seven million dollars. It's certainly the most valuable car of all time.'

'That's insane,' said Bruno, thinking it was almost obscene. 'How can any car be worth that?'

'They only made four of them. One is owned by Ralph Lauren, there's the one in the museum, a third was destroyed by a train at a railway crossing and another was lost somewhere in France during the war. It was being driven from the factory in Alsace to Bordeaux for safe-keeping but it never arrived and nobody knows what happened to it.'

'I agree with Florence,' said Bruno, taking Young's phone and looking at the car more closely. 'It certainly is beautiful. Is that the one in the museum?'

'No, that's the one owned by Ralph Lauren.' He opened another photograph of the same car in silver-blue. 'That's the one bought by the museum.'

Bruno was about to ask about the one that was lost in the war when Fabiola and Gilles descended to haul them all back to the dance floor.

4

Bruno reined in at the top of the ridge and checked his watch as he waited for Fabiola to catch up on her old horse. He was meeting Thomas and Ingrid at Fauquet's café at nine for breakfast but there was still time for a decent gallop before taking Hector back to the stables. He looked down at the familiar valley of the river Vézère, still shrouded in early morning mist. The St Denis bridge and the quayside where the vintage cars had been parked on display all lay somewhere beneath that fog. Stray tendrils were rising like wisps of steam as the first, hesitant rays of the sun peeked above the ridge and began to melt away the mist. The spire of the old church and the houses that clambered up the hill seemed to float weightlessly in the sky. His horse and dog stood still and silent as their eyes followed his gaze down into the valley until Balzac turned, hearing Victoria's hooves lumbering up the slope towards them.

'What did you think of Annette's young man?' Fabiola asked as she brought her horse to a halt beside him. Her mare, Victoria, gave a neigh of gratitude and Hector turned to rub the side of his head against hers. Sometimes Bruno thought that horses were more socially adept than many of the people he knew.

'Too soon to tell, but I liked him from the little I saw,' Bruno

34

replied. 'He seemed good-natured and friendly and he danced well. Apart from his passion for cars, that's about all I can say. But if Annette likes him, that's good enough for me.'

'I think it's more than just liking him,' Fabiola said. 'Did you see how she looked at him? I hope it works out for her. But it won't be easy, her staying here in the Périgord while he's in London most of the time. I'm sure they can have thrilling reunions at rallies and car auctions, but you don't get to know a man that way.'

Bruno looked at her with amused affection. 'Gilles was in Paris and you were down here but it worked out for you two.'

'Gilles was ready to leave Paris and join me here. I don't think that's the case for Annette and George and I don't want to see her hurt. Do you think he's ready to make some kind of commitment? Annette will need that.'

'He drove all the way down here from London to be with her, so he's obviously more than just interested.'

'That's not what I mean by commitment, Bruno. You know what I'm talking about. She seems so much more interested than he is. And he's not just good-looking, he's seriously handsome, the sort of man who's had lots of girls. Don't you think so?'

Among the many things that baffled Bruno about women was the time and effort they spent analyzing the love affairs of their friends. They seemed to make it all so complicated. Bruno liked to recall a scene from his favourite movie, Les Enfants du Paradis, when the actress Arletty turns to the tongue-tied young man who is besotted with her, lets her gown fall and says, 'L'amour, c'est si simple.' Bruno knew it was never quite so easy. There was an old Périgord proverb about love being like food; it changed with the time it spent cooking. But he couldn't see how it helped for others endlessly to pick over the passions and disappointments of their friends.

'It's early days for them,' he said. 'They met at the Angoulême rally this summer and again at the car show in Paris, so this is only their third meeting. He isn't even staying at her place.'

'They haven't been to bed together yet,' Fabiola replied. 'She's nervous about that. Annette's not very experienced and she thinks he is.'

'That's for them to work out, like it worked out for you and Gilles,' said Bruno, and looked at her steadily. 'Are you ready to ride on?'

'You aren't over your affair with Pamela,' she said, ignoring his question.

'Nor is she, so that makes two of us,' he replied, irritated and aware of a childish urge to have the last word. He certainly didn't want to pick over the bones of their parting with Fabiola. He touched his heels to Hector's flanks and his horse sprang forward. Bruno could almost feel Hector's pleasure at being unleashed, bounding almost at once into a canter, with Balzac lumbering along behind. Bruno pressed his horse to go faster to leave Fabiola's probing remarks in his wake and feel nothing but the wind in his face.

Forty minutes later, after stripping off his shirt to sluice down in the stable sink because there was no time to shower, Bruno walked into Fauquet's café. The clock on the Mairie tower was striking nine and the market stalls displaying the foods from

Alsace were already busy. Some in the crowd were eating portions of *flammkuchen*, thin slices of pastry covered with onions,
bacon and melted cheese. Bruno's mouth began to water as he
caught the aroma. He was also tempted by a stall offering bowls
of sausage chunks with *choucroute* and plastic glasses of Riesling.
But he could see Thomas and Ingrid were already installed at
a window table in the café. Before them were cups of coffee,
the local newspaper and a basket of croissants and pains au
chocolat. Ingrid was glancing through the weekly magazine of
Sud Ouest and Thomas handed Bruno the paper. It was opened to
a photograph of Sylvestre's Bugatti on the quayside, surrounded
by a throng of people.

'Your Mayor will be pleased with all the publicity,' said
Thomas. He tore off a piece of his croissant to give it to Balzac.

'I wonder if we'd have done so well if Sylvestre hadn't come
with that old Bugatti,' Bruno said, swallowing a mouthful of
croissant and regretting that he hadn't bought some hot *flamm-
kuchen* for them all. But his friends probably got enough of that
at home, he told himself.

Suddenly he caught sight of Annette half-running through
the market towards them.

'Bruno, you've got to help,' she said, bursting into the café.
'George has got a terrible migraine so he can't navigate for me
and I can't be in the rally without a co-driver. I asked Yveline
but she's on safety duty with the rest of the gendarmes. Please,
please, please will you take George's place? I won't be able to
enter the national rally unless I do well here today and there's
nobody else I can ask.'

He almost choked in surprise on his croissant. 'I'm not nearly good enough to be a co-driver,' he said, and drank some water. 'I'm not qualified, Annette. What about Sylvestre?'

'I can't ask him as he's competing with that Indian friend of his, Freddy. And you don't have to drive, just navigate for me.'

'Navigate?' he asked. 'The rally track is clearly marked. You can't get lost.'

'That's not what I mean. You navigate by telling me in advance of every bend and obstacle coming up.' From her shoulder bag she took out what looked like two rolls of paper towels on wooden handles and brandished them at him. 'I've got your track roll here. You just have to read it out so I know what's coming.'

'But I've never done this,' said Bruno. 'And the last time I drove with you I got car-sick.'

'You'll be too busy concentrating on the scroll,' she said. 'Please, Bruno, this really means a lot to me.'

He looked at the scroll, realizing that by turning the first wooden handle he could see a detailed line-by-line description of the road ahead. After the start of the rally, he read, there was an 80-metre straight on tarmac, followed by a 90-degree left turn onto gravel, then a 40-metre straight that led into a 60-degree left turn into a dip with a bad camber . . .

He recognized the descriptions, having driven the track twice and walked parts of it when checking the hay bales that would protect the spectators.

'Did you make this roll with George Young?' he asked.

'I spent days on it before he arrived, driving the route with a tape recorder and then transcribing the tape onto my laptop and finding a printer that could make a continuous roll. All you have to do is read it out.'

'I couldn't hear myself think when you drove me around that motocross track,' he said. 'You won't hear me.'

'I've got microphones and headphones in the helmets. And I know the track almost by heart. But if I don't have a co-driver I'll be disqualified.'

'I never thought of you as a man to turn down a damsel in distress,' said Ingrid, grinning at him.

'Why turn down the opportunity for a new experience? You know you'll regret it if you say no,' said Thomas, giving a grin that was the echo of his wife's.

'And she'll never forgive you,' said Ingrid.

'Right, I'll never forgive you,' said Annette, laughing as Bruno looked from one face to another and rolled his eyes. They all knew he'd have to say yes.

'Do I have time to finish my breakfast?' he asked.

'Five minutes. The rally starts at two, but they'll close the track at noon. Until then we can do test runs. We'll do one slowly so you get used to it, a second one at medium speed and then a third all out. By then you should have learned to handle the roll and judge when I need to hear your instructions.'

'So simple,' said Ingrid. 'What could possibly go wrong?'

'Only the roll can go wrong,' said Annette. 'If you lose control of the paper it unravels and piles up all over the car and blocks my vision. I had that happen once and it's not good. That's why you have to get some practice. I'll wait.'

She folded her arms and stood at the end of the table, her jaw set and her eyes fixed on him, but smiling at him expectantly.

39

He was reminded of the first time he'd seen her, in the square outside the café in her first week in her new job, showing off out of sheer nervousness by driving too fast. Annette had got a parking ticket from him and a speeding ticket from Sergeant Jules. She was only spared a charge of failing to stop at a pedestrian crossing when Florence realized it was her first job as magistrate and refused to press charges. Now she was a good friend who had learned to temper her own radical views and passion for the environment with a healthy respect for the customs and peculiarities of the Périgord. Bruno had come to admire her professionalism, and, in an avuncular kind of way – which was a new sensation for him – he was fond of her.

'This isn't your car,' he said in the parking lot, looking at the unfamiliar white Citroën DS3 festooned with advertising stickers for motor oils, car accessories and a garage in Sarlat. Annette opened the door to reveal internal roll bars forming a protective cage. 'Where's your blue Peugeot?'

'This is my race car,' she replied. 'It's a turbo, borrowed from the Citroën garage in Brive. The owner's son, Fabrice, usually drives it, but he broke his leg skiing so for once I'm being sponsored, which makes it my big chance to get into the national championship. That's why I need you. I can't give up this opportunity.'

'What happened to Fabrice's navigator?'

'That would be me. That's why I'm being given his place.'

Bruno took the helmet from the passenger seat and eased himself into the car, feeling the high sides of the special rally seat enclose him. Annette climbed in her side and showed him how the double seat belts worked, straps over each shoulder and two more for the belt, meeting at a circular lock on his belly, like the one he recalled from parachute training in the army. He put on the helmet and Annette leaned over again to adjust his microphone and plug the trailing wire into a socket between the seats. She did the same for her own audio feed and began a countdown test. He heard her perfectly and then did his own countdown and she interrupted to say it was good.

'Now try unrolling this while we're parked,' she said, putting the first roll into a bracket attached to the glove compartment. Between his feet was a second bracket and she bent down to insert the main roll. 'Just turn the handles on the top roll to feed the paper and read out the instructions to me as they come. Keep your feet braced and whatever you do, don't let your legs tear the paper or we're sunk. Try it.'

It was easy enough, sitting in the parking lot, but she kept him practising for twenty minutes before rewinding the roll, clicking in her own seat belts and then setting off for the start of the course on the road to Les Eyzies. Once on the dirt track, she kept her speed down and Bruno had little difficulty controlling the paper roll. He even had time to glance up briefly at the route ahead, checking the instructions. The special seats and the double belts kept him securely in place, even when she began to pick up speed. The strain was on his neck, to stop his head swinging from side to side as she accelerated out of the sharp bends.

'Okay,' Annette said. 'This time, don't touch the paper, just watch the road and get familiar with the track. I'll go fairly fast, but nowhere near full speed.'

She got onto the gravel track and shot away, moving slickly

through second gear and into third before braking hard for the corner and then skidding as she stepped on the accelerator. Bruno was stunned by the contrast between the sedate pace he would have driven this route and Annette's suicidal speed. Corners came up far too fast and bends were whipped through so hard he felt the safety belts cutting into his flesh as they held him in place. Trees loomed before him and he closed his eyes, sure that a crash was coming. Then somehow they were skidding sideways but still on the track and he felt the panic rising again, certain that they were about to hit a pile of hay bales. His neck ached with the strain of stopping his head jerking from side to side. He was meant to be learning the route but his senses were too overwhelmed by fear and tension for anything to sink in.

Bruno gritted his teeth; he would have to get used to this. As the road climbed up into the woods around St Cirq he felt his reactions start to adjust to the much higher speeds and to Annette's mastery of the car. He began to anticipate the corners and brace himself for the car's leap into the air when it crossed even the smallest ridge. He kept telling himself that Annette was completely in control when the rear of the car skidded sharply to one side. It was simply the way that she cornered.

'Let's do that one more time, without using the roll,' he said, when she pulled up at the finish. He heard the breathlessness in his own voice. 'I'm just starting to get the hang of this.'

Without a word, Annette clicked a stopwatch on the dashboard and set off again at speed, but this time he felt ready, his senses catching up with the sheer pace at which the inputs were coming and his body anticipating the lurches as the g-forces tried to hurl him from side to side. Somehow his brain had learned that slamming into a tree was not inevitable and that Annette would hit the accelerator just as she went into the bend rather than wait until she was coming out of it. And he knew he was recognizing bends and corners, the short straights and the dips where the car bottomed out. The feeling of panic had diminished. He felt he was back in control of himself.

'Okay,' he said when she stopped again. 'I think I'm ready to try it with the roll.'

The next trip was worse. Bruno had almost no time to glance up at the route and his eyes lost focus as the car bounced over bumps in the road or took to the air as they went over even modest hill crests. At one point when Annette braked very hard to go into a sharp right-hand bend the g-force sent the paper ballooning out between his legs. Then Bruno briefly lost his place on the roll and knew he had to keep his thumb on the paper to mark each line as he read it. Somehow he got through to the end of the ride, and as Annette braked he closed his eyes and waited for his breathing to return to normal. His hands were trembling and he felt exhausted from the intensity of the concentration.

'Not bad for a beginner, Bruno. That was under seventeen minutes,' she said. 'Now we'll do it again, only faster. If I'm going to win this thing, we'll have to do it in fifteen.'

5

Two laps into the next training session, Annette distracted him by saying, 'Someone very good is on our tail and I think I know who it is. Hang on tight.'

Bruno hadn't thought it was possible to go any faster but Annette raised her pace. Still, he was starting to anticipate each place on the paper roll by the way she shifted gears and braked and by the direction of the g-force at each bend. He learned to start reading out the next instruction as she accelerated out of each bend and to brace his legs to stop the paper ballooning when the car briefly took flight as she topped each hill.

'He's very good,' he heard Annette say as his tailbone crunched when she slammed through a dip in the road. He winced. 'He'll be the one to beat.'

Bruno saw her eyes flick to the rear-view mirror and was amazed that she could spare time or attention for anything but the road ahead. He felt he had never gone so fast in his life, and had never heard anything louder than the roar of the engine as she pushed the tachometer into the red zone. But he kept up his commentary on the road ahead and felt confident enough to take the occasional brief glance at the road.

'That was our fastest yet,' said Annette, slowing and braking to turn into the assembly area. 'I think we'll be fine. How do you feel?'

'I feel very grateful we have airbags,' he replied. 'As long as they're working I'll be OK.'

She turned to him in surprise as the car drew to a halt. 'They aren't working. We have to dismantle all the airbags for serious rally cars. Some of the jolts we take when we land after a hillcrest are shock enough to trigger them.'

Now she tells me, thought Bruno, trying to keep his face from betraying his dismay.

Half a dozen rally cars were already gathered, most of them with their bonnets up, drivers leaning over their engines. Small knots of spectators were strolling around the cars and Philippe Delaron, the local *Sud Ouest* correspondent, was taking photos, posing excited small boys against the cars.

'What about that car behind us?' Bruno asked.

'There won't be a car behind us in the rally. We race against the clock, not against each other. That would be too dangerous. Here they are now.'

A white Volkswagen pulled up sharply beside them, two figures inside, unidentifiable in their crash helmets. The driver pulled off his helmet and Sylvestre's face emerged.

'I didn't know you went in for this sport,' Sylvestre said to Bruno while waving at Annette. He called across to her, 'I bet you'll be the fastest woman on the circuit. But where's George?'

'He's sick,' she replied calmly. 'Bruno stepped into the breach. He's my secret weapon. Go too fast and he'll give you a speeding ticket.'

As Sylvestre laughed and drove off, Bruno's mobile rang. He

had to release his seat belt to get to it and saw it was Fabiola.

'I'm at the funeral parlour, looking at the late Monsieur Hugon,' she said. 'I can't see much out of the ordinary but he's been dead for at least thirty-six hours, maybe more. And the undertaker washed him down and cleaned him when he arrived, so there's no body waste to examine. There's some interesting irritation around the nose and mouth and in his throat, but it could be no more than a cold. He was certainly a prime candidate for a heart attack.'

'Gelletreau was treating him for heart trouble,' said Bruno.

'I'm not in the least surprised. In fact, I'd have been surprised if he wasn't. He's very overweight and florid so he must have had high blood pressure. There are nicotine stains on his fingers so I assume he was a fairly heavy smoker. I found a bit of bruising that could easily have happened when he collapsed. Are you sure this is a suspicious death?'

'No, I'm not sure but there are some circumstantial things that worry me.' Bruno explained his doubts about the absent files and notebooks.

'I see.' She paused and then said, 'I presume you asked for an autopsy. What did J-J say?'

'He was reluctant but said to ask if you could take a look to see if you thought an autopsy was justified.'

'Not so far, it isn't. But I'll take some swabs and get back to you. Will you be at the rally, watching Annette? I may see you there.'

'You certainly will, and you may get a surprise.' He laughed, closed the phone and looked at his watch. It was noon; there would be no more time for practice laps.

46

'Tell me what happens in the real race,' he said to Annette.

'They already drew lots and we go off fifth. That's good because the track and corners won't be too badly roughed up. There are twenty-four contestants and we start at three-minute intervals. Those who finish first and second in this regional heat qualify for the national championship. Can I buy you some lunch? I need a sandwich.'

'No thank you. I think I'd lose it on the first turn.'

'Make sure you drink some water, though. We need to meet up by one thirty. Regulations require flame-retardant gear, just in case, so you'll need to change. I've got some in the back along with George's overalls, which should fit you. Can I drop you somewhere?'

'Drop me in town. Give me the clothes and I'll change in the Mairie. We can meet there later and I ought to show my face at the Alsace market first, just to say hello to the various stallholders. You could get something to eat there.'

'Good idea, but stay away from the wine kiosk,' she said with a smile. 'I want you keeping all your wits about you, so not even a taste of Riesling, please. But I'll buy you a bottle after the race.'

The midday sun was warm and the square in front of the Mairie was full of people gathered around the dozen or so stalls. Annette paused at one that was offering embroidery and lace, oven gloves and aprons with Alsace motifs. She bought a set of tea towels, murmuring to Bruno that she felt she ought to support them. Bruno leafed through a picture book at a stall run by the Alsace tourist board, recognizing one of the old concrete forts from the Maginot line that he'd visited with Thomas and Ingrid. He pointed it out to Annette.

'That's the casemate just outside the town,' Bruno said. 'It's a museum now, with a good account of the battle that took place there. The French held out for two days. You can see it had two turrets. The Germans knocked out one with artillery and the second with an attack by Stuka dive-bombers.'

'I thought it was supposed to be impregnable,' she said.

'Nothing is impregnable. The Germans simply went around it and invaded through Belgium, while half of the French army was locked up in the Maginot line, barely able to get involved in the war.'

They walked on, glancing at a stall selling Alsace sausages and cheeses, and Bruno greeted his friend Stéphane, the cheesemaker, who was tasting the wares while chatting with his visiting counterpart. The busiest stall was the one offering tastings of Riesling, Sylvaner and Pinot Gris, and Bruno heard his name called. It was Thomas, who had been recruited to help the stallholder cope with the demand.

'A glass for you, Bruno?'

Bruno gestured at Annette behind him and called back, 'Not when I'm driving.'

Annette bought herself a *flammkuchen*. Every table on Fauquet's terrace was taken, but Bruno bought two bottles of water and he and Annette walked over to the stone balcony overlooking the river. She asked about Fabiola's call, wondering whether it could mean work for her or some other magistrate. Too soon for that, Bruno said, but told her of his concerns over Hugon's death.

'Was that an overweight, elderly man, used to work for the archives in Périgueux?' she asked. Bruno nodded. 'I knew him. We hired him from time to time to do research work for cases,

48

tax issues mainly. He was a perfectionist and had a very good reputation. I can't imagine him not keeping all his notebooks up to date.'

'His wife may have ditched them to try and avoid tax claims. But she was very open about what he was being paid for the latest job and there was a thousand euros in cash in his wallet. If she was worried about taxes I think she'd have pocketed the money before I turned up.'

'I hardly think she'd have been thinking about taxes if she walked in to find her husband dead. How long were they married?'

'Over forty years.'

'And what was he working on?' Annette finished her *flamm-kuchen* and poured some of the water onto her hands before drying them with a paper napkin.

'It's not clear, but it had something to do with the war and the Resistance,' Bruno said. 'I'll check with the relevant archives and try to find out. Maybe that's where he left the missing files and notebook.'

Bruno stood up as he saw the Mayor heading towards him, waving to friends right and left as he bustled through the crowd. He began speaking from five metres away.

'I hear you're going to be taking part in the race, so good luck to you both, but a couple of things have come up,' the Mayor said. He apologized to Annette and then took Bruno's arm and led him a few steps away, his voice dropping to a murmur.

'First, there's Jérôme's amusement park – he wants to buy some land from the town to enlarge the place and put in some new attractions. Could you go see him and get an idea if it's the kind of thing we should approve? He doesn't want to go to the expense of hiring an architect and getting a survey done if it doesn't have much chance of getting past the council.'

'Understood. I'll take a look this week.'

'The other thing is that chap with the Bugatti, Sylvestre Wémy. He buttonholed me this morning to ask for my help regarding some property his grandmother left him. You know the place, that pretty *chartreuse* on the road to the St Chamassy cemetery.'

The term meant charterhouse, Bruno knew, but in this part of France it was used for a historic building that was larger than a manor house but not quite big enough to be called a château. A *chartreuse* was usually a long, low building just one room wide, seldom more than two storeys high, but sometimes there were towers at each wing and mansard windows to allow small bedrooms in the roof. Sylvestre had turned the place into several expensive apartments and then sold them, the Mayor explained. But the inheritance was divided between him and the St Denis side of the family and some kind of family feud had now developed. Sylvestre was hoping that the Mayor might find some way to resolve matters, since St Denis stood to lose the extra property taxes and the prospect of employment for gardeners and cleaners.

'You know the family, the Oudinots. He's a stubborn old devil. Could you go and see him, Bruno, and find out what the problem is from his side?'

Fernand Oudinot and his wife Odette were in their early sixties and still ran their farm raising ducks and geese; they also kept bees and a very productive walnut plantation. Bruno knew Fernand through one of the local hunting clubs and he had a soft spot for Odette. She used her own honey and nuts to make the best *tarte aux noix* in the district, and although she had shown Bruno how to make it he could never get his pastry to turn out like hers.

'I'll find out what the problem is, but I don't want to get involved in a family quarrel,' Bruno said. 'I'm too attached to Odette's *tarte aux noix*.'

'So am I,' said the Mayor. 'But I had a call from my colleague in Alsace, one mayor to another, asking if I could help. You know how it is.'

Bruno nodded, and said, 'I've got to do this rally first but I can talk to Sylvestre later and then see the Oudinots tomorrow. They're decent people. And I'll go and see Jérôme, too.'

'There's no rush on the amusement park. If you could get us a preliminary report for the next council meeting, that would be fine.' Returning to Annette, the Mayor kissed her on both cheeks as he wished her luck in the race. 'Just don't damage our town policeman. He's got too much to do.'

'I'll do my best,' she said, looking at her watch. 'And now Bruno and I have to get into our driving clothes.' They went into the Mairie to change, Bruno using his office and Annette the ladies' room. They emerged in white Nomex overalls, all but their faces covered in the material, and got some startled glances as they walked back to the car.

'Don't forget to hit the stopwatch when we start because I'll have my hand on the gearstick,' she said.

They went through the ritual of shaking hands with the other drivers before getting into the Citroën, donning their helmets and heading for their place in the queue of cars lined up at the start. The lead car took off at the marshal's signal. Bruno felt his heart pounding as they rolled forward to the starting line. He looked across at Annette, wondering if he should wish her good luck, but settled for the all-purpose French word that team members exchanged at the start of a rugby match.

'*Merde*,' he said.

'And *merde* to you,' she replied, her voice sounding odd through the headphones. A second later the marshal's arm flashed down to release them. Bruno hit the stopwatch on the dashboard and was then rammed back into his seat by the acceleration as Annette took off faster than ever before. He started to read from his roll.

'Eighty metres on tarmac then a ninety-degree left turn onto gravel.' He remembered the phrases and the sequences as she slammed the car into a skidding turn.

'Forty metres straight to a sixty-degree left turn into a dip. Watch for the bad camber . . .'

And on it went, his body lifting and then slamming back down, jerking from left to right. He tried to brace himself with his feet, pressed hard against the bulkhead. Annette's hands were clasped on the steering wheel but his were occupied by the roll. He knew when the straights were coming and, from time to time, could risk a quick glance at the road.

'Ninety-degree right turn at the bottom of this slope and onto tarmac for two hundred metres . . .'

A blur of faces marked the turn, the onlookers safely sheltered behind hay bales. They were waving but because of his helmet he could hear nothing except the howl of the motor and the new thrust as the turbo kicked in. Then almost at once she was braking for the next bend and he was telling her to watch for the tunnel after a 30-degree right turn.

He almost lost it once when the paper ballooned up and he had to use his knees to hold it down in the well of the car, but he found his place just in time to warn Annette of the next bend.

'Beware of water in the dip at the bottom of this slope then make an immediate ninety-degree left turn going into the S-bend . . .'

As she hammered the car around the sharp turn he saw from the corner of his eye another car on its side in the ditch beside the road.

Then they were through the S-bend and onto gravel. A short straight stretch rose steeply ahead and they seemed to sail through the air for a long second before slamming down and into a 60-degree left turn with a bad camber. There were more faces and hay bales and a short straight with a banner over the road and a marshal holding a chequered flag. She went past him at high speed and began braking hard as Bruno hit the stop watch. It read 15.08. Fifteen minutes and eight seconds. Annette had said they would have to beat fifteen minutes in order to win.

6

'Great job, you're in the lead,' said a large middle-aged man with a beard, opening Annette's door and hauling her out into an embrace. Beside him was a slender youth on crutches, one leg in a cast.

'*Bonjour* Marcel, *bonjour* Fabrice,' said Annette. She took off her helmet and turned to introduce Bruno, who was still trying to sort out the tangle of his paper roll. At last he had it neatly folded back, took off his helmet, released his safety belts and clambered out. He felt light-headed and his legs were still trembling from the strain of bracing them throughout the race. He leaned against the car and waved at the two strangers, not quite up to the expected handshakes and polite greetings.

'This is Bruno, he stepped into the breach when my navigator got sick. It's his first rally,' Annette said. 'Bruno, this is Marcel, the garage owner, whose car this is, and this is his son Fabrice, who should really be driving.'

'I don't think I could do that course in fifteen-eight,' said the young man. 'You were great.' He looked at Bruno. 'Your first ride? *Chapeau.*'

'It was the car,' Annette said. 'All that power, great brakes and perfectly tuned.'

She turned to look at the large blackboard on which the times of each car were marked. They were mostly around 15.15 and one was 15.20. 15.10 was the nearest to their time. Marcel handed Bruno a water bottle and he drank gratefully, aware of other drivers and navigators in overalls staring at him curiously. He recognized one of the drivers from a rugby match in Limoges, and another one waved at him, the son of one of the big wine growers in Bergerac. Bruno waved in return and then spotted the slight figure of Félix, edging through the crowd and looking shifty as he avoided Bruno's eye.

Another car jumped over the hill towards them and raced for the finish line. Fabrice clicked the button on his stopwatch and called across, 'Fifteen-thirteen.'

'That's Montjoie over there with the blonde girl in the red jacket,' said Marcel, pointing into the distance. 'He made the national championships last year and he did fifteen-ten, so now you and Annette are the team to beat.'

'It was all Annette,' said Bruno. 'I was just a passenger. Jesus, I feel too old for this sport.'

'You're the cop in St Denis,' Marcel said. It wasn't a question. 'Was this really your first race?'

'And my last,' said Bruno.

'Not if you qualify in this heat,' Marcel replied. 'If you get into the national finals, it has to be with the same team that qualified.'

Damn Annette, thought Bruno. She hadn't told him that. 'No exceptions?' he asked, hopefully.

'Death, serious illness with a medical certificate, military orders, that's about it.'

'Then I'll just have to hope there are faster cars to come.'

'There's one who can beat you, maybe two more, and only two teams qualify.'

As Marcel spoke, Annette came around to Bruno's side of the car to hug him. He knew her well but was momentarily startled as he remembered how small she was, the top of her head barely reaching his chin. Somehow in the course of the last few hours she seemed to have grown in his mind as she demonstrated her mastery at the wheel.

Another car came across the finish line. This time the marshal at the blackboard wrote down '15.11.'

'We're still leading,' she said, looking up at him gleefully.

'Does that mean I can go and change?'

'Sorry, no. If there's a dead heat we might have to do it again. That shouldn't happen, though, because the marshals time us to tenths of a second.'

Bruno was aware of his name being called and saw a group of his friends, Thomas and Ingrid, Gilles and Pamela, Jack Crimson and his daughter Miranda, waving at him from behind the hay bales at the finish line and giving him thumbs-up. He waved back and then the Mayor was at his side.

'I hear you're in the lead,' he said.

'I'm counting on you to get me some military orders to save me from having to do this again,' Bruno replied. 'Apparently that's the only acceptable excuse, apart from death or serious injury. And shouldn't you be behind those protective hay bales with the others?'

'Rank has its privileges, Bruno. And here's the inevitable Philippe Delaron with his camera.'

With the ease of a practised politician, the Mayor insinu-
ated himself into the photo for *Sud Ouest*, Annette between the
two men, and then Philippe came forward with his notepad
as another car came over the finishing line. The marshal had
just finished writing '15.12' when he clutched at his waist and
pulled out a mobile phone. He listened briefly and then shouted,
'Ambulance,' and began clanging a bell.

'Sector seven, the corner by the sawmill at Petit-Paris, a car's
gone into a tree,' he shouted moments later at the emergency
vehicle from the St Denis fire station. Leaning out of the window
of the *urgences* vehicle, Ahmed waved acknowledgement. One of
the two full-timers on the mainly volunteer team of firefighters,
Ahmed was the senior medic. He put on his siren and roared off,
not quite as fast as the rally cars but still at a very impressive
speed. Philippe ran to his own car and followed Ahmed, again
at a speed that Bruno would have found terrifying before today.
Lespinasse followed in his tow truck.

'Don't worry,' Annette said to Bruno. 'You saw the roll bars
and security cages in the car. It's unusual for anyone to be hurt.'

The marshals halted the remaining half-dozen cars lined up
for their own runs. Last in line was Sylvestre's Volkswagen. To
Bruno's surprise, Sylvestre was the navigator and his Indian
friend Freddy was at the wheel. As he looked, Sylvestre turned,
caught his eye and gave a casual wave before rolling down the
window and calling for Annette. She strolled across, bent to
listen, smiled and backed away with a wave.

'He was just paying us a compliment on our run,' she said
when she returned.

'I'm surprised he's not driving,' said Bruno. 'He seemed to

be the kind of man who'd want to be in the driver's seat. And he was pretty quick when he caught up with us this morning.'

'Sylvestre is very good but Freddy's better. He came in second in last year's desert rally in Qatar. That's a big international event with serious prize money. And a team is a team – either one can drive. The navigator is formally known as the co-driver. That's why I could race after Fabrice broke his leg.'

'And I gather that you're stuck with me if we do qualify,' said Bruno.

'I doubt that we will. Fifteen-eight isn't really good enough. And the best we can hope for is to qualify in second place. Freddy's bound to win. Even if he weren't such a top driver with a big corporate sponsor, he's going to be the last car to race, which means he knows what time he has to beat. That's a real advantage.'

'What do you mean, a big corporate sponsor? What has that to do with how he races?'

She gestured at a large truck in the parking lot across the road with a big VW logo on its side. 'That's his support team with mechanics, spare parts and different sets of tyres for the various conditions. There's even a guy with a radio to tell him the times of the drivers who set off just ahead of him. These rally championships are big business, Bruno. Marcel isn't paying for this car himself; he's got Citroën behind him. You must have seen the Citroën advertising after they won the world rally championship. Victories sell cars.'

Bruno nodded, understanding that he was involved in something much bigger than he'd assumed when Annette had first appealed to him that morning. There was big business here and serious money, a great deal of organization and a whole subculture built around the rallies.

Suddenly, electronic feedback howled across the assembly area as the marshal at the blackboard started speaking into a megaphone. He adjusted it and the howl died. 'No injuries,' he said. 'Driver and co-driver are unhurt. The car cannot be driven so number seventeen is scratched. The race resumes.'

'What about the cars that were already on the track before the crash?' Bruno asked Annette.

'They'll have been waved down by the marshals and now they'll have to come back and run again, once the tow truck has cleared the route.'

Marcel came up to them, his mobile phone at his ear. He said 'Thanks' into the mouthpiece and looked solemnly at Annette.

'I'm not sure you're going to qualify,' he said. 'I have a friend stationed on the course with a stopwatch. Number eighteen, Rostand from Toulouse, was two seconds ahead of your time at the halfway point. Villeneuve from Cahors, number nineteen, matched your time. They're two good drivers, both in Citroëns like yours, and then there's the VW team.'

'And it usually helps to run again,' said Annette, looking crest-fallen. Marcel shrugged.

'Come on, let's take a stroll, see our friends,' said Bruno, taking Annette's arm. 'Until all the results are in, there's nothing we can do but wait.'

Reluctantly, she followed across the assembly area to the hay bales where their friends were gathered with steaming mugs. Bruno could smell cinnamon and cloves.

'I know it's not cold but Miranda thought it would be fun

to make some mulled wine,' said Crimson, holding up a large thermos flask. 'You're in the lead so you deserve some.'

'Thanks, but not yet,' said Annette. 'If there's a dead heat we may have to race again and there are some very good drivers to come.'

The marshal brought up the next car to the starting line and waved the flag to commence the run. Now Sylvestre and Freddy were no longer last in line; the three cars that had interrupted their runs because of the crash had returned to take their places at the rear. Bruno heard Fabiola and Miranda asking Annette what had happened to her English co-driver, the three women drifting away to talk among themselves. Good, thought Bruno, it will distract Annette from watching the clock.

'Do you know your face was absolutely white when Annette pulled up after her race?' Gilles asked. 'You looked like you were going to be sick.'

'I very nearly was.' With half an ear, Bruno could hear the women murmuring, picking up individual words and phrases, like 'migraine' and 'handsome' and 'serious' and 'up to him'. They were evidently talking about Annette's new boyfriend.

The next car started badly, wheels spinning as the driver used too much throttle. He must have lost a second or two.

Annette called across to Bruno. 'The start is getting chewed up. We'll have to watch that if we're told to race again.'

'Where did Annette learn to drive like that?' Crimson asked.

'Madagascar, when she was working for Médecins Sans Frontières,' said Bruno, thinking that the mulled wine smelled very inviting. 'But I think she has a gift; it seems to come naturally to her.'

At three-minute intervals, the remaining cars took off, a little slower than the earlier ones, the drivers cautious after seeing the first wheelspin. Then they began to come over the hill to the finish line. The first one was clocked at 15.10, the next one was 15.09, and then Freddy in his VW hit 15.03, beating Annette's time by five seconds. The VW pulled over and Sylvestre and Freddy clambered out, their fists pumping the air, and ran to embrace one another at the front of their car.

Annette was still in second place, but then the last car of all now passed the finish line, timed at 15.08. The marshals began to confer. Annette had one hand to her mouth, the other hand clutching Fabiola's arm. Bruno felt himself being caught up in her excitement. Would they have to race again?

Sylvestre strolled across to join them. Bruno shook his hand and murmured congratulations. Annette was now bouncing up and down on her toes as she waited for the marshals to act. Finally one of them turned to the blackboard. Annette's name remained in second place as the marshal filled in the tenths of a second. Annette had been timed at 15.08.2. Her rival for the vital second place came in at 15.08.4.

'We did it!' she screamed and turned to jump into Bruno's arms, her small body trembling with emotion as she planted a smacking kiss on his cheek. 'We're in the national championship!'

Bruno forced himself to smile as he hugged her and pretended to be delighted, although inside he felt a foreboding that was mixed with dismay. Once had been more than enough. Their friends clustered around slapping them on the back and cheering. Philippe Delaron was taking more photos.

'Thanks,' Bruno said to Crimson. 'I hope there's enough of

that mulled wine left in the thermos for me to have a glass or two. In fact, give me two glasses, there's someone I should talk to.'

He took the glasses across to Sylvestre, who was leaning against his VW, eyes closed and head back, enjoying the last of the autumn sun.

'Congratulations again,' said Bruno and handed him a glass. 'Where's your partner?'

'Freddy is in the marshals' tent doing the paperwork.' He took the wine, sniffed it, sipped and then nodded his thanks.

'I heard from the Mayor that you're having some problems with your property here and he's asked if I could look into it, see if we could help.'

'I'd be very grateful,' Sylvestre said, his manner suddenly businesslike. 'There's one of those foolish family feuds that's made worse by jealousy. My grandmother had a brother and they shared the family property here when their parents died. It's a pleasant little château with about fifteen hectares of land. Since my grandmother moved to Alsace when she married, she couldn't use the farm and she agreed with her brother to split the estate. She got the *chartreuse* and garden and her brother, my great-uncle Thibaut, got all the land. She didn't bother to get a formal easement from her brother giving her a right of way onto the property.'

Bruno nodded sympathetically, thinking he could guess what was coming.

'It was fine as long as Thibaut was alive, but when Thibaut's son Fernand learned that our side of the family was becoming wealthy through property investments, relations cooled a bit.

When my grandmother died it got worse. Fernand asked for the return of some of the family furniture she'd brought to Alsace when she got married. Naturally we discussed it the next time we came down to stay at the house. We were very polite and friendly but we said no. Our grandmother had wanted the furniture to stay with her grandchildren. The family feud began and pretty soon it began to escalate. You know Fernand keeps geese?'

Bruno nodded. 'So do I, just a couple. They're pretty common in the countryside around here.'

'Yes, but they're very noisy. When we said no, Fernand moved a couple of hundred geese to within about five metres of the back of our house, on land that was his. They started cackling just after dawn and it went on all day until nightfall. That was the end of our vacation, and for about ten years we didn't bother coming down here. But on principle we determined to keep the house. We paid the taxes and then five years ago my mother came down for the twin town reunion, staying at a hotel. She went to see the house and hired a local company to come and do maintenance, repaint the place, repair the roof and so on. She tried to see Fernand but he wouldn't let her into his house.

'Two years ago, I came down with her and saw the possibility of converting the house into three really nice residences, selling them and washing our hands of the place and of the other branch of the family. My mother refused. It was her family inheritance. She died last year and I telephoned Fernand to invite him to the funeral but he slammed the phone down on me. Then I wrote to him, saying what I proposed and that I'd send the builders in, put a swimming pool where the vegetables used to be and fix up the garden. He wrote back saying he had no objection to any building works I proposed. So I wrote thanking him and went ahead, putting over a hundred thousand euros into the conversion. When I came down this time with Freddy, I parked the car, unpacked and went to see Fernand, hoping that we'd be putting the feud behind us.'

'But it didn't work out like that.'

'No, he met me on his doorstep, didn't invite me in, and then gave me a nasty smile as if he'd been looking forward to this moment. He asked how I intended to sell these conversions when he wouldn't allow any of the new owners to cross his land to get to the place. That was when I found out there was no right of way.'

'He can't stop you getting access to your land.'

'He doesn't have to. I can use a small and very narrow dirt track, but I can't sell them as luxury holiday homes if that's the only way in. And then this morning, Fernand fired the second barrel. The geese are back.'

7

When Annette came back from the caravan that served as the office for the rally, she was hanging onto the arm of George Young, who was beaming, evidently delighted at her success. He seemed to have recovered from his migraine, if that was what had caused him to miss the race, and shook Bruno's hand to congratulate him.

'This calls for a celebration,' he said. 'My treat – but where can we go around here, Bruno?'

'Didn't the Mayor say there was going to be a special *marché nocturne* tonight, in honour of the race?' Annette asked. 'I'm sure lots of the other drivers will be there so I wouldn't mind going.'

'I've never been to one,' said Young. 'Let's do it.'

This was fine with Bruno, who had been a fan since the first night market had been launched nearby in the hilltop village of Audrix. The local farmers were invited on Saturday evenings in summer to sell their produce from stalls erected around the village square, which the Mairie filled with tables and benches for the public. It had begun modestly with pâtés, salads and strawberries, foie gras and cheeses, a stall that grilled steaks and lamb chops, and another selling wine by the bottle. It proved highly popular with the locals as well as tourists and quickly expanded to include *haricots couennes*, beans cooked with pork rind, as well as pommes frites, omelettes and soups. Then a local farm began offering snails in their shells with butter and garlic and the Mairie rebuilt the village's old stone baking oven in the village square to produce fresh bread and pizzas. By the end of the first season, local bands and singers were performing, there was a donkey cart to take children around the village and it was hard to find a place at the tables. By the second year, half the villages of the Périgord were offering similar events.

St Denis, never a town to rush into things, watched and waited. Bruno and the Mayor and their friends sampled the other markets, observed what worked and what didn't, and carefully planned their own version. They didn't want loud rock music since they had learned that the diners liked to hear themselves talk. They decided to offer folk singers, jazz groups and ballads until ten o'clock and then a disco took over so people could dance. Bruno and the Mayor had tasted the cheap plonk sold at inflated prices in other markets, so they insisted on offering only good local wines and kept a close eye on the prices. With the local butcher they set up a proper barbecue that produced steaks, lamb, chicken and fish. Huge cauldrons were brought in to cook *moules marinières* and paellas. Bruno persuaded his friend Stéphane to bring his cheese stall, the Vinhs to offer their Asian food, and Fauquet to keep his café open until midnight and to make vast quantities of his own ice cream.

They had brought Florence into their plans from the beginning, since she had persuaded the local education authorities that the best way to teach environmental sciences was to have schoolchildren run their own small farm at the *collège*.

It was doing well enough to provide the night market with eggs, chickens, tomatoes, courgettes and lettuces. Florence also insisted on proper plates, glasses and cutlery rather than the plastic forks and paper plates and arranged for the use of the *collège*'s industrial dish washers. The older schoolchildren earned pocket money for setting up the tables and benches in the town square. Since Florence reckoned that the children should learn to prepare the food they grew, she had set up a voluntary cooking class in the *collège* kitchens after school hours. Now the youngsters had their own stall offering the pâtés, lemon tarts, apple pies and brownies they had made.

Bruno was happy to agree. He was proud of the town's night market and had been planning to take his guests from Alsace. 'It's a warm enough evening,' he said. Usually the events were held in the tourist season of June, July and August, but this was an unusually warm autumn.

'And it's going to be a spectacular sunset,' said Young, looking at the scattered low clouds in the west, already touched with pink and gold as the sun began its slow decline.

'We arrange those specially for occasions like this,' came a new voice, and Yveline from the Gendarmerie joined them, embracing Annette and adding her own congratulations. She was in uniform, with the two white stripes of a lieutenant on her shoulders. 'You'll have to show me how to drive like that.'

'Please don't,' said Bruno. 'My nerves couldn't stand it.' He introduced her to George Young as Annette's friend. 'Are you on duty this evening or can you join us at the *marché nocturne* in town?'

'I'm on duty but I can take a meal break, and I'd probably

take a stroll around the market anyway.' She glanced at Bruno's fire-retardant driving clothes, smiling as she raised an eyebrow. 'Will you change or will you be eating disguised as a snowman?'

'You're right, I've got to change, but first I'd better tell my friends from Alsace where we'll be. You'll enjoy meeting him, Yveline. He's another *flic*, municipal police like me.'

'*Merde*,' she said, rolling her eyes. 'Just what we need, another cop like you.'

After calling his friends, Bruno steered Young towards Monique's, the new wine bar on the Rue de Paris, to wait while he and Annette changed in the Mairie. As they came out, they ran into Florence, who was supervising her pupils as they unloaded crockery and cutlery along with some of their pies and pâtés from the back of her car. Annette invited her to join their table for dinner.

'I'd love to. Another of my pupils is babysitting my kids this evening,' Florence replied. 'But I may have to be up and down a bit since I'm supposed to keep an eye on the youngsters.'

'I may have to take a turn at barbecue duty,' said Bruno, glancing across to where Valentin, the town butcher, was manning the grill. The tables in the square were beginning to fill and Florence and Yveline sat at one to reserve places for them all. Annette and Young went to collect plates, glasses and cutlery from the stall run by Florence's pupils. Bruno bought a bottle of white wine and another of red from Raoul at the town vineyard's stall and took them to the table where Thomas and Ingrid had just arrived. He introduced them to Yveline and went to place an order for the meat.

Young joined Bruno at the barbecue, carrying plates and

insisting on paying the bill. 'I've ordered a small steak and a lamb chop for each of us, but chicken for Annette,' Bruno said.

When they returned to the table with the loaded plates, the Baron had joined them, bringing a double portion of mussels cooked in white wine for the table to share. Yveline had already bought salad and *pommes frites* for everyone and Florence had ordered apple pies for dessert. Bruno poured the wine and offered a toast to Annette. Thomas went for more wine and Ingrid came back from Stéphane's stall with some goat cheese and Cantal.

'What's it like, being married to a policeman?' Florence asked Ingrid. 'Do you worry about what might happen to him?'

'Of course. But it's what he wants to do, or rather, he did, until these new rules and management systems came in. Now they have targets and quotas for arrests and Thomas agrees with Bruno that's no way to judge police efficiency. He's thinking of taking early retirement.'

'He's not the only one,' Yveline chimed in. 'They're turning us into not much more than traffic cops, with a set number of arrests to make each month or you get marked down on your annual efficiency report. That's not why I joined the gendarmes. It's all right for Bruno, he works for the Mayor, who likes the way Bruno operates. He hardly ever has to make an arrest.'

'That can work in a small town like St Denis where I know everybody,' said Bruno. 'It wouldn't work in a big city.'

On the stage, Arlette, a newcomer to St Denis who had recently joined the Mairie as an accountant, was adjusting the microphone as she settled on a stool and began to play some classical guitar music. The sun was setting, streaks of rosy pink and red alternating with the scattered lines of cloud, and the old stone of the Mairie had turned into a rich gold. It was that brief moment of twilight before someone turned on the lamps over the diners, and Bruno murmured to himself one of his favourite words.

'*Crépuscule*,' he said as he looked at the red sheen of the setting sun on the bend of the river, not aware that he had spoken aloud until the Baron repeated it back to him.

'*Crépuscule*, one of the loveliest words in our language, for one of the loveliest times of day just as it gives way to night,' the Baron said softly, gazing at the shifting planes of red and crimson light on the river. 'Sitting here, with wine and food and surrounded by friends as generations must have done before us in this very place, makes all the world's troubles seem very far away. Sometimes I imagine the prehistoric people sitting here on the river bank, sharing their roast mammoth or whatever it was, and watching the sun go down just like us.' He raised his glass. 'I drink to them, whoever they were.'

'I never thought of you as such a romantic,' said Bruno.

'When you get to my age, you'll realize that we men are the real romantics. Women are much more practical; they have to be.' The Baron paused, turning his head to look at the stage. 'Who is this girl playing guitar? She's good.'

Bruno explained, and as he spoke, Arlette ended the piece, put down her guitar and picked up a lute. She was a tall, slim young woman but seemed to have a wiry strength. She bent to raise the microphone higher and announced she intended to play an old medieval song by one of the troubadours of the region, Bertran de Born, a twelfth-century knight who had been lord of the castle of Hautefort. She began to pick out a delicate but haunting melody on the lute.

Suddenly to the surprise of all at the table Young rose to his feet and began to sing in a fine tenor voice, but in a language that Bruno could not understand, although it seemed distantly familiar. He heard the Baron mutter that it was old Occitan, but then all fell silent as Young sang through to the end, Annette gazing up at him entranced and then bursting into applause, in which other tables joined. Ingrid called out 'Bravo,' and Valentin the butcher banged his tongs against the grill and demanded an encore.

'Another?' Arlette called down to him from the stage.

'*Mon chan fenisc ab dol et ab maltraire,*' Young called back, and she nodded and began to play again, a slower song that sounded like a lament.

Bruno had applauded politely with the rest, but while he respected the antiquity of the music and the tradition it represented, it was not much to his taste. Annette clearly delighted in it and in Young, but except for their common interest in motor sports he seemed an unlikely partner for her. Annette was fair-haired, slim and pretty and looked much younger than her years. Bruno would have thought Young was the type to be attracted by a more dramatic, assertive type of woman, one of those leggy blondes who liked fast cars and discos. Maybe there was more to him than that, but again Bruno wondered if Young knew of Annette's father's wealth.

'Where did you learn that?' Annette asked as Young sat down, kissing him on his cheek. 'You were brilliant.'

'I read Romantic Languages at university, and Bertran de Born was required reading,' Young said, laughing as he picked up his wine glass. 'I'm not a great fan, all that glorifying of wars and battles and how he loved to fight and see men die. One of his poems was about Richard Lionheart, to tell him there was too much peace about and it was time for some more battles.'

'We have an early start tomorrow to get back to Alsace, so for us it's time for some sleep,' said Thomas, rising. 'Thank you all for a very fine weekend and you'll always be welcome to visit us.'

8

Bruno was in his office after saying goodbye the next morning to Thomas and his wife before they set off on the long drive home to Alsace. He was going through routine paperwork when his desk phone rang. Grateful for the interruption, he answered and recognized the voice of the manager of the local supermarket.

'Another shoplifting case, caught on the security camera,' Bruno heard. 'You can probably guess the identity of the youngster who did it?'

'Félix again?' Bruno said with a sigh.

'Right, and as you know, it's not his first time. We're holding him here in my office with our security guy and we'll wait for you.'

'I have to contact his father first, then the youth services people. You know the rules for juveniles, whatever your cameras might show.'

'I know these damn rules only too well, Bruno. How are we supposed to deter these youngsters if we treat them with kid gloves?'

'Come off it, Simon. You've got the lowest shoplifting rate in the *département*. I'll be there as soon as I can. What was he stealing?'

'A set of stereo headphones.'

To double-check on Félix's age, Bruno first went to the dusty room filled with old files that the Mayor called his archive and pulled out the large ledger that recorded the town's births and deaths. He saw that Félix would not be sixteen for another ten days and, as Bruno suspected, he had to be treated as a minor. He returned to his office and called the youth services in Périgueux but no one was available to talk to him. The receptionist said they were overworked and understaffed and he should use someone from the social services at his own Mairie to sit in for the preliminary questioning. Bruno called Roberte from the Sécu team to ask if she was free to join him.

The rules on dealing with minors were strict and on the whole Bruno thought they made sense. The magistrate who usually dealt with juvenile cases was Annette, as the most junior in the office. He called her and explained. Her office was in Sarlat but she was in a meeting with a lawyer in Les Eyzies. She could join him at the supermarket within the hour.

Félix's father wasn't at home but Bruno knew he could find him in the town's second café, which had off-track betting and TV sets permanently tuned to horse racing. He rounded up the father and Roberte from the Mairie and headed for the supermarket.

Félix was slumped on a chair in the corner of the upstairs office. He was wearing jeans that were too short for him, an old denim jacket and a T-shirt. His trainers had seen better days, one sole repaired with duct tape. The security man, Bertrand, whom Bruno knew from the rugby club, was standing over the boy. He was wearing a single earphone in one ear with a flesh-coloured wire leading from it and disappearing under his collar. That was new, thought Bruno. Simon, the manager, was behind his desk. Four TV screens on the wall showed images from the security cameras. A fifth TV stood on a filing cabinet.

Félix looked up at the new arrivals, his lip curling in a sneer at the sight of Bruno and his father. Bruno tried to remember what it had been like to be almost sixteen, and to have no money when prosperous schoolmates were buying CDs and fashionable clothes and seemed to have endless supplies of one-franc pieces to put into pinball machines.

'You should be at school, Félix,' he began after the usual greetings. 'Would you like to tell me what happened?'

Félix shrugged and turned away to look out of the window.

'Answer the policeman, you little jerk,' said Félix's father, stepping forward aggressively. Bruno put a restraining hand on his arm.

'Simon, do you have a statement?' he asked.

'Mine and our security guard's statements are already typed up, signed and witnessed,' said Simon, handing the sheets of paper across his desk, confident in his familiarity with the procedure. 'You realize that I have no latitude in these cases. Company policy is that all shoplifters must be pursued to the limit of the law. And it's not the first time with this kid. I've made a copy of the video tape for you, but let's take a look at it.'

The TV screen on the filing cabinet flickered into life, showing a washed-out image of the aisle containing CDs, DVDs and electronic equipment.

'We have one fixed camera here and another for alcohol, since they're the two high-value zones. The other cameras are on swivels so they can monitor different aisles,' Simon explained. 'The boy came in just as we opened at eight-thirty, when there's always a bit of a rush, as he well knows. He probably thought he could slink out without us spotting him.'

'I wanted to get to school,' said Félix in a low voice, the first time he had spoken. He was looking out of the window at the parked cars as if these proceedings had nothing to do with him. His arms were folded protectively across his chest.

The screen showed a modest throng of shoppers walking along the main aisle, and then a thin youngster peeled off and went into the electronics aisle, straight to a section with stereo headphones. He pulled down three or four, examining them in turn. Then he turned his back to the camera while appearing to replace the headphones, walked quickly to the end of the aisle and turned left past the microwaves and coffee-making machines.

'I was watching the camera, spotted Félix and thought he was behaving suspiciously,' said Simon, reading aloud from his own copy of his written statement. Bruno recognized the wording. It came straight from the template given to all the store managers by the company's legal office.

'So I used the radio to alert Bertrand, the security guard, who was standing by the entrance. When Félix walked through the checkout without paying, Bertrand stopped him and asked him to come to the office. The boy tried to run out of the store but Bertrand caught him by his jacket and these headphones fell from under his arm where he'd hidden them. The retail price is €39.99. Bertrand then made a citizen's arrest and we called you at once.'

'Anything to say, Félix?' Bruno asked.

'Ask him why I took that brand of headphones,' said the boy, still gazing at the world beyond the window.

Bruno looked questioningly at Simon, who shrugged. 'Maybe he liked the colour. I don't know.'

'Is it the best brand or the most expensive?'

'No, it's a mid-price model. Some are over a hundred euros.'

'Why did you take that brand, Félix?' Bruno asked.

'Because it was the brand I used to have. I bought them here a week ago with money that I earned chopping wood. Ask my mother, she'll tell you.'

His father grunted something that might have been agreement. Bruno knew that Félix's mother worked at weekends cleaning houses, as well as cleaning at the *collège* during the week. He could imagine that the boy's only pocket money would come from odd jobs he found through his mother.

'So what happened to your old earphones?'

Félix continued to stare out the window. 'Tell him to ask his son.'

The plot thickens, thought Bruno. Simon's son, Tristan, was the same age as Félix but one class ahead at the *collège*, since Félix had been held back a year to resit after failing his exams. Tristan was big for his age, a forward on the school rugby team that Bruno trained. He was strikingly good-looking, with clear skin and curly fair hair. When he began playing rugby his mother had badgered Bruno about the game being too rough and could Bruno guarantee that her son's features would not get damaged. But Tristan's manners did not match his looks. He was brash, noisy, and inclined to throw his weight about. Bruno had warned him several times about dirty play and he'd noticed that while most of the good young rugby players seemed popular with the local girls, Tristan was an exception. They steered clear of him. Bruno looked quizzically at Simon, whose face had gone red.

'Let's talk privately,' Bruno said, and led Simon out into the corridor and then to the staircase where they would be out of earshot.

'Could Tristan be involved in this in some way?' he asked. 'I'm trying to understand why Félix said we should ask him about the earphones.'

'I don't see how,' Simon replied. He wouldn't meet Bruno's eye.

'Has Tristan got earphones of his own?'

'Yes, a much better set, he got them for his birthday.' Simon paused and then sighed. 'But I confiscated them last week because he wasn't doing his homework.' He looked up at Bruno. 'When they get to that age, it's not easy to discipline them.'

Bruno nodded sympathetically. Simon was a slim man, shorter than Bruno, and about the same height as his wife. She was a good-looking but burly woman, an aggressive tennis player with a loud voice who seemed to change her hair style and colour almost every week. Their son took after her, rather than Simon. Tristan was already bigger than his father and probably stronger.

'So if I went to the *collège* and searched Tristan, do you think it's possible that I'd find Félix's earphones on him?'

'Look, Bruno, this kid Félix has been in trouble with the law before. My son has never been caught doing anything wrong. You'd have no right to do that, none at all.'

'I know your son. I'm his rugby coach and I've seen him behaving badly on the field too many times. It's very unusual

78

for anyone to be sent off in *collège* games but it happened to him twice last season. You know I've threatened to drop him from the team unless he starts to control himself?'

'No, I didn't know that,' Simon said, sounding tired.

'Do you think your son is a bully?'

'It's just his age, high spirits, he'll settle down.'

'Let's hope you're right,' Bruno said. 'But it looks to me as if your son took Félix's headphones and Félix came in today to replace them from the store run by Tristan's father. He might even have seen it as a kind of justice. Does that sound plausible to you?'

'It was still shoplifting, and anyway, the procedure has started. We can't drop it now.'

'Of course you can. I can take care of Bertrand and Roberte from the Mairie. Even if you go ahead, Félix is still a few days short of sixteen. As far as the law is concerned he's a juvenile, so nothing is going to happen to him, except that the very word "justice" will leave a nasty taste in his mouth. But he's not going to get off lightly. I'll go back in there, take him home with his dad, put the fear of God into him and search his room. If there's any more evidence of shoplifting, I'll throw the book at him.'

'What about Tristan?'

'You're his dad, that's up to you,' said Bruno. 'But if you want to go ahead and press charges against Félix, I think I've got reasonable cause to haul your son out of his classroom and search him for those headphones. That would be a case of theft, probably theft with threats of violence. And your son has passed his sixteenth birthday, so in the eyes of the law he's an adult. Do you really want me to do that?'

Simon closed his eyes, his mouth working. He seemed about to speak but then stopped himself and clenched his jaw.

Bruno decided to use his last weapon. He spoke so quietly that it was almost a whisper. 'I don't think your wife would like that.'

Simon took a deep breath, looked at Bruno and shrugged. 'Okay, I'll drop the charges. And I'll pay for the headphones. But if that kid ever comes in this store again, we'll film his every move.'

'You're right,' said Bruno, knowing it was time to leave Simon with some shred of self-respect. 'And I'll make sure Félix knows that. And we both know you're doing the right thing, Simon. You're a good man.' Bruno slapped him gently on the shoulder. 'I'll take him off now and search his room and make sure he never gives you reason to regret this.'

'Regret what?' came a familiar voice and the sound of high heels on stairs as Annette appeared. She was wearing her usual working uniform of dark blue suit and white blouse buttoned to the neck, a black leather briefcase in one hand.

She greeted Bruno and held out her hand to Simon. 'Monsieur,' she said.

'Congratulations on your success in the rally, Mademoiselle,' Simon said. 'I saw the report in the paper today. But your photo did not do you justice.'

'Whereas mine showed me scared to death,' said Bruno, smiling. 'I think we're almost done here, Annette. Simon here, the store manager, has decided not to proceed with charges against the boy. But I thought you and I should at least visit his home and see if there's any evidence of other thefts. I can explain the details later.'

He led the way back to Simon's office, introduced Annette, thanked Bertrand and Roberte and said he'd drop her back at the Mairie now that the magistrate was present. No need, she said, she'd take the opportunity to do some shopping. Félix was staring wide-eyed at Annette, as if awed to be in her presence. He must know about her success in the rally, Bruno thought. He took Bertrand aside and said the store manager would explain the agreement they'd reached. Bruno turned back to inform Félix and his father that he and the magistrate were going to search Félix's room at home. He showed everyone out into the corridor, picking up the set of headphones from Simon's desk and slipping them into his pocket as he said to Simon, 'Since you're paying for them . . .'

Bruno took Félix's father in his police van and Annette followed with Félix. Bruno used the drive to explain that he'd persuaded the store to drop charges on account of Félix's age but on the condition that there was no other evidence of shoplifting.

'He's a bit of a handful, that boy,' said his father, lighting a cigarette as they drove. He had lit one earlier as soon as they were out of the supermarket. Bruno plucked it from his hand and threw it out of the partly open window. 'Not in a police van,' he said. The man shrugged, coughed and opened the window fully to spit. 'His mother can handle him but he never listens to me.'

'Maybe that's because you don't have a job and you're never at home, always in the café,' said Bruno.

'There aren't any damn jobs, not for someone my age, not anymore.'

'Your wife finds work to do, and so does Félix. Lots of old

81

people would pay a few euros to get their wood chopped, their gardens taken care of.'

'Is this about me or about my son?'

'Both. If your son is getting into trouble, and we both know it's not the first time, it's your job to take an interest. You could steer him back onto the straight and narrow, set him a good example. What was your job when you worked?'

'Storeman at the sawmill, until they closed it. I had that job for nearly thirty years, ever since I came out of military service.'

'Which unit were you in?'

'Infantry, 110th regiment, based in Germany at Baden-Baden.'

Bruno had been based there for a few months after finishing basic training, before he went on the course for the combat engineers. There had been over fifty thousand French troops stationed there at the time, including the headquarters of two army corps before the army finally withdrew from German soil in 1999.

'Not a bad posting,' said Bruno. 'Did they give you conscripts the extra money for being outside of France?'

'Not much, but yes, a few of those Deutschmarks. I remember a bar we used to go to, Chez Hannes it was called, run by a big German guy who'd been in the Foreign Legion, always ready to tell a few war stories. He'd been in Indo-China and Algeria.'

'I've been there,' Bruno said, remembering. 'If I remember rightly Hannes was as bald as a badger but he had one of those big handlebar moustaches and he'd sing "Le Boudin" when he got drunk.'

'That's right, the old Legionnaires' marching song. *Putain*, I

can see the old bastard now with all those tattoos on his arms.'
He laughed, his eyes lively as he remembered. 'Hard as nails,
Hannes was. You should have seen him throwing people out
when there was a fight. I wouldn't have wanted to be on the
wrong end of one of his punches.'

They drew up outside Félix's home, an old public housing
block of four stories and no elevator.

'Did you ever tell Félix about those days, what it was like
when you were young and in the army? He'd probably be
interested.'

The man looked sideways at Bruno, then nodded grudgingly
before climbing out of the car and lighting another cigarette.
Bruno sighed as Annette parked behind him. He'd talk to the
manager of the retirement home, see if there were any odd jobs
that could be found for an unemployed ex-soldier.

Félix had a small room to himself. It contained a single bed,
a small chest of drawers, a rickety card table and a chair. The
floor was covered in linoleum, holes patched with duct tape.
Two hooks on the back of the door provided the only place
to hang clothes. On the walls was an array of photos cut from
magazines of sports cars and horses. There was no laptop, no
radio, and Bruno knew Félix was one of the few *collège* students
without a mobile phone. The room smelled stale with an overlay
of dirty socks. Bruno checked the drawers and found T-shirts and
threadbare underwear, another pair of jeans. One drawer contained about a dozen apples and the waste-paper basket revealed
several cores. On the card table was a pile of schoolbooks and
beside them two dog-eared issues of *Cheval* magazine, lacking

their covers. Bruno looked up; the covers had been attached to the wall with sticky tape.

'Obviously he likes horses and cars,' said Annette, looking around. She closed the door behind her. 'Are you going to tell me what happened here? I'm called to a shoplifting case with a juvenile and suddenly it's all dropped.'

Bruno explained and brought out the headphones. 'Do you think I should give them back to him?'

'No, I think you should get the bully to return Félix's own phones. In the circumstances, you're pushing your legal rights in searching this boy's room. If the father hadn't allowed you inside I think I'd have stopped you. And I don't see any evidence of other shoplifting here, except maybe those apples.'

'You're right. But this kid is going to get into more trouble unless somebody sets him straight, and pretty soon. Next time he'll face juvenile detention,' Bruno said. Annette made a face, evidently disapproving of the tougher new laws Sarkozy had brought in.

'I've never been able to get through to the boy, not through rugby or tennis or anything else, and I don't think his dad has much of a relationship with him,' Bruno went on. 'Félix is a loner, scrawny, small for his age, with no friends that I know of, a bit of a victim.'

'If he'd been arrested, we could have got him assigned to community service,' Annette said. 'That could have helped, got him started on something that might lead to a job and a bit of self-respect. But now that the case has been dropped, there's no cause to arrest him.'

Bruno nodded. 'I'm wondering if these pictures of horses

tell us something. Maybe we could steer him into work that way.'

'You mean Pamela's riding school? It's worth a try.' She looked around the drab room, wrinkling her nose. '*Mon Dieu*, how the other half lives.'

9

Fernand and Odette Oudinot lived in a cottage that had once belonged to one of the farm workers employed by the owners of the *chartreuse*. With a lot of hard work they had transformed it into a welcoming and attractive home. They had turned the attic into a large bedroom with its own bathroom, and downstairs they had knocked down walls to make two large rooms, a huge kitchen and a separate dining room where Bruno had sometimes been a guest. They had also created a large archway into the connecting barn where in the past tobacco plants had been dried. The lower part of the barn was now a vast living room, 12 metres long and 5 metres wide. Its large, double-glazed windows gave spectacular views down the slope where Fernand kept a small herd of cows, some for dairy and others for veal. Fernand had done most of the conversion work himself. Upstairs were three guest rooms, each with its own bathroom.

At the other side of the large vegetable garden, and far enough removed to be almost out of earshot, was another barn where the geese, ducks and chickens were kept at night. Beyond them stood a *pigeonnier*, a tall tower which still housed pigeons for the family pot, a large pond and two hectares of land where the birds roamed free. Then came the orchards and the walnut plantation, and just over the brow of the slope was the *chartreuse* that belonged to Sylvestre.

The whole place was a tribute to the ability of the farmers of the Périgord to adapt. It was hard to make a living from ducks and geese alone, so Fernand's dairy cows brought in a little extra money and the calves he raised were known to produce the best veal in the district. In the summer, the three guest rooms were rented by the week for farm vacations. The guests ate with Fernand and Odette, roamed the farm and enjoyed the countryside. Odette cared for her bees and cooked endlessly, making jams and her splendid pies and tarts to sell in the market along with her honey. From her vegetable garden came strawberries and courgettes, tomatoes and aubergines, peppers and every other vegetable Bruno could think of. What wasn't eaten by the paying guests was pickled, preserved and put into jars to be sold in the market in winter. And with all of this, Odette still found time to cultivate the daffodils that made the hillside dance in spring, and the roses that she'd trained to wind prettily around the doors and windows of her cottage. It made a splendid palette of colours in summer with the sunflowers that flanked the guests' barn and a lower meadow filled with wildflowers where her bees and hosts of butterflies feasted.

Fernand and Odette had made their home and farm into one of the better-known places in the Périgord. Hardly a tourist brochure was printed without a photo of their ducks and geese in the shadow of the *pigeonnier* or their garden with the rose-covered cottage behind. It was every city-dweller's fantasy of the French countryside, and the rural heritage that most French people still held dear and to which every French politician paid homage. The Mayor's own campaign brochures featured him smiling as he picked tomatoes in Odette's garden or sat on the terrace helping Fernand shell walnuts. This was the image of *La Belle France* and a promise that some core of that grand tradition was still to be seen and enjoyed.

'*Bonjour*, Bruno,' Odette said, wiping her hands on an apron and advancing to kiss him on both cheeks. A plump and motherly woman, Odette's own rosy cheeks were as round as two little apples. She smelled of flour and jam and good cooking. Behind her on the giant stove sat four large copper pans, each bubbling with black currants, and on the kitchen table stood an army of empty jam jars waiting to be filled. '*Tu as mangé?*'

Bruno grinned at the traditional farm welcome, the eternal question, 'Have you eaten?' It was an invitation as much as a welcome, and Bruno loved to eat in this friendly home, staring down at the grazing cows and the ducks and geese waddling among them.

'I'm on duty today so I can't stay, Odette, much as I'd like to,' he said. 'Is Fernand around?'

She directed him to the workshop, a lean-to attached to the barn for the ducks and geese. Fernand was using a small circular saw to cut logs for the winter, and stacking them neatly under the eaves of the barn. When he saw Bruno he pushed his protective goggles up onto his bald head, shook hands and said with his bright blue eyes glinting, 'Time for a *p'tit apéro*? I keep a bottle here that Odette's not supposed to know about. You can tell me about the race. I saw it in the paper.'

'Not this time, Fernand. It's business, although very unofficial. The Mayor got a call from a Mayor in Alsace about this trouble with your cousins over the *chartreuse*. He's tied up today with the regional council meeting or he'd have come himself, but he asked me if there's anything we can do to help.'

'It's a family thing,' Fernand said. 'I can't say I'm happy about the way the row built up, but I don't want to see the old family house turned into some fancy berth for rich tourists.'

'You have a few tourists here yourself.'

'Yes, but what we do is tourism on the farm, eco-tourism they call it these days. The kids get to play with the ducks and chickens, see the cows and calves, pick vegetables for their lunch – it's educational. He wants to do something very different, make a fortune by selling off these luxury apartments. It's crazy; this is the countryside, not the heart of Paris. Besides, there's some bad blood built up between us over the years.'

'How do you mean? I thought you and your elder sister agreed to divide it, she got the *chartreuse* and you got the land.'

'Yes, but we had a verbal agreement that we'd try to keep it all together in the family, not start selling it off. The Alsace family used to come down here every year, and we'd light the fires, air the beds, take care of the garden, get a meal ready to welcome them.'

'What went wrong?'

'It was money, of course. When our parents died, and they died within three weeks of each other, there was this land and a fair bit of money saved up. I was under-age but I wanted to stay with the farm, so my great-aunt agreed to let Jeannot, our neighbour, take me on as an apprentice and he and I farmed this land together. The idea was that I'd take over the farm when I came of age. That was fine, just what I wanted. But then she came to me and asked if she could use the money to invest in some business project that she and her husband had back in Alsace. She promised to pay me back, with interest, and got a *notaire* to make it all legal.'

'And did she pay you back?'

'Oh yes, in cash and right on time, but she paid me only three per cent interest a year at a time when inflation was roaring away. And she used our money, my money, to help her new family buy back the aerodrome which eventually made them millionaires. I'd just married Odette and I had a row with my aunt at the wedding when I said I wanted to be paid with an allowance for inflation as well as the interest. That was when it started. She said a deal is a deal and there was nothing in the contract about inflation. Anyway, it went on from there, me and Odette struggling to build this farm up and make ends meet, while she and her family up in Alsace were buying fast cars and fancy clothes. And she took all the family furniture although half of it was mine.'

'What would it take to settle this?'

'They've got all the money in the world. It wouldn't hurt them to let me have the *chartreuse*, as compensation for all the money I lost through inflation and the interest I lost along with it. I sat down one night and worked it all out, using the government's own inflation figures. Last time I looked it was close to half a million euros they owe me. And I'm not asking for anything that's not mine by right. So if they think they can make some more money from this place, they'll have me and my rights to reckon with. And it's not just me, it's our Martine. All this will be hers when Odette and I are gone, and I'd like her to have the *chartreuse*.'

Bruno nodded, Martine was a late child, a woman who must now be in her thirties who'd gone to the *lycée* in Périgueux and then to university in Bordeaux. The last Bruno had heard she'd joined some high-powered business in Paris.

'Is she still in Paris?' Bruno asked, thinking she might be prepared to reach some sensible settlement with Sylvestre.

'She's based in England now, got her own business helping French companies get established in London. She's doing very well, employs three or four people,' Fernand said proudly. 'She was always good with languages.'

'Didn't she get married, must be ten years ago or more, just about the time I got here and took this job?'

'She married a business colleague from Paris, but it didn't last. I never took to him. She's divorced now, no kids, more's the pity. Odette can't wait to be a grandmother. And I'm not getting any younger. I'd like to have some little grandson to take this place over one day.'

'Do you see much of her?'

'She's here now, just came for the week on one of those discount flights from London that come into Bergerac. Only cost her fifty euros, there and back. She's off seeing some old school friends in Périgueux but she'll be back for dinner. Come and join us.'

Bruno had to decline, citing a previous engagement. He left his car outside the cottage and Fernand led the way through the walnut plantation.

'I watched the parade of old cars the other day but I was sorry we missed your race. We were having lunch with friends in Rouffignac. But I saw that white Jaguar again as we were driving there. It shot right past me.'

'The E-type?' Bruno asked. 'Are you sure?' That was Young's car. Why was he driving around when he was supposed to have been laid low by a migraine? Maybe he wasn't as attached to Annette as she liked to think.

'Oh yes, and it was the same driver, the fair-haired young chap.'

They walked on over the brow of the hill. Strolling through the geese to the wire fence Fernand had erected just a few metres from the rear of the *chartreuse*, Bruno saw the building had two wings enclosing a large courtyard with a handsome old tree in its centre. About thirty metres beyond the archway that led into the courtyard was a separate gatehouse. The main house was about fifty metres long, with mansard windows in the roof.

'He's turned each wing into a separate house and he plans to keep the gatehouse for himself,' said Fernand, over the noise of the geese. 'I've fenced off his land from mine, so you'll have to walk around from here and get to his house by the dirt path that leads off from the road.' He opened a small gate in his fence to let Bruno out of the goose enclosure and back into the walnut plantation.

'Any message for him?' Bruno asked.

'Tell him to pay me what his family owes and I'll remove the geese and sell him an easement for an access road. I'll even put up with him living in the gatehouse.'

It was a pleasant stroll through the trees and out to the

single-lane tarmac road. Deep potholes suggested heavy use by trucks coming with building materials for Sylvestre's conversion. The path that led off to the *chartreuse* was muddy and narrow, marked by ruts that had been filled in with gravel. Trees and bushes on each side had been battered by the truck traffic. Nobody interested in a luxury home would want to arrive this way. And the closer Bruno approached, the louder the cackling of the geese became.

Once past the path, Bruno whistled in admiration and pulled out his mobile phone to take some photos. To his left was the two-storey gatehouse with a four-by-four vehicle outside. The place was about the size of Bruno's cottage, big enough for at least two generous bedrooms upstairs. Straight ahead, the stone archway led into the courtyard with another four-by-four vehicle parked in the shade of the central tree. The *chartreuse* itself was a fine building, with two white pillars supporting a porch at the main door, tall French windows to either side and mansard windows on the floor above. The barns to each side of the courtyard had also been given French windows and the walls of local stone had been cleaned and repointed.

As he advanced he saw to his right an all-weather swimming pool with a sliding glass roof where somebody was swimming laps. Behind the pool rose a handsome stone *pigeonnier* just beyond a terrace. A long stone building, evidently newly built and topped with solar panels, seemed to be the pool house. Expensive deckchairs lined the length of the pool. On a terrace between the pool and the house stood a large wooden table and chairs where Sylvestre was sitting opposite an elegant dark-haired woman in jeans wearing large sunglasses. As he approached, Bruno saw a tall, slim bottle that signalled an Alsace wine on the table, along with green-stemmed glasses and a large ashtray.

'*Bonjour*, Bruno, this is an unexpected pleasure, and congratulations again on your race,' said Sylvestre, rising and speaking loudly above the geese. 'Do you know my cousin Martine? Will you join us in a glass of Riesling?'

'I'm glad to see at least two members of the family are talking,' he said, and turned to Martine. 'I've just been to see your mother and father. Your dad's very proud of you and your career in London.'

'Did he add that he can't wait for me to drop it all and start giving him grandchildren?' she replied, an edge to her voice as she stretched out a lazy hand to be shaken.

She took off the sunglasses, a graceful gesture that revealed an attractive face, and gave him a lopsided smile. Her voice was lower than he'd expected and her accent pure Parisian. Her dark hair fell gracefully to her shoulders from a side parting. Expensively cut, Bruno guessed. She'd inherited her father's eyes, bright blue and twinkling, and her mother's full mouth and good cheekbones. Her most prominent feature was an imperious nose that some would have found too large. Bruno thought it gave her face character. He glanced at Sylvestre; he had the same nose. It must be a family trait.

'Your father said something about wanting grandchildren to inherit the farm. He's right to be proud of it and the business he's built with your mother,' Bruno said. 'But the Mayor thinks everybody's inheritance could be improved if the two wings of the family could reach an agreement. He's hoping for a reconciliation because he likes Sylvestre's project. He thinks it will bring more tourists and maybe a few more jobs for local people.'

'The Mairie is already enjoying the new property taxes I'm paying,' said Sylvestre. He gave a short, barking laugh. 'If anybody can reach a settlement, it will be me and Martine.'

'You've made the place look great,' said Bruno. 'I wish you luck, and if I can help in any way . . .'

'Thanks, but let's not talk of that now.' Sylvestre poured a glass of wine and pushed it across to Bruno. 'I don't think you were there the other day after the parade when we got talking with your doctor and that Green council member, Alphonse, about electric cars. He was wondering if I could help organize a special race for them in the Vézère valley. Martine's in public relations and she has some ideas about getting sponsorships to help make it happen.'

'I imagine your Tesla would start as the favourite,' said Bruno. 'Talking of that car, where is it?' He looked around.

'There's no way I'd bring it up that rutted path. The truck with the Tesla and the Bugatti is in the secure parking lot of that logistics company in Le Buisson. I hired the Range Rover to get into my property and to get around.' Sylvestre gestured to the vehicle parked in the courtyard behind him. 'Alphonse said he'd talk to the Mayor, and he called me this morning to say the Mayor is interested in the idea.'

'The Mayor has become an enthusiast after the Concours and yesterday's rally,' said Bruno, as a splash came from the pool and Freddy hauled himself out. He was thin and wiry, with black hair spreading down from his chest and into his trunks. He grabbed a towel from one of the deckchairs, put on a towelling robe and came to shake hands.

'You're a brave man,' said Bruno. 'It's too late in the year for me to go swimming in the open air.'

'The pool is heated by those solar panels,' said Freddy, in good French but with an accent Bruno didn't recognize.

'How are you enjoying the Périgord?' Bruno asked. 'Is this your first visit?'

'I like it a lot, all those old castles. And it's very green, a pleasant change after living in the Emirates. Excuse me, I should go and change.'

He nodded courteously and left, and Bruno noticed that he headed for the gatehouse rather than the main building.

'Perhaps I could come and see you about the electric car rally idea,' said Martine. 'My father tells me you're the Mayor's right-hand man.'

'No, that's his deputy, Xavier, the *maire-adjoint*,' said Bruno. 'I'm just the municipal policeman, but I'd be happy to make an appointment for you to see the Mayor. It's this family feud that brings me here. Your father seems to be open to some kind of financial settlement . . .'

'He is,' said Martine. 'But every time he meets Sylvestre all the old family resentments come out and he starts demanding the return of a grandfather clock and some bed of my great-great-grandmother's and talking about historic inflation rates. If there's a deal to be made, Sylvestre and I will do our best to reach it and then it will be up to me to sell it to my father.'

'Which way did you come here?' Sylvestre asked, and Bruno

explained how he'd walked through the woods from Fernand's home.

'So he didn't steer you the other way around, where you'd have seen a perfectly good road that goes around his walnut trees and comes out by my swimming pool. That's the logical way to get here, but he's fenced it off.'

'The law gives you a minimum right of access to your property,' said Bruno. 'You could turn that rutted path into a decent gravel road and it would make for a handsome approach.'

'Minimum is the word, not even two metres wide, and since it's not my land I can't make it into a paved or tarmac road. Still, I'm going to put down the gravel. But that doesn't solve the problem of the geese. Even with double glazing and earplugs, they wake me at dawn and it goes on all day. It's enough to drive me crazy. I'd never be able to sell any of these apartments.'

'That reminds me of a tourist who came to the Mairie to lodge a complaint about the house he'd rented for a week,' said Bruno. 'It was just on the outskirts of St Denis and the people in the houses on each side kept chickens. The tourist wanted me to find some way to silence the cockerels who woke him at dawn every day.'

'What did you say?' Martine asked. She'd been raised in the country herself and sounded amused.

'I asked him why he'd come to the French countryside where cockerels were to be expected. And he should count himself lucky that the neighbours didn't raise geese or donkeys.'

'Peacocks are the worst of all,' she said. 'Their screams sound like someone's being murdered.' She turned to Sylvestre. 'Don't worry, I won't suggest my father should get some peacocks – as long as you're prepared to be reasonable. In the meantime, just to show good will, I've brought you a peace offering.'

Sylvestre sat up when she reached into her shoulder bag and brought out a sheaf of photocopies of handwritten pages that looked as if they came from a private journal or diary.

'It's about that Bugatti you're interested in,' she said. 'It's the unpublished memoir of an RAF bomber pilot shot down in 1941. He was rescued by someone driving a car that sounds like the Bugatti that obsesses you. When the airman died, his family sent his unpublished memoir to the Imperial War Museum in London. I'd been working with them on getting French sponsors to help promote a new exhibition about French escape routes for downed pilots, which is how I heard about it.'

She handed the pages across to Sylvestre, who took them as if receiving some holy relic and began quickly scanning the pages.

'Is this about the Bugatti that disappeared in the war when being driven to Bordeaux?' Bruno asked.

She looked at him in surprise. 'You know about it, too?'

'I just heard about this lost Bugatti at dinner the other day after the Concours d'Elégance when people were talking about the most valuable cars in the world. I didn't know it was that famous.'

'I'd never heard about it until I was doing some business with the new Bugatti headquarters in London and Sylvestre let them borrow his old sports car for the launch of their showroom,' she said. 'Once I heard his name, I realized that we were cousins, even though we were on opposite sides of the family feud, and I introduced myself. We met for lunch and he told me of his interest in the lost Bugatti.'

'This airman says he was hit by flak after bombing the Michelin plant in Clermont-Ferrand, lost an engine and the crew had to bail out,' said Sylvestre, lifting his head from the pages, his eyes alight with excitement. 'He was picked up by someone in a black Bugatti who didn't give his name but said he'd been a pilot in the First World War. He drove very fast and dropped the airman at a château where the family spoke English. They put him in touch with some people who had access to an escape route to Spain over the Pyrenees. He says it was called the PAT, after some British naval officer named Pat O'Leary who had helped to start it.'

'Any route from Clermont-Ferrand to Bordeaux would probably have come through this region,' said Bruno.

'The driver sounds as though it could have been Robert Benoist,' said Sylvestre. 'He won the French, British and Italian Grands Prix and he went on to win Le Mans and run the Bugatti racing team. Who else would they trust to get the Bugatti to Bordeaux?' He turned to his cousin, his eyes shining. 'This is amazing, Martine. I won't forget this.'

10

Back in town, Bruno turned down the Rue de la Paix and pulled into the parking lot by the river. It served the amusement park, still open despite the end of the school summer holidays thanks to the continuing good weather, and Bruno had long considered it an eyesore. At the far end of the park was a stretch of scrubland, almost a field, between the windmill and the campsite further downriver. That would be the place to park cars, tucked well back so they didn't spoil the view of the river from the other bank. Whatever Jérôme said about his plans for expansion, changing the parking area was going to be Bruno's first recommendation to the Mayor.

Bruno had visited the place twice, once as a new arrival in St Denis, and more recently when he'd taken Florence and her young children there as a treat to ride the carousel, to eat sausages smothered in mild mustard and ketchup inside a baguette and to watch him win each of them a stuffed animal at the popgun range. She had ignored the children's pleas to see the burning of Joan of Arc and the guillotine beheading Marie Antoinette, the park's two more renowned attractions, and marched them into the water garden to eat their sausages and paddle in the shallow streams. When Bruno had seen it, the burning at the stake had been mildly impressive, thanks mainly to the clothes worn by the figure of Joan. They were fashioned from a special kind of paper that burned furiously with a bright flame, like the blonde wig which ignited in a suitably dramatic manner as a bell tolled, black smoke poured out and the visitors were moved out to make room for the next batch.

'They're banning Joan,' said Jérôme when Bruno went into his office. 'They've been at me for years about it, first for the smoke and then for the asbestos used to make the model. And now the new Prefect is pro-Green, so I'm sunk. I have to think of something else and I remembered an idea my father always wanted to do.'

A burly man in his forties with a long, thin nose and a sales-man's easy patter, Jérôme was a member of the town council who was usually at odds with the Mayor over anything that might increase his taxes. The Mayor in return kept a beady eye on any of Jérôme's more imaginative plans for new exhibits and had memorably vetoed the scheme to re-enact a black mass being performed on the naked form of one of King Louis XIV's mistresses.

'He dreamed it up in the Seventies, when I was still a kid, and the small farms around here were closing down or being brought together into bigger units and all the old rural life was disappearing. Dad thought people would like to see how it used to be. So he had this idea to re-create a nineteenth-century village with its schoolroom, blacksmith, apothecary and basketweaver, people dressed in period costume, making knives and spinning wool and weaving cloth on looms.'

'I think the Mayor would prefer that to the black mass,' said Bruno as Jérôme unrolled a large blueprint that more than covered his desk.

'I'd put a waterwheel in here in a little cut I'd make in the river bank and use that to grind corn, then we can sell both the flour and the artisan bread we'd make. We'd let visitors try their hand at using scythes to cut the hay – under close supervision, of course. At the far end beyond the windmill I'd have a traditional farm with ducks, geese and chickens, a petting zoo for the kids with some sheep and dwarf goats and a display of traditional farm implements, including horse-drawn ones. My dad had started collecting some. We'll have a restaurant called the Old Farmhouse Kitchen and I want to start a brewery. I'd keep the existing amusement park, minus poor old Joan, of course, and build this new village on that land beyond the windmill. What do you think?'

'I think the Mayor will like it. I certainly do, and it would mean some new jobs in season.'

'About five or six jobs, I reckon, but if it works well, it could be more. The thing is, Bruno, we can promote it as educational. School trips could come here and bring in business outside the school holidays.'

'You'll need more parking space. Could you use some of that land beyond your windmill, over by the campsite?'

'That makes sense. Yes, why not?'

'So tell me, how are you going to replace Joan of Arc, and how do you get that effect on Marie Antoinette's neck when her head rolls into the basket?'

'For Joan, I'm going to build an exhibition of nineteenth-century clothes with a small photo studio attached so people can dress up and have their photos taken, singly, couples, the whole family. But Marie Antoinette is a trade secret.'

'Come on, Jérôme, I worked out that you have a small pump in there that shoots out the fake blood, but it's the neck that interests me.'

'It's spaghetti in tomato sauce behind a sheet of glass, but don't you agree it looks good? I came across it in England when I went over for a rugby international. I saw people eating it on toast in a café and couldn't believe my eyes. Spaghetti and toast, those English will eat anything. And they sell it in cans. But I realized it was just the thing for Marie's neck so I brought some cans back.'

Bruno took his leave, telling Jérôme to drop off a copy of the plans at the Mairie. His working day was over, his horse needed exercising and he had to pick up his dog. And tonight was the regular weekly dinner with his friends. He found himself smiling as he drove up the familiar road, imagining their reaction when he told them of Jérôme's use for tinned spaghetti.

His affair with Pamela might be over, but Bruno always enjoyed the approach to what he still thought of as Pamela's house, even though she no longer lived there. Gilles and Fabiola had bought it, and Bruno continued to keep his horse, Hector, in the adjoining stables along with the old mare, Victoria. And his dog Balzac often spent the day there with Hector, who had known him since he was a puppy. Gilles was waiting for him, the horses already saddled. Hector nuzzled at Bruno, expecting his usual apple. Bruno gave it to him as he stroked Hector's smooth neck. Balzac put his paw on Bruno's foot by way of greeting and Bruno gave him his biscuit. The basset hound wolfed it down and then darted around the horses' legs, eager for his customary run.

Bruno donned his riding boots and hat as Gilles explained that Fabiola would meet them at Pamela's riding school where there was a new horse she might buy. Gilles had just started learning to ride, so Bruno checked the saddle girths and kneed each horse gently in the stomach so he could tighten the straps a notch. They set off side by side at a sedate walk, Balzac trotting ahead.

'Do you remember Annette's English boyfriend talking about the Bugatti the other night, the one that's worth millions?' Bruno asked. 'Something has come up that might make a story for you.' He explained what he'd learned from Sylvestre about the downed British airman and his handwritten memoir.

'Robert Benoist?' Gilles exclaimed. 'I've heard of him, a hero in both world wars and a Resistance leader. I'm pretty sure he was arrested and shot. They held a special race in his name in the Bois de Boulogne in Paris after the war. There's a plaque about the race in the Bois. I'd better go and see Sylvestre, it's the kind of story *Paris Match* loves.'

Gilles had taken a buyout at the magazine after getting a book contract and deciding to leave Paris to be with Fabiola, but he still wrote articles for them as a freelancer.

'Ready to start riding?' Bruno asked. 'We'll start with a trot and then go into an easy canter along the firebreak.'

He set off, holding Hector back from the gallop he was expecting, and glanced behind to see Gilles riding well. Balzac was trotting at Bruno's side, looking up from time to time as if waiting for the pace to pick up. Bruno now loosened the rein and let Hector canter up the shallow slope that led to the forest and the long firebreak that would take them to Pamela's riding school. At the start of the firebreak, he reined in.

'Wait a few seconds after I set off and let Victoria set her own pace. She's too old for gallops but Hector's impatient for his run.' Bruno's horse was tossing his head, eager to go, but Bruno kept him circling until he saw Gilles understood. Balzac was already fifty metres ahead, looking back to see if Bruno was coming. 'I'll rein in at the far end and wait for you. We're not in a hurry so there's no need to rush.'

He loosened the reins, bent down in the saddle and let Hector bound forward, moving almost at once into a stretching run that swiftly became a gallop. The trees blurred away on each side and Bruno narrowed his eyes against the rush of wind as Hector's hooves drummed on the turf. Within seconds, Balzac was left behind and Bruno felt the familiar strain in his thighs as he bent far forward, his rump clear of the saddle and his horse moving as if he could run for ever. All too soon the end of the firebreak loomed ahead and he sat back in the saddle, taking deep breaths as Hector slowed. He turned to see Gilles cantering easily in the distance with Balzac bouncing valiantly along beside the horse. As they came closer Bruno smiled at the way Balzac's ears flapped like some primitive set of wings.

'You're riding well,' Bruno said. 'You're better than me when I was a beginner. Pamela says you have a natural seat.'

'I certainly enjoy it. Just wish I'd started when I was younger.'

They walked the horses down the bridle trail that came out on the ridge above Pamela's new place and paused, looking down at the half-dozen children on ponies walking around the sand-floored ring. Jack Crimson's daughter, Miranda, sat on her white mare in the middle of the ring as she watched them circle.

Pamela was in the paddock, standing by a low hedge over which two older youngsters were taking turns to jump.

'It looks busy,' said Gilles. 'And Fabiola's here already; there's her car, though I don't see her.'

'Probably trying out the new horse,' said Bruno, looking down at the freshly painted doors and windows of the office and stables. The old house Pamela had bought along with the riding school still looked down at heel, but Bruno could see men working in the emptied swimming pool repairing the leaks, and the shutters on the *gîtes* gleamed with new paint. There was a lot of work to be done to get the *gîtes* ready for the next tourist season and for the moment Pamela and Miranda, along with Miranda's children, would all be living in the main house. Bruno admired the courage of the two women, each of them determined that their hard work and energy could make a success of what had been a failing riding school. Pamela had a good track record, having made a success of renting out the *gîtes* at her former house. Miranda had her father's money behind her, which didn't hurt.

As Bruno and Gilles walked their horses past the apple orchard towards the stables they heard a shout and saw Fabiola cantering towards them on a dappled grey mare with a distinctive, darker mane. The mare was smaller than Victoria, Bruno saw, probably a good size for Fabiola. She reined in beside them, and edged her mare forward alongside Gilles so she could reach over and touch his hand.

'I'd kiss you but I think we both might fall off,' she said. 'You too, Bruno, consider yourself kissed. How was your ride?'

'Wonderful, perfect autumn weather, a good gallop and Gilles is riding well. How's the mare?'

'Perfect, but I'm not sure I can afford her after we pay the mortgage on the new house,' Fabiola said. 'We might have to wait until next summer when we start getting some money from the rentals. They want four thousand for her and she's six years old. She's a Spanish horse, Andalusian, but bred in France. Pamela thinks she can get the price down a bit and she might buy her if I don't. But enough of that,' she went on. 'Bruno, I've got some good news, well, maybe not good, but you'll be pleased to know I'm recommending an autopsy on Monsieur Hugon. I've already told J-J.'

'What?' Bruno almost jumped in his saddle from surprise, startling his horse. He took a moment to calm him.

'The autopsy might not tell us much, because if it's what I think it is, detection after this amount of time won't be easy,' she went on. 'I've warned J-J that it's a risk and I've also asked him for a forensic check on the room where the body was found.'

'What do you think it was? Poison?'

'It's possible, only possible, that cyanide was either put into his drink or sprayed straight into his face. But it's not easy to be sure. Cyanide traces dissipate very fast after death and then human tissue can produce cyanide gas as part of the decomposition process.'

'What kind of drink? Could it have been coffee?' Bruno recalled the three dirty coffee cups in the sink. His wife had said they were her best cups and had been surprised that Hugon had used them. Could he have been killed by his visitors?

'Yes, indeed,' Fabiola went on. 'Half a gram of potassium cyanide is usually fatal, and in crystallized form, mixed with sugar or artificial sweetener, the victim is unlikely to detect it.

You don't need much, less than the amount of salt you'd put on your *pommes frites*. Or it could be delivered by a spray, which could be indicated in this case by the irritation around the victim's nose and mouth.'

'Isn't cyanide a controlled substance?' Gilles asked. 'You can't just go into a pharmacy and buy it.'

'No, but it's used a lot in the metals industry and in electroplating and by some photographers. I can think of several workshops and garages in town that would probably have it. You even find it in some fertilizers,' she said. 'And it isn't hard to make for anybody with a basic knowledge of chemistry. I could make enough for a fatal dose from heating green almond shells and then running the hydrocyanic gas that's released through a solution of baking soda. It would be even stronger if I excluded air when I heated the shells and replaced it with an inert gas like helium or nitrogen. I could even do it through heating polyurethane. Some fire victims actually die of cyanide poisoning from the polyurethane in a mattress.'

Bruno stared at Fabiola, stunned by the contrast between what she was saying and the bucolic scene around him, the autumn countryside and the laughter of children in the riding ring, the snorting of the horses and Balzac's busy foraging beneath the apple trees.

Fabiola followed his glance and added, 'You could even make cyanide from apple pips, if you had enough of them. One of my teachers in medical school had a grisly sense of humour and used to talk of ways to commit the perfect murder. Cyanide was his top choice, especially for anyone with heart or respiratory problems. It works by stopping the body from processing oxygen.'

'Why is it hard to detect?' Bruno asked.

'It breaks down so fast. The usual toxicology tests don't work too well just one day after death and they're almost useless after two days. If Hugon drank it in coffee, we might get an indication from signs of burning in the oesophagus or stomach. If he was killed by a spray, then we'll have to use a new technique, by looking at his liver cells with a bio-marker called ACTA, which stands for aminothiazole and carboxylic acid. We don't have that capability in the Bergerac lab so the body would have to be examined in Bordeaux.'

'What made you think of cyanide?' he asked.

'I found a trace of potassium on the nasal hairs and something else that I think might be DMSO, dimethyl sulfoxide. DMSO is a terrifyingly efficient way of carrying cyanide into the body. It's not toxic itself but it will dissolve potassium cyanide to make a liquid that can poison you through your skin – even through gloves. It's known in chemistry labs as "liquid death". That's why I recommended an autopsy and a full forensic check of the room where the man died.'

Bruno's mind was racing. Who had a motive to kill Hugon? His wife was in the clear; her alibi in Sarlat had been confirmed. Bruno had spent part of the afternoon on the phone with the Périgueux archives and the Resistance archives at the Centre Jean Moulin in Bordeaux, trying to trace the subjects of Hugon's research. In Périgueux, it turned out, Hugon had been working on property-tax records and files for registered foreigners in the *département* in the pre-war years. In Bordeaux he'd called up files covering the earliest years of the Resistance, from 1940 until the end of 1942, when German forced-labour requirements sent floods of young Frenchmen fleeing into the Maquis, hiding in the woods. In both places, Hugon was well enough known that he was allowed to roam at will through the stacks, so not all his searches could be traced.

'Are you going to buy the horse?' Gilles asked Fabiola, jerking Bruno from his thoughts.

'If Pamela can get the right price, or if we can reach an agreement that we buy her jointly, put her to a stallion and then I get the mare and Pamela gets the foal.' Fabiola turned to Bruno. 'Pamela plans to buy mares so she can get them to breed more cheaply than by buying new horses.'

They rode down to the stables to greet Pamela and Miranda, and by the time they had unsaddled and brushed down the horses, Crimson had arrived in his vintage Jaguar with the Baron. They carried the half-case of wine they had brought into the old house and put it on the kitchen table next to the Baron's ancient iron cooking pot in its box of hay to keep it warm. Beside it were stacked two cans of the Baron's home-made pâté, a large apple pie and a wooden platter crammed with small rounds of *Cabécous* goat cheese, a wedge of Stéphane's *tomme d'Audrix* and a cylinder of English Stilton that Crimson had bought on his last trip to London.

The dinner to be prepared was a new ritual that had begun when Pamela and Miranda had first moved to the riding school, and Bruno, Florence, Fabiola and the Baron had taken turns to bring dinner for the two women. The evenings had been so enjoyable that now each week they held a similar dinner, with each of the friends taking turns to provide the food and wine. It had proved to be the perfect way for Pamela and Bruno to end their affair but maintain their friendship, the fellowship of the group easing them through the transition. It probably also helped, Bruno thought, that no new woman had come into his life to take her place. There had been a moment when he thought it might happen with Nancy, an FBI agent with the Embassy in Paris, after she'd been wounded in an anti-terrorist operation. There'd been talk of Bruno's joining her in Florida as she convalesced, but it never happened. He'd heard she'd left the FBI and was now running for Congress.

This evening was the Baron's turn to prepare the main course to feed all of them, plus the children, and since Crimson claimed to be a hopeless cook, he provided the wines from his well-stocked cellar. They were now so accustomed to preparing the meal that they fell automatically into their usual roles. Fabiola polished the wine glasses and set the table and Miranda's father decanted the wines before starting to slice the big circular *tourte* of fresh bread. The Baron opened his cans of pâté, explaining that he'd brought one of venison and one of rabbit. Pamela went to the vegetable garden to pick lettuce for the salad while Bruno and Gilles took the big plastic *bidons* to the spring that burbled from the hillside to bring back some water. Meanwhile Florence, who had now joined them, and Miranda bathed their children and prepared them for bed, but they would eat with the adults before heading upstairs to snuggle into the old feather beds that had come with the house.

It was the kind of evening that Bruno most enjoyed. It felt like being part of a family, with friends and good food, the presence of children, even when they squabbled, and the comforting knowledge that this had taken place last week and the week before that. Above all, he could expect to be with these same people the following week and countless weeks ahead. Strange, he thought, that they never ran out of things to talk about; local politics, the economics of riding schools, the merits of local vineyards and the best way to prepare various dishes.

As he and Gilles staggered back with the now heavy *bidons*, Bruno wondering as he always did how to run a pipe system down to the house from the hillside, they ran into Pamela with her lettuces. He asked her to wait a moment when they reached the house and explained his concern for young Félix and his interest in horses. Could she find a use for the youngster around the stables, perhaps in return for riding lessons?

'If he's prepared to muck out the stables, I certainly could, but he doesn't sound like an attractive youth or even particularly trustworthy,' she replied. 'Still, bring him round and I'll take a look at him. How's he going to get here?'

'I'll take care of that,' Bruno said. He'd taken some garden waste to the *déchetterie* that weekend and seen an old bicycle that Jacquot, the custodian of the recycling centre, had salvaged. He'd found it to be in working order and put it to one side. Bruno had already called Jacquot to say he had a use for it.

Inside the large kitchen, where Crimson had lit a fire in the elderly wood-burning iron range that stood against one wall, the Baron was explaining to the freshly bathed children the art of making a cassoulet Périgourdin.

'Down in Toulouse they think they know about cassoulet, but we know better,' he was saying as he lifted the lid on the pot to let them smell the rich aroma. Four pairs of young eyes followed his every move. 'A real cassoulet has to contain stuffed neck of duck and some duck sausage and I like to add some *manchons* of duck as well, because my grandmother always did. A cassoulet is always based on white beans with onions and tomatoes. It's fine to add some ordinary pork sausage as well, as long as it's been made with plenty of garlic, but without the duck it's just a pale shadow of a true cassoulet. It also needs to cook very slowly, which is why I made it this morning and left it cooking in the haybox all day.'

'Time to eat,' called Pamela, putting out a bowl of *cornichons* to go with the pâté. Crimson poured them each a glass of white Bergerac from Château Montdoyen and Miranda gave the children water from the spring. Pamela began carving slices of pâté, Florence passed her the children's plates and Bruno handed out the bread.

'I can hardly wait for your cassoulet, Baron. It smells magnificent,' Pamela said. '*Bon appétit* to all.'

11

Next morning, after an early ride with Hector, Bruno picked up the elderly bicycle from the *déchetterie* and arrived shortly after eight at the block of flats where Félix lived. He walked up the stairs with Balzac at his heels and tried the bell. He heard no sound of ringing and no one came to the door, so he began knocking. After a moment Félix's mother opened it wearing a wraparound apron over her working clothes. She invited him in for coffee.

'I heard you sorted things out for Félix at the supermarket,' she said, leading him into a cramped kitchen before putting the kettle on and washing a bowl at the sink. Even after all the years in St Denis, she still spoke with a West Indian accent. 'Thank you, we don't seem able to do much with him.'

'Unless you do, he's going to get into real trouble,' Bruno said as she spooned a coffee-chicory mixture into the bowl from a jar and poured in hot water, followed by a splash of milk. 'I saw from the pictures in his room that he likes horses.'

'Horses and cars, anything mechanical, but it's mainly cars he likes. I sometimes think he only likes the horses because it gives him something to talk about with his dad, but he's always liked animals. He's one of those boys who collect stray dogs.

They always follow him home, but we could never afford to keep one.' She looked down at Balzac and smiled. 'Would your dog like a bowl of water?'

'Yes, please,' he said, knowing that people with little money took pride in offering something to others. 'That would be very kind.'

She washed another bowl at the sink, filled it with water and bent to give it to Balzac, who gave her hand a tentative lick. She fondled his ears as Balzac drank. 'We used to have a dog when Jacques was working.'

'Is Félix up yet? He's got to get to school.'

'I get him up very soon, so he comes with me when I go to work.'

'Perhaps you could wake him now. Tell him I'm here and want a word with him before school.'

When she left, he took a sip from the mixture she called coffee and grimaced. Rather than offend her he poured most if it down the sink and ran the tap for a moment. After a couple of minutes Félix appeared, his face washed and his hair wetted down, wearing the same clothes as the previous day.

'*Bonjour*, Félix. How are you?' Bruno asked.

The boy shrugged. 'OK.'

'I see from the pictures in your room that you like horses.'

Félix shot him a wary look. 'Don't mind them.'

His mother handed him a bowl of the chicory mixture and the heel of what looked like the previous day's baguette. The boy looked down at Balzac and tore off a piece of the stale bread to give to the dog. He dunked the rest of it in the muddy brown liquid and began his breakfast. His mother gave him a nudge, and he said grudgingly, 'Thank you for helping yesterday.'

'How would you like to learn to ride?'

'What?' His head jerked up and he swallowed some food the wrong way, choked and coughed to clear his throat. He looked up. 'Ride a horse, me?'

'You'd have to work hard instead of paying for it, but do a good job and there might even be some pocket money in it. But if you do a bad job, or don't turn up for work on time, it's over.'

'How d'you mean?'

'The riding school near Meyrals is looking for a part-time stable boy. They're prepared to give you a trial. You spend Saturday mornings and some evenings cleaning out the stables and putting hay in the horses' mangers and they'll get you started, learning to ride.'

'That'd be great.' His eyes lit up, but then they dulled again. 'How'd I get to Meyrals? It takes two hours to walk there. What time would I have to start?'

'You'd have to be there by eight on the dot.'

'I'd have to leave before six.' He looked down at his shoes. 'I could run part of the way.'

'Can you ride a bike?'

'Yes, but I haven't got one.'

'Your mother says you like mechanical things. Could you fix up an old bike?'

'Depends what state it's in, but probably. I used to help Edouard fix his bike at his dad's garage. That's where I learned to ride one.'

Bruno nodded. That was interesting; he hadn't known that

Félix was friendly with the garage owner's son. Edouard was a good kid and a fine rugby player. He'd flattened Bruno with a hard tackle in the last juniors' match against the old men. Bruno suppressed a smile at the memory and led Félix and his mother downstairs, where he pulled the old bike from the back of his Land Rover. 'Could you fix this one up?'

Félix lifted the front wheel, squeezed the tyre with his fingers and then spun it. He tugged at the loose chain and tested the brakes, his movements deft and confident. He put the bike down and used his hand to wipe dust from the seat.

'It's working already but I could probably clean it up and tighten that chain. It could do with a good going-over.'

'You fix it up as best you can and I'll lend it to you,' Bruno said. 'Then after school today, we'll go to the riding school in my car and if they like the look of you, they'll give you a chance. You'd better shower and get into some clean clothes before you go. I'll pick you up here at five. If you aren't ready and looking present-able, the deal's off. If the school decides after they try you out that they don't want you or if you don't turn up on time, I take the bike back. It's on loan, it's not a gift. So rather than leave it out here at night, you might want to keep it in your room.'

'Can I take it up now? And could I meet you at the garage instead of here? Edouard has some tools I might need.'

Bruno nodded and held the door open as the boy shouldered the heavy old bike and staggered up the stairs. When Félix had gone, he looked at the boy's mother. 'I'll need you and your husband to make sure the boy gets up on time every Saturday and that he takes care of that bike.'

'I understand,' she said, squaring her shoulders before she

went on. 'He was always little for his age, that's why he gets bullied a bit. It was fine while Edouard was in the same class, they got on well together, but Félix failed his exams and was kept behind for a year.'

Félix trotted out through the door of the apartment house, shaking his hands as if he'd just washed them. He grinned at Bruno and gave Balzac a pat before he set off with his mother for the *collège*. Bruno watched them go and then led Balzac into his Land Rover. He would go to Fauquet's café for a decent cup of coffee and a croissant before he started work.

From his office in the Mairie, Bruno called Annette to tell her that Pamela was prepared to give Félix a chance at the stables and then asked if her English boyfriend had been serenading her with his troubadour songs. His name is George, she retorted, and said he'd been on good form the previous evening when they'd gone for dinner in Sarlat. She sounded happy about it, so Bruno didn't mention that George had been seen driving his E-type when he was supposed to be too sick to be in the rally.

He also briefed her on Fabiola's decision to call for an autopsy on Hugon. She might want to warn the Procureur that there could be a murder inquiry to organize, and certainly an inquest into Hugon's death. He promised to send her a report later that morning. Then he began to check his emails and found one from the Mayor, who had attached a copy of a memo from Alphonse suggesting that the Mairie look into the possible benefits of organizing a rally for electric cars. The Mayor asked for Bruno's views.

He raced through the rest of the emails, at least half of them from garages trying to sell him a rally car. He supposed they'd seen Philippe Delaron's race report. Another one came from the Périgord rally club saying that he'd omitted to sign up for membership before competing, which meant they could annul the result unless he paid them a retroactive registration fee of fifty euros. He forwarded that one to Annette and was just finishing his report on Hugon's death when the Mayor's secretary, Claire, slunk into the room in a new dress rather too tight for her generous frame.

'A Mademoiselle Oudinot to see you,' she said, somehow putting salacious meaning into the words. That would be Fernand's daughter, Martine, obviously reverting to her maiden name since her divorce. He asked Claire to show her in and to make two cups of coffee from the Mayor's own blend, not the usual sludge from the communal pot.

'This is business, Claire,' he said briskly, hitting the 'Save' key on his report. 'The Mayor has become a rally enthusiast after the weekend and we're counting on my visitor to help.'

Martine was dressed for business in a dark skirt and blue pin-striped blazer over a white blouse. Her hair was severely pulled back into a tight bun in a way that did little for her looks, Bruno thought. She was wearing lipstick and a little more make-up than the previous day and was carrying a slim briefcase in black leather. He stood up to receive her, shook hands across his desk and sat down gingerly, trying to avert the usual squeak from his elderly chair. As always he failed.

'I've put some thoughts down about this electric car rally we talked about yesterday,' she said, her tone cool and professional. He found it slightly intimidating, reminding him that she was probably an expert at presentations such as this, accustomed to dealing with corporate clients with big budgets. And he was a country policeman. She pulled a folder from her briefcase and he cleared some space for it on his desk, opening it to see a neatly printed sheaf of papers headed 'The Lascaux Green Grand Prix'.

'Obviously we will need sponsors to finance this, and I've listed those I think most likely to be receptive to the idea. We'll need your Mayor's influence to get the other communes to co-operate, along with the regional council. I thought we could use the word Lascaux in the title, since that's the most famous name in the region and it should also guarantee support from the tourist board. Calling it Green helps us promote the environmental benefits of electric cars. The combination of the most modern form of transportation with the prehistoric art of Lascaux makes a neat juxtaposition.'

Bruno sat forward, resting his arms on the desk, trying not to show that he was impressed. Equally, he sought to damp down his interest in Martine as a woman he found attractive, despite the deliberately impersonal way she was dressed. Odd, he thought, for a woman who specialized in public relations not to exploit her looks. The Martine he had seen at Sylvestre's house had been striking and evidently confident of her allure. Perhaps it had been deliberate, a ploy to win Sylvestre over to her hope of ending the family feud. If so, Bruno thought with a touch of disappointment, she'd felt no such need to look her best for him.

'This is my list of what needs to be done, by the Mayor, the regional council and other interested parties,' she said briskly. 'It will be my job to recruit the sponsors. I know several of the key figures in the various firms I've listed and it's an area where I have a lot of experience. Here's my CV with a list of references from companies I've worked with.'

Martine then handed him a map that showed the route she suggested for the race, starting at the parking by the Lascaux exhibition centre, passing through the heart of Montignac and across the narrow stone bridge leading out of the village. The route then turned off through the picturesque village of St Léon-sur-Vézère, past the Château de Losse and up around the prehistoric park of Le Thot. It took the curving hill road after Tursac, turned off to swing around the Château de Marzac and then returned to the main road through the long, narrow street of Les Eyzies. From there it took the long straight to the turn that led to the Grotte du Sorcier and through the woods to come down through St Denis with the finishing line at the far side of the bridge.

'You'll see that I've tried to include as many tourist sites as I could,' she said. 'But I'm sure we can adapt the route if there are any I forgot or any communes that we need to add for political reasons.' She smiled at him, a sudden hint of playfulness in her eyes. 'We certainly don't want any of the mayors to feel left out.'

'I'm proposing three different kinds of sponsor, starting with the various car companies themselves along with Electricité de France and all the renewable energy companies we can recruit,' she went on. 'The second tier would be governmental, the European Union's energy and environmental commissions and equivalent bodies from France. The third tier would be the international public, starting of course with every school in the Périgord, since we promote this race as being about their future.

We challenge every schoolchild to donate five cents towards the cash prize we offer to the winner of the race – the publicity value will far outweigh the money we raise that way.'

She handed him another sheet of paper from the folder. 'Here's my marketing plan for targeting these different tiers. You can see that my preliminary calculations suggest that with my estimated income target of three million euros the race should cover its costs and make a modest profit. Naturally that will go to financing green energy at all the other tourist sites in the region, starting with the Lascaux cave itself.'

She sat back, her hands in her lap and her back straight, the very image of the professional businesswoman. But her face was not quite impassive; there was a slight lift to one eyebrow, Bruno noted, as if daring him not to be impressed.

He sat back, blinking partly in admiration, partly in surprise at the figures in her proposal. 'This is admirable, Martine. You must have put a lot of work into it and you didn't have much time. It's obviously a very professional piece of work.'

'I'm glad you think so,' she said coolly. 'Here's a note on my proposed terms. We will need to establish a non-profit foundation to administer and run the overall project. The foundation will contract with my company for the exclusive marketing rights, from which I will take an agreed percentage of all the outside funds that we raise under my plan. Fifteen per cent is the usual rate in the public relations industry. I will also organize and commission all the advertising, to include press, broadcasting and electronic media, and take the standard ad agency rates.'

Bruno scribbled down notes as she talked. He looked up. 'Your fifteen per cent of three million euros would net you four hundred and fifty thousand. We could never sell that to the council. Once the press got hold of it they'd all be thrown out at the next election. The average income per head in this commune is less than twenty thousand a year.'

'But I don't get a penny unless I make this work by raising the money,' Martine countered swiftly. 'I'll have to invest my own money in that. That's my risk.' She sat back, her eyes blazing at him. For a moment he thought she was going to walk out. Instead, she sipped at her coffee and gave him a crisp smile.

'You said you were impressed by my proposals. These aren't just ideas, Bruno, it's a serious marketing plan. What's more, I'm a woman from a local family and I want this to work.'

'Yes, I said I was impressed and I am.' He knew he was dealing with an experienced businesswoman who must have met similar hesitation when prospective clients saw the bill. Bruno felt out of his depth, but he knew his local politicians.

'I was impressed first of all by your understanding that we'd need to get the enthusiastic support of all the local communes, which means their mayors and councils,' he told her. 'I know you were born and raised here but you don't live here. I do and I know these people, their concerns and the kinds of budgets and payrolls they are accustomed to dealing with. They simply won't understand these fees you're proposing.'

She was looking at him thoughtfully.

'I'm sure you have a plan B,' he said. 'And you probably have it in your briefcase ready to show me, because the one thing I'm missing here is what happens after the race. This can't be just a one-off event, because if it works half the regions in France will be fighting to stage their own race. We need a long-term plan. If this is going to work, it will be because the Vézère valley becomes a household word for racing, like Le Mans or Silverstone or the Nürburgring.'

'I agree. There's a note on the list of prospective sponsors that says we're looking for a five-year commitment. That means it will be the biggest boost to the tourism industry this region has ever had,' she said firmly. She was still full of confidence and showed no sign of backing down from her fees. After a moment, she smiled at him. 'Your mayors and council members will all see that, or they will when we explain it to them. You can sell this project, Bruno. My dad says they trust you.'

Bruno smiled inwardly. She was changing her approach from combative one moment to appeasing the next. Didn't she know that every policeman in France had learned to play good cop, bad cop within months of starting the job? Bruno might not know much about business negotiations, but he knew how to get what he wanted from interrogations, and this meeting wasn't so different. He returned her smile and sat forward. His hands were relaxed on the desk and he opened them, spreading his arms so that his body language suggested agreement and understanding.

'Yes, Martine, you may be right about that. And I recognize that you're an expert in your field and you're probably worth every cent. But you don't want these people whose support we need to think you're being greedy. You have to make this about them and their valley and their local businesses. Right now, I'm worried that they'll take one look at your proposed terms and decide that it's all about you.'

She raised her eyebrows and leaned forward, resting her chin on her hands and gazing at him with interest. 'So, as the local expert, what do you suggest?'

'Don't try to take all the money up front. Delay the payments. Cut your fee to two per cent the first year, and raise it in stages for subsequent years. That gives you a stake in the project's long-term success.'

'I'll then have skin in the game,' she said. 'That's the current business-school jargon for sharing the risk.'

'I wouldn't know,' he said. 'Around here we'd say bread today, jam tomorrow.'

'Very well,' she said, stretching out her hand. 'Three per cent the first year, five per cent the second year, seven the third and then ten per cent thereafter.'

He held up a hand. 'You mentioned you would expect the standard agency rate for all advertising. I don't know what that is, but we'd better have it on the same sliding scale.'

She withdrew her hand a little, and eyed him, considering. Ah, he thought, she's playing the silence trick, putting pressure on me to fill it. But he knew how to do that.

'Of course, all of this is notional until I take you in to convince my Mayor, and then we'll have to introduce you to all the councils in the valley to make your presentation. But on that basis, sliding scale for both fees and advertising commissions, you'll have my full support.'

He held out his own hand. 'Do we have a deal?'

She remained still but she did something with her eyes that made them unreadable. 'What about you?'

Bruno raised his eyebrows. Could she possibly be thinking he would take a bribe? He stared at her levelly and said nothing.

'What's in this for you?' she said, cocking her head as though simply curious. 'Would you want to be hired as security consultant?'

'I'm the chief of police for St Denis, so I'll do that anyway as part of my normal work,' he said. 'I believe we can make this work for the good of my town and the whole valley. That's enough for me.' He paused. 'There's just one more thing.'

She arched her eyebrows. 'And what is that?'

'If we shake hands on this, I'll take you to lunch, then we go to see the Mayor.'

Without a smile or any other visible expression on her face, she reached forward, took his hand and shook it once. 'Agreed.'

Then she smiled, and suddenly she looked like a different woman, still entirely professional and businesslike but very much more human.

12

Even though Martine had relaxed sufficiently to loosen her hair from its bun so it floated free, the lunch had been a mistake. Bruno was too well-known to be permitted an undisturbed meal with an attractive stranger. Ivan himself came from the kitchen to hover and to be introduced. He was followed by Bruno's hunting partner Stéphane, Julien, from the town vineyard, and Rollo, the headmaster at the local *collège*. Then Dr Gelletreau arrived, declaring proudly that Martine had been one of the first babies he had brought into the world after opening his practice in St Denis. He promptly sat down at their table.

Once they had finished Ivan's *plat du jour* of *steak-frites* and returned to Bruno's office, Martine took from her briefcase the thinnest laptop he'd ever seen to amend the papers outlining her terms and printed them out at Bruno's desk. After a brisk hour of discussion with the Mayor, Bruno excused himself when his mobile rang with the special tone that signalled the Brigadier's office. With the sense of foreboding that always came when he heard from this powerful official in the Interior Ministry, Bruno took the call in his office.

'*Bonjour*, Bruno,' came the Brigadier's crisp voice, sounding suspiciously affable. 'I'm calling to let you know there's a serious operation coming onto your patch. We're giving full support to a multinational operation that's being led by Eurojust. It has to do with money-laundering, probably to fund terrorism, and there's a Périgord connection. It's being led by an old friend of yours, Commissaire Perrault. It seems you parted on difficult terms, so she asked me to smooth the way.'

'Would this be connected to the operation in Luxembourg that went wrong?' Bruno asked, remembering the gossip he'd heard from J-J.

'Where did you hear about that?'

'Just a rumour among cops. Commissaire Perrault used to serve down here, you'll recall. She has a lot of friends in the region.'

'Sounds like our friend Jean-Jacques has been indiscreet again. It wasn't serious, just one of those usual bureaucratic disputes. It just delayed things a bit, but it's all being straightened out now.' The Brigadier's tone changed, becoming brisk again. 'I'm sure you'll be entirely professional and give her your complete cooperation. I'll fax the usual letter to your Mayor. And remember, Perrault is in charge and she'll call you in a few moments.'

It had been a long time since Bruno had thought of Isabelle as Commissaire Perrault. Even after the passing of time and the pain she had caused him, his heart still skipped a beat at the thought of her. The Brigadier's 'usual letter' attached Bruno temporarily to the minister's staff. The letter to the Mayor, Bruno's nominal boss, was simply a formality. If the Brigadier chose, he could activate Bruno's reserve status in the French army and place him under military discipline. That would be disagreeable, but coming under Isabelle's command would be disagreeable in a different and deeply personal way.

During the passionate summer months of their affair he would have called her the love of his life, and the intensity of the attraction and the physical passion remained. But for Isabelle, her career in Paris and now at Eurojust in The Hague took a higher priority than the love of a simple country policeman in the Périgord. If she had stayed as a detective in the Police Nationale in Périgueux, she would by now be the heir apparent to Bruno's friend Jean-Jacques, and they might have stayed together and fulfilled Bruno's dream of a family of his own. He had resigned himself to losing her. But during one of those occasional reunions when they had not been able to resist one another, she had become pregnant and had chosen to abort the child without telling him until the deed was done.

Biting his lip, Bruno went down the old stone steps of the Mairie into the fresh air and walked to the centre of the bridge to stare at the river and tell himself he was no longer in Isabelle's thrall. He could go for a week or two without even thinking of her, but then something – a song or a place or even the way some woman turned her head – would summon the memories. And now Isabelle was coming back into his life. He let out a long sigh and headed across the bridge to the open parkland behind the medical centre, waiting for her call and wishing Balzac were with him. Balzac, who had been Isabelle's gift to him after the death of Bruno's first dog, was just as attached to her as his master.

His phone vibrated and he braced himself before answering.

'*Bonjour*, Bruno, I hope you're well,' came the familiar voice, dear but disturbing. 'Are we secure?'

'The button on my phone is green. We're secure. The Brigadier said you were running a multinational operation. What's up?'

'Money-laundering with some Arab connections and links to terrorist financial networks. The Brits, Germans and Belgians are involved and the Americans are in the loop. There's now a Périgord link, so I'll be coming down to maintain the surveillance. We've been monitoring two principals and their mobile phones show them moving around St Denis.'

Bruno felt he knew what was coming. There were not many people newly arrived in St Denis with international financial connections. Was it Sylvestre or Martine or both?

'The names are Sylvestre Wémy, a French citizen, and Farid Iqbal, born in India but travelling on a Portuguese passport after buying his citizenship with a million-euro investment. Do you know anything about them?'

'I was sitting by their pool yesterday and racing against them in a rally the day before that,' he replied, enjoying the gasp of surprise he heard down the phone. 'Sylvestre owns property here and Farid, who calls himself Freddy, won the rally. Apparently he also won some big race in the Middle East. Sylvestre is from a rich Alsace family and owns a showroom in Dubai selling classic cars. He has a grandmother who was born in St Denis. How can I help?'

'You already have. We didn't know Farid was a racing driver. The car business is how they manipulate the money. I'll be arriving tomorrow or the day after with a surveillance team – if the Brigadier and I can clear the paperwork in time. Plotting their phone locations on a map, we think they're in a large three-sided building with a farm nearby but no real access road and no other neighbours.'

'That's the house Sylvestre inherited from his grandmother. The nearby farm belongs to another wing of the family and they're at loggerheads over the inheritance. Audio surveillance won't be easy because the farmer is trying to drive them out with hundreds of cackling geese.'

She laughed, a sound that touched his heart. 'We usually use bailiffs; driving people out with geese sounds very Périgord. Do they have any other visitors?'

'Not at the moment, except for another family member who's trying to settle the feud. Martine Oudinot is her maiden name, aged somewhere in her thirties. She's divorced so might have a different name and is now based in London where she runs a PR company. I can email you her mobile phone number. She was there at the house when I called on them yesterday.'

'Thanks and it's good to be working with you again. I'll call to say when I'm arriving. And be careful not to do anything that might alert them. So far we're just monitoring them.' She paused, as if about to hang up, and then in a different tone of voice, she asked, 'How's Balzac?'

Bruno smiled at the question; they would always have Balzac. 'He's in great form. He runs after me when I'm riding and he's learning to hunt. But there's a lot of puppy left in him – he still rolls onto his back for a tummy scratch whenever you stroke his ears.'

'I'll look forward to that – and remember that some of the truffles he finds will be mine,' she replied, chuckling, and he thought he could imagine the grin on her face. 'Take care.' She closed the connection.

He smiled as he closed his phone and there was a spring in his step as he returned across the bridge to collect his van. He had time to call at Lespinasse's garage before picking up Félix for his interview at the riding school. Young Edouard Lespinasse, who had protected the boy from the bullies, was probably the nearest Félix had to a friend. That made him a potential ally to steer Félix into a better life.

The garage was for Bruno one of the symbols of the way St Denis was being forced to change. Just like Delaron's photography shop, which had been rendered obsolete by the ubiquitous camera phone, Lespinasse's garage had closed its gas pumps, unable to compete with the cheaper prices at the supermarket. Even the Mairie, which had long used the garage to refill its various vehicles, including Bruno's police van, had worked out they could save nearly a thousand euros a year by using the discount pumps. And the traditional work of local mechanics had been eroded by the new generations of cars that needed less servicing and rather the skills of a computer technician. So Lespinasse had reinvented his business as a place to restore old cars and Edouard had developed a useful sideline in tuning motocross racing bikes and restoring old motorbikes. Spending two days a week at the technical school in Périgueux and four days a week at the garage, Edouard was becoming as good a mechanic as his father, and would get formal qualifications when he completed his technical course. But Bruno still felt a pang as he pulled into the garage and saw the gaps where the pumps used to be.

'*Salut*, Bruno,' said Lespinasse, emerging from beneath the bonnet of the Jaguar E-type that Annette's boyfriend had been driving. He extended his forearm to be shaken, sparing Bruno his oily hand. 'You did well at the rally. If you want to take up the sport, I've got a useful little Peugeot that would do you well.'

'One rally with Annette was enough for me,' he replied. 'What's wrong with the E-type?'

'Nothing, but I offered to give it a tune-up just for the pleasure of working on the car. It's a bit different from Jack Crimson's old model. The owner is coming back to pick it up tonight at about seven. I'll have it purring by then.'

'Is Edouard around?' Bruno asked. Jean-Louis gestured to the rear garage where the motorbikes were kept and Bruno found Edouard and Félix working together on the old bicycle rescued from the dump. The bike had been transformed, cleaned and polished, the chrome on the handlebars sparkling, and the chain tautened.

'I'm impressed,' said Bruno after greeting them. 'You guys have done a good job.'

'Félix did most of it,' said Edouard. 'He just needed to borrow some of my tools.'

Bruno checked his watch and looked at Félix. 'If you leave now, you'll be at the stables in half an hour or so. I'll see you there. I just want a word with Edouard first.'

Félix set off, pedalling hard, and as they looked after him Edouard said, 'He told me what you did at the supermarket.'

'I remember doing something of the kind for you a few years back, when the head teacher caught you pinching his prize tulips.'

'I remember,' Edouard said, grinning. 'It was Mother's Day.'

'It turned into father's day pretty fast when I took you back to your dad,' said Bruno. 'I could hear your howls as I drove off.'

Edouard laughed. 'Dad always had a strong arm. The spanking probably did me good. Listen, Félix is a good kid at heart, but he's always been too scrawny to play any sports and he never really fitted in. That's why he always got bullied.'

'I gather you helped protect him from the worst of it.'

'There wasn't much I could do, once we were in different classes. And you know how kids can be. His mother being a cleaner at the school made it worse. Even the girls would ask him when he'd be washing the windows, teasing him. I tried telling him to make a joke of it but he didn't really know how to handle it.'

'Has he got the makings of a mechanic?'

'He knows his way around an engine and he's helped me strip a gearbox. But he's not what I'd call a natural, you know, like some people can just listen to an engine and know what's wrong.'

'Like you and your dad,' said Bruno. 'It must be in the blood.'

'He'll do well with the horses,' said Edouard. 'He always got on well with animals, and I know he likes being at that little farm the new teacher started at the *collège*.'

'We'll see,' said Bruno. 'I'm glad he's got a friend in you, even though I know you're busy with the tech school. Are you enjoying it?'

Edouard nodded. 'There's a couple of teachers there who really know what they're doing. One of them was a merchant seaman, working on engines on the Corsica ferries. He's great on diesels and the technical drawing, and the electrics guy is brilliant. We do a lot on car computers because he says that's the future.'

He paused, evidently with something else to say but choosing his words with care. 'I'll keep an eye out for Félix, but it's not like there's any work for him here. So far my dad is just making ends meet. Maybe if this classic car business picks up after this weekend . . .'

'I understand,' said Bruno. He'd never assumed that the small garage could afford another employee. 'I'd better get along and see how Félix does with the horses.'

At the riding school, Pamela told Bruno that Félix was doing well enough to be invited back to work on Saturday. They left Félix loading hay into the stable mangers with a pitchfork. Pamela took Bruno for a stroll around the paddock where Miranda was teaching three little girls to trot on their plump ponies.

'The boy's not frightened of the horses, they seem to know he's comfortable around them and he's a willing worker. That new Andalusian that Fabiola is interested in can get a bit lively, and he did well to calm her. What do you think I should pay him? I can't afford minimum wage.'

'Pay him in riding lessons and maybe after a while you might want to give him some pocket money. But don't give him too much. I'd say ten euros for a Saturday should do it.'

'You'll have me arrested for exploiting child labour,' she said with a laugh. 'The occasional ten euros won't break me. And what if I paid him in kit? I've got an old pair of riding boots that should fit him and the last owners left an assortment of riding caps and jodhpurs in the tack room.'

'I think he'd be delighted. But don't give it all at once. Dole it out, make him know he's got to work for his rewards.'

'Like I did with you, you mean?' she said, turning to him and smiling as she took his arm. 'You were very patient with me. It's one of the reasons I always knew you'd be good with horses.'

'You said once that I was the first man you'd been with since your marriage broke up.'

'It's true, and I'm glad it was you, Bruno. I just hope Miranda finds someone as kind. She's the sort of woman who really needs a man in her life, and it's been hard on her, being left with the children.'

Bruno looked at her, startled. Surely she couldn't be hinting that he should take the role. Pamela knew him well enough to read his thoughts.

'*Mon Dieu*, not you, Bruno!' she said, laughing. 'Miranda would be quite wrong for you, although I can see many a man would find that plump, pink innocence rather enticing. She'd try to domesticate you and bring you carpet slippers. You'd be driven to drink within weeks.'

Bruno paused, wondering what to say, and finally came out with something that sounded lame, even to him. 'She has a new life now, new friends, the riding school to run.'

'That's the problem. The riding school takes all her time in the days and the children fill the evenings and weekends. It doesn't leave much time to be out and about and meeting new people. Maybe you could talk to her father, tell him to start throwing some more of his parties.'

'I have enough on my plate without getting involved in match-making,' said Bruno, although mentally he was running through a list of the few unattached men in the district. They turned back to the stables, where Félix was whistling as he hosed down the yard in a pair of rubber boots that looked much too big for him. He looked up as they approached and his face turned solemn as he addressed Pamela.

'I've given them all hay and water but I thought I'd stay to help the girls unsaddle the ponies,' he said. 'Is that okay?'

Pamela nodded. 'That would be fine, Félix. Will we see you on Saturday morning? We start at eight to get ready for the first lessons at nine.'

'Sure, I'll be here,' he said cheerfully, his eyes shining. 'But can I also come back tomorrow after school?'

13

Bruno pulled in at Lespinasse's garage just after seven and heard the deep and potent roar of a perfectly tuned engine. Young was in the driving seat and Jean-Louis stood proudly alongside as Young smiled his appreciation at the work that had been done.

'Would you like to come for a spin?' Young asked Bruno.

'Very much.' He climbed inside, surprised at the size of the steering wheel and the old-fashioned knobs and switches on the dashboard. He enjoyed the deep leather seats and the wood trim. He felt very low to the road.

'The only new element is the safety belts,' said Young. 'They weren't required when this was built. Where shall we take her?'

Bruno took him up the winding hill road that led to Boutenègre and then through the woods to the long, straight stretch between St Cirq and Les Eyzies. As soon as they reached the straight, Young dropped into second gear and the acceleration hit Bruno like a punch in the back. He glanced at the speedometer, indicating a much slower speed than he'd have imagined. Then he suddenly realized it must be marked in miles per hour. By the time he had calculated they were doing a hundred and eighty, Young was slowing for the tight bends that led to the bridge over the river and the narrow main street of Les Eyzies.

'Glad to hear your migraine cleared up so fast,' Bruno said, as the sound of the engine diminished to a throaty murmur. 'I had to stand in for you at the rally and Annette scared the wits out of me. Now it seems I'll have to do it all over again.'

Young apologized, saying some vital business had come up.

'To do with Sylvestre?' Bruno asked, thinking of Isabelle's call.

'In a way.' Young glanced at him sideways. 'How did you know?'

'Pull in here on the right,' Bruno said. 'We'll never hear each other once we're on the road. You and Sylvestre seem to be interested in the same car, the one whose picture you showed me.'

'Did he tell you about the Bugatti?' Young asked. 'Damn him, he may have all the money but it's my family.'

'How do you mean, your family? Did they own it? I thought you said it was lost in the war.'

'It wasn't lost. It disappeared,' Young replied. 'Anyone who finds it will make a fortune, and my family was very much involved with that car.'

Young explained that his great-grandmother's brother had been William Grover-Williams, a British racing driver who lived in France, married a French wife and worked and raced for Bugatti in the 1930s. He'd been born in France in 1903, where his father had bred horses. At the age of sixteen, he'd talked his way into a job as chauffeur for William Orpen, a British artist who had been commissioned at the end of the First World War to do portraits of the participants at the Versailles peace conference. Grover-Williams fell in love with Orpen's mistress, a Frenchwoman named Yvonne Aupicq, and later married her. In 1928, he won the French Grand Prix and the following year, in a Bugatti 35B like the one owned by Sylvestre, Grover-Williams won the first Monaco Grand Prix. Bugatti hired him as a regular driver, along with his friend Robert Benoist, who went on to win the first twenty-four-hour race at Le Mans. Grover-Williams also acted as a salesman for Bugatti and was allowed to drive the now-missing Atlantic model around Paris.

'One of the few remaining photos of the car from the period shows Yvonne standing by the car with her dogs, Scottish terriers,' Young said.

'So driving is in your blood,' said Bruno. 'No wonder you're so passionate about cars.'

'Grover-Williams was a hero in our household. My mother was his great-niece, although she was born after the war and never met him. And he was a real hero in the Resistance with Benoist.'

During the war, Williams had volunteered to join SOE, Britain's Special Operations Executive, an underground organization that sought to recruit, arm and train Resistance fighters in occupied Europe. He and Benoist had built the Chestnut network in and around Paris, using their racing connections to arrange parachute drops of arms.

'That's where things get murky,' Young said. 'The official record says Grover-Williams wasn't parachuted in from England until early 1942, by which time the famous Bugatti had disappeared.'

As Hitler planned the German invasion of Russia in June 1941, a crash programme to build more weapons took over the Bugatti factory in Alsace, Young explained. The cars and some of the machine tools the Nazis did not need were evacuated to Bordeaux. In February 1941, the factory records showed that the famous Bugatti Atlantic left for Bordeaux. But it never got there.

'Was Grover-Williams driving it?' Bruno asked.

'It's not clear. The official records suggest that he was undergoing training in England until early 1942, but we have family letters that say he went to France in early 1941 on some secret mission, and some of his French friends remember seeing him in Paris with Benoist around that time.'

Somewhere between Alsace and Bordeaux, the car had disappeared. Both Grover-Williams and Benoist were arrested by the Gestapo and later died in concentration camps. Nobody ever knew what happened to the car, nor whether either of the two racing drivers was at the wheel when it vanished.

'So you're here looking for the car? I imagine you're not the first to try to track it down. But is there anything to suggest it still exists?'

'I found something interesting in the family papers, a reference to friends Grover-Williams trusted, a British family living in a château in the Périgord, at Rastignac. I heard about an old woman who worked at the château as a maid during the war. I've been trying to see her for weeks. I finally got the call that she would see me on the morning of the rally. That's why I had to let Annette down and leave you in the hot seat. I'm sorry.'

Bruno wondered why he hadn't told Annette the truth, but instead he asked, 'And did this old woman know anything about the car?'

'Not a thing. She seemed baffled by my question. She said everybody else who had wanted to talk to her asked only about the valuable paintings that had been in the château. Apparently the Nazis took them and burned the place down. It looks pretty good now, though.'

'Did the château seem familiar?'

'Yes, but I couldn't place it.'

'We call it the French White House. The design was copied by the architect of the one in Washington. Ours is the original, although the Americans don't believe it.'

'Well, it was a wasted day. And I'm sure Sylvestre will be miles ahead of me. He's got the money to hire professional researchers.'

'So you're competing?' Bruno noted that reference to professional researchers. There were not many of them in the region, other than the late Monsieur Hugon. Could Sylvestre be his mysterious client?

'Absolutely, we're competing,' said Young. 'I suggested we join forces but Sylvestre just shook his head and smiled in that infuriatingly superior way of his. I thought my bit of family knowledge might give me an edge.'

'What do you know about Sylvestre and his friend Freddy?'

'That he's rich, does well in his classic car business, particularly since he and Freddy launched the new showroom in Dubai. And Freddy is a hell of a driver. I don't know Sylvestre that well. When we meet, usually for a meal or a drink when he comes to London, we talk about cars. But he's never asked about my personal life.'

'Does he know of your link to Grover-Williams?'

'Not from me. It's the only advantage I have so I've kept it to myself. But that Rastignac connection doesn't seem to be getting me very far.'

'There's somebody else in on the hunt now,' said Bruno. 'A journalist friend of mine who sometimes works for *Paris Match*. His interest is the story rather than the car, but he picked up something that seemed to interest Sylvestre.'

Bruno told Young of Martine's memoir from the downed RAF bomber pilot who was picked up and helped to escape in the Bugatti by someone who sounded like Benoist. But it might have been Grover-Williams.

'How did you learn that,' Young asked eagerly. 'Did Sylvestre have a copy of this memoir?'

'Yes, and he seemed excited by it, which makes me think he hasn't found any sign of the car itself. He's still looking for clues.'

'Just like me,' said Young. 'But when we last spoke, he had that cat who got the cream expression on his face, as though he knew a lot that I didn't. But then he often looks like that.'

'This all happened seventy years ago,' Bruno said. 'Even if you find the car hidden in some abandoned barn, won't it be rusted away by now?'

'Depends on how carefully it was stored, and it was made of a special alloy, part magnesium, so rust wouldn't have been a problem. But magnesium has a low ignition point, which explains why they couldn't weld the car and had to use rivets instead. There's a long ridge running along the roof where the rivets held the bodywork together.'

'Still, the chances of finding it must be pretty slim,' said Bruno. 'And it's even less likely that it would be in a fit state to be restored.'

'We only need to find three out of five items,' said Young, ticking them off on his fingers as he spoke. 'There's the engine, the chassis, the transmission and the front or rear axle. With three of those, it counts as a restoration. And with that car's legend, it's worth thirty or forty million, maybe more.'

'Maybe you should talk to my reporter friend,' said Bruno. 'I don't think you're going to get very far on your own.'

Bruno directed Young towards Gilles's home. Careful of his car's suspension, Young went slowly up the long approach on the dirt road. He stopped as they topped a gentle rise to see the old farmhouse in the gentle hollow below. It was flanked by two barns that Pamela had converted into self-contained *gîtes*. The buildings formed a natural courtyard, dominated by an old ash tree in the centre, and a vine-covered terrace made a charming spot for dining in summer. Two embracing wings of poplars were set back from the house, and the way the farm blended into the landscape made it seem both peaceful and welcoming.

They found Gilles at work in the spare bedroom of the main house, which he had turned into his study, lining the walls with bookcases and filing cabinets. Beneath the window he'd installed a big old dining table as a desk. To Young's surprise, on a bulletin board where Gilles had pinned notes, business cards and photos of Fabiola was attached a printout of the car Bruno had first seen on Young's mobile phone.

Bruno introduced the two men and, over a glass of wine, Young explained what he knew of the lost Bugatti and his family connection. Gilles had been researching on the internet and had downloaded from the Imperial War Museum in London a copy of the memoir by the downed RAF pilot. Young scanned it quickly, requested an atlas and asked if the Michelin factory at

Clermont-Ferrand was inside the territory administered by the Vichy regime. Bruno confirmed that it was.

'So if the car picked him up near Clermont-Ferrand, the direct route to Bordeaux would come through the Périgord,' said Young.

'The best road would go through Terrasson and Périgueux,' said Bruno. 'That would take him right past the Château de Rastignac.'

Young quickly told Gilles of his fruitless visit to interview the former maid.

'Let's be frank about this. My interest is the story, which is a pretty good yarn even if we don't find the car. People always like mysteries,' Gilles said, looking at Young. 'But what about you? Is your real interest the car or the money it might make?'

'The money would be fine, but I probably wouldn't get much more than a finder's fee,' Young replied. 'Ownership will be a legal mess. I imagine Bugatti would have a claim, but they were wound up decades ago and I don't know if the new Bugatti company would have any right to the old assets. The heirs of the driver might have a claim, depending on the contract he had with Bugatti to deliver it. The owner of whatever place it might be hidden would want at least decades of storage fees. And even if it is found and can be restored, full restoration costs would run into the millions.'

'In that case, why not broaden the search by publicizing it?' Bruno asked. 'We could bring in Jack Crimson, whose contacts might find something in the SOE archives. You might consider asking Florence and her computer club to trawl the internet for links to any of the people or places connected to

Grover-Williams. And why not get *Sud Ouest* to run a story and see if any new information turns up? It might mean you'll have to share any finder's fee.'

'Let's not bring *Sud Ouest* into this, they're competition,' said Gilles. 'At least wait until I run the story in *Paris Match.*'

Young looked uncertainly from Bruno to Gilles, obviously unsure how much to trust them. Bruno didn't know much about Young, but if Annette liked him, Bruno was prepared to give him the benefit of the doubt. What Bruno couldn't say was that Sylvestre and Freddy were the targets of Isabelle's operation, which made them serious suspects. And if Sylvestre had indeed been in the market for a professional researcher there was a chance that they might be linked to Hugon's death.

'If we make the search public through the press, how might the money be shared out?' Young asked. He looked from Bruno to Gilles and back again, an appeal in his eyes. 'Please bear in mind that I've lived with this story since I was a boy. I can't tell you how many times I sat at my mother's knee, hearing about this ancestor of ours, one of the great racing drivers as well as a Resistance hero. What I'm trying to say is that this is very personal for me and I've put a lot of time and effort into it. So however the money gets shared out, I think I should get half.'

'That's not just greedy, it's premature,' said Gilles. 'We don't know what else we'll find out, or who might contribute crucial new information.'

'I'll be frank,' Young said. 'The money is quite important to me but it's not the only thing. If I get credit as the man who played a key role in finding the lost Bugatti, that would really

146

make my name and also allow me to give old Grover-Williams his due.'

'I can see that,' said Gilles. 'He and Benoist both deserve to be better known, and that's one thing I can contribute.'

'Yes, but as you said, it doesn't matter to you whether the car is found or not. You still have your story.' Young gave Gilles a hard look.

'It's a much better story if it is found,' said Bruno, trying to still the sudden note of hostility that was developing between the two men. 'Why don't we ask Annette to adjudicate anything to do with money? We each know her and trust her.'

Young gave a long sigh. 'Okay, but I have real doubts about doing anything that might bring Sylvestre into this. I don't trust him and I'm sure he'll have thought through all these questions about ownership and he can afford the best legal advice. He might even have found some way of buying the rights to any Bugatti lost in transit during the war.'

'I understand that,' said Bruno. 'But once this search goes public, you and he are on an equal footing. You'll get the credit in *Paris Match* as the man who launched this search and you're also the relative of Grover-Williams. It will be your story, not his.'

Young sipped at his wine, looking solemnly at each of them in turn. Then he put out his hand towards Gilles and said, 'In that case, I think we have a deal.'

14

Young dropped Bruno back at the garage to pick up his police van and Bruno drove home to change, check his ducks and chickens, and take Balzac for a brisk walk through the woods. It was in the stillness of the trees that Bruno did his best thinking. He liked this time of year when the first leaves had begun to fall but the canopy above him was still golden brown, tinged with red where it caught the last rays of the setting sun. The birdsong was changing as the summer migrants moved south and the hunting season had opened. He had not been out yet, preferring to wait until the weather grew colder and Balzac's training had progressed. Bruno whistled, and the dog came to heel at once, but he was still learning the whistled notes that sent him skirting right or left before driving Bruno's much-desired *bécasses* back to his master. Young as he was, Balzac seemed fearless, ready to chase away even a big fox. Feeling a sudden burst of affection, Bruno kneeled down to stroke him and tell him what a fine hunting dog he would be.

As he walked back, he thought of his next steps. Isabelle's investigation into terrorist finance was beyond his skills. He'd leave that to her. But the death of Hugon was his business. He would need to ask Sylvestre about Hugon. Even if he denied knowing the man, Sylvestre's face might show some reaction. He should ask Madame Hugon if she'd ever heard the name, and whether any new mail had arrived for her husband since his death. He needed to ask other members of the history society whether Hugon had talked about his latest research job. The euro notes in Hugon's wallet were new; the numbers might be traced back to the bank where they were issued. J-J could take care of that. But first he should do what he could to help Isabelle.

Back at his home, he went to a locked cupboard in his barn and took out two battery-operated surveillance cameras that he'd recuperated from one of the Brigadier's earlier surveillance operations at a local château. He'd always thought they might come in handy some day. Then he called Isabelle.

'Where are our two suspects now?' he asked.

'Their phones show Sylvestre in Trémolat and Farid in central Sarlat, each in a fixed location, so I assume they're having dinner. But it might be another day or two before I can get down,' she replied. 'This is turning into a real mess. Since we've been using the Americans' TFTP we have to go through all kinds of hoops to abide by European rules on data sharing with the US.'

'What's the TFTP?'

'Terrorist Finance Tracking Program. They've got the best data on money movements, but in order to use it both we and Europol are required to verify each individual case and ensure every request we make is necessary and tailored as narrowly as possible to minimize the amount of data collected. It's crazy – we're all fighting the same people. In the meantime, whatever surveillance we can mount depends on you and Jean-Jacques.'

'Leave it with me and let me know when you get here,' he

said. 'But if you can monitor their movements by their phones, what else do you need?'

'We need to know about any visitors or meetings they have, that's the priority, along with the licence plates and registration numbers of whatever vehicles they're using. We want to know if they're visiting internet cafés to use an email address we don't know about.'

'OK. I might be able to help with the vehicle numbers. I took some photos of the place where they're staying on my phone and their rental cars were parked there. Your technicians should be able to blow up the images. I'll email them to you. Is Jean-Jacques providing any support?'

'He's trying but he's short-staffed as it is. I know you'll do your best and, thanks, Bruno. Give Balzac a hug for me.'

She hung up and before setting off Bruno mentally reviewed the map of the region that he carried in his head. He couldn't use the direct road that led to Sylvestre's place in case he or Freddy returned early and saw his car. Nor did he want to alert Fernand by using the access through the Oudinot farm. There was a hunting trail he knew that went close enough, so Bruno loaded Balzac into the passenger seat of his Land Rover and headed down the lane, through St Denis and out on the road to Le Buisson. When he got to the distinctive bend in the hunting path he pulled out his map and a compass to check the bearing to Sylvestre's house. Ten minutes later, Balzac snuffling at his heels, he reached the road and saw the *chartreuse*, illuminated by a porch light.

He took one of the cameras from his rucksack, checked the new batteries and the data stick he'd installed to record the images, and used the same black masking tape he'd used to seal the casing against rain to fix it into the fork of a tree. He juggled it until the lens had a clear view of the muddied track that led to the lodge and courtyard. He put the second camera at a spot where it had a view of both the pool area and the path that Oudinot had sealed off. That would have to do. He checked that neither camera was visible from the road or the house, led Balzac back to the Land Rover and returned to St Denis. Back in town, his phone was showing four bars of reception, so he sent the photos of Sylvestre's place to Isabelle.

There were only two customers left in Ivan's bistro, strangers who seemed to be speaking English. Ivan looked at his watch when Bruno came in with Balzac, gestured him to a seat at the bar and poured out a generous glass of scotch. 'I've got some tuna salad left, a slice of apple pie, and you can share the nasi goreng that Mandy's making for us. That suit you? What about your dog?'

'*Santé*,' said Bruno, taking a sip of the scotch. 'That all sounds good, and just a bowl of water for Balzac, please. I fed him before I left home. How's Mandy?'

Ivan invariably returned from vacation with a girl he'd met, and usually found one whose cooking skills could enlarge his own repertoire. There had been a Belgian girl who broke his heart, but left him with half-a-dozen ways of preparing mussels and the recipe for a thick chicken stew called Waterzooi. A Spanish girl had introduced St Denis to gazpacho and paella, and the departure of the German girl with her Wiener Schnitzel was sincerely mourned by Ivan's customers – he could never get the breadcrumb coating quite right without her expert assistance.

His last vacation to South-east Asia had raised hopes among the townsfolk that he'd return with a Thai woman who would broaden his menu yet further. Instead he'd fallen for Mandy, a breezy Australian who could wipe the floor with Bruno at tennis. She was working with Ivan while awaiting approval for her application to study at the wine school in Bordeaux. Having spent a year in Indonesia before meeting Ivan on the beach at Kota Bahru in Malaysia, she knew how to prepare a range of Asian foods.

One memorable evening Mandy had produced for Ivan's regulars a *rijsttafel* of a dozen different dishes: chicken in peanut sauce, caramelized beef rendang braised in coconut milk and chillies, duck roasted in banana leaves and pork braised in sweet soy sauce. There had been different kinds of noodles, rice and spring rolls. While the names of the various dishes escaped him, the meal had lasted for hours and Bruno had never forgotten it. Tonight's nasi goreng, which Mandy translated as fried rice, was rice with salted dried fish, prawns, hard-boiled eggs and shallots, all generously flavoured with garlic and tamarind. Bruno had eaten it before and enjoyed it.

'Mandy's fine, but what about you? Tell me about this new girlfriend of yours, Martine.'

'Not a girlfriend, just a local woman back for a brief visit to her folks,' Bruno replied. 'She's going to be helping us set up a new rally for next year, so it was a business lunch, at least until Gelletreau decided he wanted to join us and tell stories about her childhood measles and whooping cough.'

Balzac padded across to greet the middle-aged couple who had finished their meal. They made much of him before calling across to Ivan for the bill in broken French, and Mandy came out from the kitchen to say goodbye to them. But first she introduced them to Bruno, saying they were Americans from California on vacation. Bruno's English had improved in his time with Pamela and it was fluent enough, if full of mistakes. He was able to ask where they had been so far and they enthused about their visit to the Lascaux cave earlier that day. Like most local restaurants, Ivan kept a stand by the door filled with tourist brochures and Bruno pulled out one for them that listed the main attractions. They left, promising to return for another of Ivan's meals. Ivan steered Bruno to a table set for four and went into the kitchen to fetch the tuna salad.

The nasi goreng was delicious and the apple pie came with a generous scoop of vanilla ice cream. The three of them were chatting over coffee when the door opened and a very late customer came in. Bruno turned to see it was Martine, looking dressed to kill in a little black dress beneath her stylish raincoat, but her jaw was set and her eyes were angry.

'I need a drink,' she began. 'Bruno, I'm glad to see you here because it's you I'm looking for. Sorry if I'm interrupting but I need to talk about Sylvestre.'

'Sit down, join us,' he said, pouring her a glass of wine and then helping her take off her coat. 'This is Ivan and Mandy and my dog is called Balzac. Have you eaten?'

'Yes, thanks,' she said, leaning down to fondle Balzac, who always had a soft spot for women. Maybe it was something about their scent, Bruno thought, as he caught a hint of Martine's vaguely familiar perfume.

'A dog like this is just what I need to calm me down,' she said

153

as Balzac licked enthusiastically at her hand. 'Sylvestre took me
to the Vieux Logis in Trémolat, but other than the food it was
a wretched evening. That bastard said he was offering a settlement, but what he wants is just outrageous. Now I know why
my dad can't stand the man. He had the nerve to tell me that if
he doesn't get his way he'll bankrupt my parents with lawsuits.'

Briefly Bruno explained the family dispute to Ivan and Mandy,
who wanted to know what Martine had eaten at the Vieux Logis,
a famed local hotel whose restaurant was said to be on the verge
of winning its second Michelin star.

'The food was great – foie gras, *coquilles* St Jacques, roast veal
with truffles – but it nearly turned to ashes in my mouth,' Martine said. 'He even tried to buy me. Would you believe that he
promised me fifty thousand euros in cash if I could persuade
my parents to sell the surrounding land to him at ten per cent
above market price. We were waiting for the dessert, but at that
I threw my napkin in his face and walked out. I would have
thrown my wine after it but the glass was empty.'

'I wish I'd seen that,' said Mandy, laughing. 'I enjoy a good
scene in a restaurant.'

Martine turned to Bruno. 'Remember that Indian friend of his
at the *chartreuse*, Freddy? Do you think they're gay?'

'I have no idea, but the more I hear about Sylvestre the less
I like him,' Bruno replied. 'If he's being aggressive with you,
it's time to counter-attack. We can check in the morning but
I'm pretty sure the land around his *chartreuse* will be zoned for
residential use, since there are already buildings there. Your dad
can apply for a construction permit to build half a dozen very
cheap bungalows for social housing all around the *chartreuse*. He

doesn't have to build them, just get the permit. It's his land. He could use it as a threat. The cottages would destroy Sylvestre's views and his setting, and when he hears the term social housing he'll fear the worst.'

'You mean he'll imagine being surrounded by unemployed families and immigrants with lots of children who'd sneak into his swimming pool and puncture the tyres on his car?' asked Martine, her face lighting up with a mischievous grin. She might sound like a Parisian businesswoman but he was beginning to recognize the depth of her Périgord roots.

Bruno grinned back at her. 'You said he gave you his proposal. Did you have an alternative plan to make to him?'

'Yes, I spent a lot of time talking my dad into it, and put the plan to Sylvestre over dinner. I suggested that we all cooperate to develop the *chartreuse* and our farm as a unit for eco-tourism. Sylvestre would contribute the house and we'd contribute the farm. We'd create a new company in which we held equal shares and the company would pay my parents a salary for running the farm. There wouldn't be a cost because the farm makes a good income as it is, but my parents aren't getting any younger and this way we could run the whole thing as a commercial enterprise.'

'It sounds very reasonable, and when your parents retire you could hire a young couple to take over the farm,' Bruno said.

'Exactly. I thought it was a decent compromise, but Sylvestre turned me down flat and said the only deal he'd accept was one that let him buy the land around the *chartreuse*. That was when he tried to bribe me. Frankly I don't think I could bear to work with him at all.'

She turned to Mandy and Ivan, who had been following the exchange with interest. 'Sorry to inflict my family feud on all of you. I must be spoiling your dinner, but I'd much rather be here drinking house wine with you three than eating Michelin-starred food with that greedy boor of a cousin of mine. Thanks for letting me get it off my chest.'

'Not at all, it's been interesting,' said Ivan. 'We'd better think about closing up for the night and we'll look forward to seeing you again and hearing the next episode in the family saga.'

'Maybe the best plan is to bring your cousin to eat here and I'll put some ground glass or something in his food,' said Mandy. They all erupted in laughter.

'If Bruno hadn't heard that, I might take you up on it,' said Martine, before standing up. 'Maybe it would be better to sprinkle a heavy dose of laxatives over it, preferably just before he goes off to race one of those fancy cars of his.'

Ivan waved aside Bruno's attempt to pay for his meal. Bruno thanked him and left a 10-euro note as a tip. He helped Martine back into her coat as they said goodnight. Escorting them to the door, Ivan noticed that a light rain was falling. He handed Bruno an umbrella and said to return it sometime.

'Where's your car parked?' Bruno asked her, opening the umbrella and holding it over their heads. Balzac was looking up at them, wondering what these humans planned to do. Bruno was asking himself the same question.

Martine gestured down the street. Then she looked at him, flashing that mischievous grin again. 'Good thing I rented a car – otherwise I wouldn't have been able to walk out on Sylvestre.'

Bruno laughed, took her in the arm that wasn't holding the

umbrella and leaned forward to kiss her goodnight on both cheeks. To his surprise, as he drew back she leaned forward and kissed him firmly on the mouth, her lips surprisingly soft and a sound like a purr coming from deep in her throat. It only lasted a moment but it touched him. It had been a while since he'd kissed a woman like that.

'That was a lovely surprise,' he said as she pulled back, smiling at him. 'Just as lovely as the sight of you when you walked into the bistro. You took my breath away.'

'It was so good to see your friendly face after my wretched evening,' she said, taking his hand. 'Come on, you and Balzac can walk me to my car. Unless, that is, you want your friend Ivan to keep on watching us.'

Bruno turned to see Ivan locking up while giving Bruno a wink, Mandy standing beside him grinning as she made the thumbs-up sign.

'Our shameless behaviour will be all over St Denis by lunch-time tomorrow,' said Martine.

'Sooner than that,' said Bruno as they walked on, huddling together beneath the umbrella. 'They'll talk about your loose Parisian ways, taking time off from Michelin-starred restaurants to lead the innocent town policeman astray.'

'Innocent, hah! You forget I was born here,' she said, just as they reached her car. 'They're more likely to talk about the wicked policeman and the helpless maiden.'

15

The next morning Bruno took Hector on an unusual route, a bridle trail that ran past the village of Audrix and then through the woods that led to St Chamassy. From there it was an easy canter to the ridge above the Oudinot farm. He dismounted to go through an old-fashioned wooden gate whose catch was too low to reach from the saddle and walked Hector the rest of the way. He put Balzac on a leash, knowing that otherwise the ducks and geese would be too great a temptation, then hitched Hector to the fence around the sheltered vegetable garden and loosened his saddle, casting an envious eye on Odette's still healthy crop of lettuces and tomatoes, and knocked on the kitchen door. Martine opened it and her face lit up with pleasure before she glanced down at her dressing gown and carpet slippers, put her hands to her hair and said, 'Oh no, Bruno, you could have given a girl notice.'

'You look wonderful,' he said, but she was already bending down to welcome Balzac, who was clearly delighted to renew the acquaintance.

'Come in, Bruno, come in, we're just having breakfast and there's lots of brioches left for you,' called Fernand as Martine darted through the archway to the living room and up the stairs.

Bruno took a seat and Odette poured him coffee and pushed towards him a plate of brioches, still warm from the oven.

'I always make them for Martine,' she said. 'They're her favourite, ever since she was a little girl.' Alongside the brioches was a bowl of fresh butter, probably churned by Odette, and pots of homemade jams.

'She never eats all the ones I make, so maybe your dog would like one.' Without waiting for his reply she handed Balzac a brioche, probably the first he'd ever tasted, and he took to it gladly, wolfing it down in two bites and looking up hopefully for more.

'Sorry to call so early but I heard that your compromise offer to Sylvestre went nowhere and I thought I'd better ask what you plan to do next,' Bruno said. 'I have to report back to the Mayor – you know he's taking an interest.'

On the ride over, Bruno had wondered how to advise the Oudinots, now that Sylvestre was heading into serious legal trouble. But that was not something he could reveal to them.

'Martine talked me into making that compromise offer, but it doesn't surprise me that Sylvestre turned it down flat,' said Fernand as Odette brought a pot of fresh coffee. 'And would you believe he tried to offer Martine a bribe of fifty thousand euros to reach a deal she could get me to swallow? It's shameful, trying to turn her against her own parents.'

'I gather he's trying to buy some of the land from you, which would at least mean you need have nothing more to do with him,' said Bruno. 'How much is he after?'

'He wants all the land up to the ridge, about three hectares in all, which would give him that land where I've put the geese and about a hectare on each side of his buildings.'

'Construction land is going for about eight euros a square metre these days,' said Bruno. 'But most of the land you'd be selling is too hilly to build on. And forest land is barely a thousand a hectare. You cold squeeze three or four units of social housing onto the flatter bits, but that's all. And if he's prepared to pay another fifty thousand on top, that would add up to a decent offer.'

'That's just what I was saying when you arrived,' said Odette, looking crossly at her husband. 'But he won't have it. And it's not as though you were using that land for anything. It's just patchy woodland.'

'I grant you that a direct sale would mean we never have to deal with him again, but it leaves out all the other matters I was telling you about,' said Fernand stubbornly. 'There's the loan to his grandmother, the interest they never paid, the family furniture they took. And since he really needs that land I won't sell it for market price. He'll make money from the timber alone. No, I'd want a fifty per cent share of the timber sale.'

'Say you ask him for forty thousand euros for the land plus the fifty he offered Martine,' said Bruno. 'Add it up, throw in ten thousand for the timber and you're getting to a nice, round number, a hundred thousand.'

'That's exactly what I told him this morning,' said Martine, making an entrance in jeans and a black turtleneck sweater, her hair brushed. Bruno's glance lingered on her, remembering how soft her lips had been the previous evening.

'I'll have to talk to him, but I'm pretty sure the Mayor would support that,' Bruno said. 'It's a very good price and would settle the feud. What's more it would spare you those lawsuits

Sylvestre's been threatening. That's an aggravation and an expense you don't need. Shall I tell the Mayor you're thinking about it?'

Fernand looked unhappily at his wife and daughter and then back at Bruno. 'You can say I'm thinking about it, but I'm not making any promises. And this is my decision to make, not for the womenfolk.' He rose and headed for the door, taking a jacket from a row of coathooks. 'I'd better go and see about the geese.'

Bruno rose as well, but as the door closed, Odette said, 'He'll come round. I know him, he just said that to save face.'

Bruno nodded and said to Martine, 'Do you want to say hello to my horse before I head back?'

'Love to,' Martine said and plucked a carrot from the vegetable basket as Bruno kissed her mother goodbye and thanked her for the delicious brioches. 'I've never met a horse yet that didn't like carrots.'

'Do you ride?' he asked, as they left the house.

'Not for years, but if I'm coming back here more often I'd like to take it up again.' She stopped in her tracks as they turned the corner and saw Hector lift his head from grazing as they approached. 'He looks magnificent. What's his name?'

'He's called Hector and he's got his eyes on that carrot.'

Without a trace of hesitation Martine advanced on the horse and began stroking his neck as she fed him the carrot. Bruno joined her, patting his horse's neck but keeping his eyes on Martine's profile. She might have changed out of her dressing gown, but she hadn't bothered with any make-up. Her complexion didn't need it. Hector had finished his carrot and was enjoying Martine's gentle scratching of the soft flesh under his jaw.

'Would you be free to join me for dinner this evening?' he asked.

'Love to, so long as it's not a fancy restaurant. I had enough of that last night.' She turned from Hector to look at him, mischief in her eyes again. 'And if we go back to Ivan's the gossips will never stop. I'm surprised some busybody hasn't already called my mother.'

'I thought I'd cook for you and you could see my place.' He held his breath as he waited for her reply.

'I'd like that,' she said, serious now. 'But I'd better be home early otherwise my mother would probably start planning a wedding and naming her first grandchild. And you should know that's definitely not in my plans. I love my mum and dad but they drive me crazy sometimes. You heard that stubborn old dad of mine – not a decision for womenfolk.'

Another independent woman intent on her own career, Bruno thought. Why is it they're always the ones I'm attracted to?

'In that case we should start early, about seven, so you can be home by ten or so. Do you know where I live or should I pick you up?'

'Your place is out on the Rouffignac road, one of the turn-offs after that prehistoric burial site at La Ferrassie, isn't it?'

'That's right,' he said, wondering how she knew that. She must have been making enquiries. 'There's a stone tower for electricity just opposite the turn-off. Drive up the lane, turn left through the woods and you'll see my house.'

'That will be something to look forward to,' she said. 'I'm spending the day calling on all the mayors from here to Montignac to try to persuade them to back the electric rally. Your

Mayor set it up. I'll see you at seven.' She leaned forward to give him a quick kiss on the lips and then bent to stroke Balzac as Bruno tightened the saddle and swung himself onto Hector.

'You look very dashing on horseback,' she said and waved him goodbye. He resisted the temptation to rear Hector up onto his hind legs and leap into a gallop and trotted sedately off with Balzac jogging along behind.

When Bruno got to the Mairie, the Mayor called him in to show him the fax from the Brigadier requesting Bruno be given a temporary assignment to his staff. The Mayor, who hated emails, had been delighted to learn that the Brigadier considered faxes more secure. He signed it with his fountain pen and handed the fax to Bruno, telling him to file it with the earlier ones.

'What can you tell me about this operation he wants you for, Bruno?'

Bruno explained briefly, and then described the failure of his efforts to help Sylvestre and Oudinot reach a settlement over the *chartreuse*.

'You seem to have developed a friendship with Martine,' the Mayor said, with the hint of a twinkle in his eye.

'News travels fast.'

'Madame Lespinasse was putting the cat out last night and saw your fond farewells. She told Fauquet at the café and now it's all over town.'

'Between you and me, Sylvestre is one of the targets of this money-laundering operation I've been hauled into. Not that I'll be doing much, just helping with the surveillance. I think we're still a long way from making any arrests. Knowing the Brigadier, he'd rather monitor them and track down all their contacts as opposed to locking them up.'

'Is he coming down himself to run this show?'

'No, it's a Eurojust operation, so Inspector Perrault will be taking charge.'

'You mean Isabelle? I hope that doesn't cramp your style with Martine. I liked her very much when she explained her plans for this electric car rally. She's a smart woman, probably another high-flyer like Isabelle. You do like to live dangerously, Bruno, when we've all these fine farmers' daughters yearning to settle down.'

'That's why you are now happily settled down with a Franco-American historian with a professorship at the Sorbonne,' Bruno replied. 'Jacqueline is hardly a farmer's daughter.'

'*Touché.*' The Mayor smiled. 'But unlike you, I'm too old to interest them. What about Hugon? Any progress there?'

'An autopsy is being done with an eye on possible cyanide poisoning,' Bruno said. 'We haven't had the results yet but Jean-Jacques is now involved. I've made the usual inquiries but I'm having trouble in identifying Hugon's last research job. Jean-Jacques is getting one of his experts to crack Hugon's password and get into his computer.'

'Have you asked any of his friends at SHAP? You remember Doumergues, the retired history teacher from Sarlat, the one who gave us that monograph about the lost artworks of Rastignac? It might have been before your time. He was probably Hugon's closest friend and he called me the other day asking about the funeral. I suppose the autopsy will delay that. But you might want to give him a call and see if he knows what Hugon was up to. I must say Hugon being poisoned sounds very unlikely, unless it was his wife, of course.'

He gave Bruno the telephone number and Bruno went back to his office to make the call. After explaining the background, he told Doumergues that the police were investigating whether Hugon's death had been suspicious.

'Goodness, that doesn't sound like Henri. And he was on fine form when I last saw him, like a dog on the trail of a good scent. He wouldn't say much about the job he was doing but he certainly picked my brains clean about Rastignac.'

'What did he want to know?' Bruno asked, remembering that the château of Rastignac was the place where Young's research had drawn a blank.

'You know about the paintings that disappeared: seven Cézannes, five Renoirs, four Manets, three Toulouse-Lautrecs, a Matisse and one of Van Gogh's Arles paintings?'

'I thought they were destroyed when the Nazis burned the place?'

'Not according to the maid, who says that before the fire began she saw German soldiers taking tubes wrapped in tapestries out of the château and loading them into trucks. She thought they were wrapping the paintings, the entire collection of the Bernheim family, who had a famous art gallery in Paris. The Bernheims thought the paintings would be safe with their friends the Lauwicks, the Anglo-American family who owned the château. But it wasn't the paintings that Henri was interested in, it was their friends, particularly any English friends. The

165

widow Lauwick's daughter had married an Englishman named Fairweather and they had lots of English friends, one of them a famous racing driver.'

'Would that have been Grover-Williams?' Bruno asked, sitting up in his chair.

'Yes, how on earth did you know that? And Henri asked me the same question. Young Jacques Lauwick worked at *Vogue* magazine and knew all the fashionable people of Paris, and Grover-Williams was part of that beau monde. He and his wife stayed at Rastignac before the war.'

'Did the Lauwicks have any connection to the Resistance or to any escape networks to help Allied pilots who'd been shot down?'

'Not that I know of, but if you have any names I can look up the copy I made of the château's guest book.'

'A British naval officer called Pat O'Leary,' said Bruno, looking in his notebook. He heard a jolt as Doumergue's phone was placed on a desk or table, followed by the squeak of a filing cabinet drawer and the rustling of paper.

'No, nobody of that name,' Doumergues said when he returned to the phone.

'What about Robert Benoist?'

'The racing driver? Yes, he was there before the war with Grover-Williams.'

'Did you ever hear anything about a car being hidden at or near the château?'

'That's what Henri asked me. No, I heard nothing about that, and I interviewed all the surviving people who had worked there during the war, before the Nazis burned the place down. They used phosphorus, you know, and the fire burned for five days. A terrible thing.'

Bruno carried on with his questions but Doumergues knew no more. Bruno thanked him, and promised to let him know when the date for Henri's funeral was set. Then he called the curator at the Centre Jean Moulin, the Resistance archive in Bordeaux, to ask what was known about an escape route known as PAT.

'It was named after Lieutenant-Commander Pat O'Leary of the Royal Navy, but that was a ruse to disguise the founder's real name,' the curator replied. 'He was a Belgian army doctor named Albert Guérisse and he got more than six hundred people out across the Pyrenees before being arrested by the Gestapo. He was sent to the Natzweiler concentration camp in Alsace but he survived the war. It was a dreadful place, where they gassed over eighty Jews just so they could obtain their skeletons for some awful anthropological museum that Himmler set up in Strasbourg to demonstrate the alleged inferiority of the Jewish race.'

Bruno shuddered but pressed on with his inquiry. 'Do you know of any connection the Belgian doctor might have had to the château at Rastignac?'

'Not offhand, but if I look it up will you tell me the whole story next time you're in Bordeaux?'

'Yes, and I'll buy you lunch while I tell it,' Bruno replied. '*Au revoir*.' He put the phone down and called Jean-Jacques.

'I'm on my way to Hugon's place now with my forensic team,' came the familiar cheery tones. 'The widow is driving from Sarlat and will meet us there. If you joined us we could have a walk in the garden and go over a few things together.'

'There's more than that to discuss,' said Bruno. 'We may have a suspect, or at least someone we need to question. I've worked out who was Hugon's mysterious last client.'

'I should be there in about half an hour,' said J-J and closed his phone.

Bruno had a few minutes before he would have to leave. As he was about to call his police friend Thomas in Alsace he remembered something, called up the photo of the famous Bugatti that Young had sent him and printed out two copies. One was for him, the other for the collection on Félix's wall. Then he called Thomas, who started to thank him for a pleasant stay in St Denis. Bruno cut him short.

'This is urgent, Thomas. We're on a murder investigation, involving that researcher whose death took me away from the vintage car show after the parade. You remember. It seems his last mystery client for a big research job was your Sylvestre, which makes him our top suspect. We'll be bringing him in for questioning. I need to know everything you can tell me about him – the gossip, the rumours, everything.'

'*Mon Dieu*, are you sure about this, Bruno? Sylvestre's a big man around here, wealthiest family in town, a big employer at that garage of his.'

'If you want confirmation, I can get the chief of detectives for our *département* to call you if you like. He's leading the inquiry.'

'*Merde*, where do I begin? Well, I told you about the airfield so you know where his family money came from. It must be twelve, thirteen years ago as a young man straight out of business school that he started this classic car business. I think it began as a hobby, but he saw the possibilities and then opened his garage and began hiring top mechanics and buying up old cars to restore them.'

The boom in old cars hadn't really taken off then, Thomas explained. Sylvestre's big breakthrough came with two Mercedes from the 1930s that he found at an estate sale of some French general who had died. The cars were probably loot from the war. He got them cheap, fixed them up and the local paper reported that he got over a million for the pair of them at an auction in Germany. He went on from there, specializing in old Mercedes. He travelled all over Europe looking for cars in Italy, Spain, Scandinavia and then eastern Europe – places where the classic car business was in its infancy. Then he opened his showroom in Dubai.

That had been in 2007, just before the financial crash. The next year, the rumour was that Sylvestre was in real trouble, all his money tied up in stock he couldn't sell. He had to lay off some of his mechanics. The banks wouldn't lend him any cash to tide him over. He tried to sell some of the family's property holdings but there were no buyers. Then Sylvestre suddenly obtained some finance, waited out the recession, and when the oil price went up his Dubai business turned into a gold mine.

'He's the last of his line, which makes him the most eligible bachelor in Alsace,' Thomas went on. 'He lost his parents when he was at university. They were both on board that Concorde that crashed at Charles de Gaulle airport. So now he owns all the land and property and the car business. He's got thirty mechanics working for him and his collection of old cars is said to be worth more than all the other property investments he inherited.'

'Any idea where he found the money when he needed it?'

'Not for sure, but there were rumours about some big Arab investors he'd got to know in Dubai. I don't know if it's true or if he found a bank to bail him out. Sylvestre had a lot of contacts in the financial world from his time at business school, INSEAD, in Fontainebleau.'

'What do you know about that Indian friend of his, Freddy. How long has he been around?'

'I think he was involved in the Dubai venture from the beginning. He's here in Alsace from time to time, and some people think that he and Sylvestre are a couple but I don't believe it. Sylvestre's always been a man for the ladies. A couple of years ago there was a story that he was getting married to one of those titled German girls, a Gräfin or something with a von in her name. One of those glossy celebrity magazines had some paparazzi photos of them together on a yacht in Monaco during the Grand Prix. I don't know if anything came of it. I'll ask Ingrid, she knows more about those things.'

'Thanks, Thomas, that's very helpful, and I'll be sure to keep you informed of where we're going with this.'

'Please do; the Mayor will need to know if it looks like our town's leading citizen is about to get arrested. Meanwhile I'll keep this under my hat. And I'll call you after I talk to Ingrid.'

'Right, give her my best.'

Madame Hugon was standing in the front garden when Bruno pulled up in his car. J-J had not yet arrived. He got out to greet her and she said, 'I'll miss this garden. I planted those roses and laid out the flower beds. But I can't stay here after this. Suspicious circumstances! It's the last thing I ever expected to hear about Henri, such a gentle man. We had our differences but we were married a long time and got very used to one another.'

'I know, I'm sorry to cause you this extra trouble,' he said. 'There may be nothing to it. You know how the police like to be sure.'

She nodded solemnly and then J-J's car arrived, the forensic van close behind, and J-J clambered out shouting, 'We've driven past this damn place twice already and if I hadn't seen your police van we'd have gone past again.'

'Commissaire Jalipeau, this is Madame Hugon,' said Bruno.

'My apologies, Madame, and my condolences. Forgive my little burst of temper. May we come in? We'd better dress up first.'

He handed Bruno a snowman, police slang for the white paper overalls that forensics rules required, and pulled one from the back of his car to squeeze into it, grumbling about its inadequate size. Bruno and the rest of the team followed suit.

'Do I have to wear one of those ridiculous things?' Madame Hugon asked. J-J replied that so long as she wasn't going into the room they were interested in, she needn't bother. Her own traces would be all over the house anyway. Yves, the head of the forensics unit, led her to his van to get an oral swipe for DNA and to take her fingerprints.

She finally led them in, and Bruno noticed at once that the place had been cleaned, or at least the dirty crockery in the kitchen had been washed and put away and there was a smell of cleaning fluid in the sitting room.

'Have you cleaned the study as well?' he asked.

'No, I couldn't bring myself to go in there again,' she said. 'It's as he left it, or rather, as you left it. I cleaned the rest of the place the other day after you were here. Then I went back to my sister in Sarlat. I couldn't bear to sleep here.'

'Did you touch his clothes?'

'Yes, I bundled them all up into a couple of suitcases and took them to *Action Catholique*. I checked there was nothing in the pockets, of course. There were just some papers, a supermarket bill and some receipt from the post office.'

'What kind of receipt? Do you remember? It could be important,' J-J asked sharply.

'I'm not sure, but it looked like the kind of thing you get when you send something by registered post. Henri was always careful to do that when sending reports or papers to his clients.'

'What did you do with it?'

'I must have thrown it away, maybe threw it into the fireplace or the bin. I really don't know. Do you need me any more or may I go back to the garden? It's painful for me to be here.'

'Of course, Madame,' J-J said. 'Could you let us have your birth and wedding dates, please? We'll try those for the computer password, otherwise we'll have to resort to special measures.'

She wrote them down for him on a pad, added her husband's army number from his military service and went back to the garden to sit on a wooden bench, a balled-up handkerchief in her hand.

'Poor woman,' said J-J. He stood in the doorway after Yves opened the study, put the laptop into a plastic bag and handed it to one of his colleagues, who took it to the van. Bruno leafed through the mail that Madame Hugon had piled onto a hall table. There was an electricity bill, a couple of catalogues and a history magazine wrapped in clear plastic with Monsieur Hugon's name in the address box.

'I'll check the fireplace, you check the garbage,' J-J ordered, and Bruno took a large plastic sheet from the pile of evidence bags that Yves had put by the door and emptied the contents of the kitchen bin onto it. Mercifully, there was little but orange peel and a banana skin, coffee grounds and some screwed-up papers: a supermarket bill, a bill from a coffee shop in Sarlat, and a post office receipt for registered mail, sent by Monsieur Hugon to a Monsieur F. Iqbal, *poste restante*, Strasbourg central post office.

'Bingo,' Bruno called to J-J, who hurried into the kitchen at a speed that belied his bulk.

'What have you found?'

'Sylvestre's business partner, Freddy, the Indian racing driver, was Hugon's client, sure enough.' Bruno showed him the postal receipt. 'I'm sure he and Sylvestre are in this together and they hired Hugon to find out about the lost Bugatti. Who but Hugon's client would take away all the research notes and notebooks about the job? And who but the killer would have come here to Hugon's house to take them?'

'I thought you were supposed to have searched this place when you first came here,' said J-J.

'I just had suspicions at the time,' Bruno said defensively. But the suspicions had been his, so it was Bruno's responsibility to make sure all the evidence was gathered. 'You're right, I'm sorry. I should have looked more carefully. No excuses.'

'So now you want to arrest them?' J-J asked.

'We have to question them. This makes them our prime suspects.'

'Okay, I accept that. But we're not sure it's a murder yet, not until the Bordeaux lab confirms Fabiola's theory about cyanide poisoning. I'm hoping to get something from them by the end of the day, but it could be later.'

'So then do we bring them in?'

'Maybe so, but let's think this through,' said J-J. 'Consider the relative importance of a case of local murder here in your little commune against a case of international terrorist finance. What is the Brigadier going to say if you derail the whole investigation by arresting Sylvestre tonight? What's Isabelle going to say when you torpedo the first big investigation she has led for Eurojust?'

Bruno bit his lip in frustration, understanding that again J-J was right, even though holding back went against all his instincts.

'And if you're convinced this is a murder, what do we do then?'

'Then we tell Isabelle and the Brigadier, and you know as well as I do what they'll say. They'll tell us that we can always bring the murder charge once their operation is complete, but for now, terrorism trumps murder. And both the minister of justice and the minister of the interior will agree with them, and so will ninety-nine French citizens out of every hundred, me included.'

16

He might not be able to arrest Sylvestre, Bruno reflected, yet the fact that Oudinot was now considering a sale of some land to his estranged relative gave him the perfect excuse to call at the *chartreuse*. First he went home to clean and tidy the place for Martine's visit, to put some more wood into his stove and to set the table for dinner. Most important, he had to decide on the meal he would prepare.

Martine was born and raised in the region, so truffles and foie gras would be too routine. And her mother would certainly have prepared a classic series of dishes to welcome Martine's return, as the farm produced ducks and geese and raised some of the best calves in France. Fernand had been the man who had taught Bruno how to recognize a classic veal calf, raised only on its mother's milk. First, he said, peel back the calf's eyelid and if you see any red veins in the eyeball, it is no longer being raised *sous mère*. To be sure, Fernand had continued, while steering Bruno to the back of the calf, raise its tail. Fernand had then leaned forward and used his thumbs to prise open the calf's bottom. 'Look at that,' he said. 'Not a single red vein to be seen. That's the kind of calf you want.'

He didn't want to serve a heavy meal, so that excluded beef

and lamb, which left fish. Bruno called his friend the Baron, a devoted fisherman who was an infallible source of fresh trout, and asked if he planned to fish that day.

'I was in the boat with Antoine this morning and we got some lovely young trout,' came the reply. 'Better than that, we went afterwards to that little stream that comes down near St Cirq and got enough *écrevisses* to feed half a dozen. Do you want to join us for dinner?'

Bruno savoured the idea of cooking the wonderful local cray-fish. 'I can't, Baron. I've got a date tonight, but I'd love to buy enough for two from you.'

'Who's the lucky girl? I heard you'd been seeing Oudinot's daughter, the one who went to Paris.'

Bruno laughed, shaking his head. 'Can't keep secrets in St Denis! Yes, that's the one. I was going to grill some trout but now I'm thinking of *écrevisses à la nage*. When can I drop by and pick them up?'

'Any time this afternoon. I'll be working in the garden. I'll save you a dozen. What do you plan to drink with them?'

'I was thinking of a bottle of Pierre Desmartis's Cuvée Quercus.'

'A fine choice, but what do you plan for the rest of the meal?'

'A zabaglione for dessert, with my own goose eggs. And to begin, you remember that Dordogne food fair we went to in Périgueux, when that friend of mine from Neuvic gave us each a can of the caviar they're making there? I haven't used it yet, so I thought I'd make some blinis and serve that as a first course.'

'Don't forget a glass of ice-cold vodka to go with the caviar. That should do the trick. And you might try using Monbazillac instead of Marsala for the zabaglione, it works very well. Are you going to serve it on its own?'

'No, I was going to poach a couple of pears and throw in some fresh blackberries. There's still lots of them in the hedge.'

Bruno put a bottle of vodka in his freezer and sat down at his laptop to search for something on the web about Freddy. He knew a fair amount about Sylvestre but nothing about Freddy. Isabelle had given his real name as Farid Iqbal, so he entered that name, along with 'Dubai' and 'car race'. Most of the sites that came up were in Arabic but there were a couple from an English-language paper, *Gulf News*. He clicked on the first and found a photo of a beaming Freddy on the winner's podium at a race track in Dubai that described him as a well-known sports enthusiast and businessman, running the classic car auctions in the region.

The second article was an interview with Iqbal when he and Sylvestre had opened their showroom in Dubai and staged the first of their auctions. Freddy described being born and brought up in Ahmedabad, in Gujarat state in India, the son of a successful businessman who had sent him to school in Switzerland, where he'd been introduced to go-kart racing. He began to win races and was placed third in a European championship race when he was just fifteen. Then his parents were killed in a Hindu–Muslim riot that lasted three days and resulted in over a thousand deaths in Gujarat in 2002.

'My parents were martyred in a Hindu pogrom and it was then I understood the great responsibility of being a Muslim,' Freddy said in the interview. 'That is why I am so much at home here in Dubai among the faithful.'

Bruno sat back, thinking that Isabelle's connection of the car auctions to terrorist financing suddenly made sense. He could see how it might work. Sylvestre sold cars to wealthy Arabs who then registered the cars in the Emirates. They could transfer legal ownership of a valuable car to someone with terrorist connections who then exported the cars back to Europe to be sold at another of Freddy's auctions. The proceeds would be legal and the money whitewashed. Bruno scrolled down through more websites but learned only that the total sales at Freddy's most recent car auction had topped ten million dollars.

He put Balzac in the van before setting off for Sylvestre's *chartreuse*. He'd found that people tended to be more friendly and talkative when his dog was present, and pondered how far he should go with his questioning. Should he ask Freddy what was in the envelope Hugon had sent to him and whether he knew of Hugon's death? Should he ask Sylvestre if he and Freddy had been the clients for Hugon's search for clues about the lost Bugatti, or would that alert them too soon? He decided to play it by ear.

There was nobody in sight when he arrived, but one Range Rover was parked in the courtyard and another by the gate-house. He knocked there first and after a moment heard an answering shout. A few seconds later Freddy opened the door, wearing shorts and a sweat-drenched T-shirt.

'Sorry, I was working out on the rowing machine,' he said, and glanced briefly down at Balzac, who was wagging his tail in friendly greeting. Freddy didn't react to Balzac's overtures and looked back at Bruno. 'You need to be fit to be a racing driver. What can I do for you?'

'Is Sylvestre around?'

'He's in the main house but he's on the phone to China. It's about opening the Shanghai showroom next month.' He was standing in the doorway, one hand on the door as if impatient to get back inside and close it.

'Will you be going, too?'

'No, I have business in the Gulf.'

'I can wait until Sylvestre's free,' Bruno said. 'Is he likely to be long?'

Freddy shrugged. 'Who knows? He's been on that call half an hour already.'

Trying to find a way to prolong the conversation, Bruno said, 'You told me the other day you liked the castles that you'd seen here in the Périgord. Which ones have you visited?'

'I haven't really visited them, just seen them while driving around. There was one on the cliff overlooking the Dordogne. I remember Sylvestre saying the English had it and the French built another castle on the other side of the river. And I saw one by the road on the way to Sarlat and another one from the autoroute on the way down here.'

'Do you have castles like that in India? I remember Sylvestre saying that was where you were from.'

'Yes, of course.'

'I wanted to ask you about that Tesla you were driving,' Bruno said, trying a new line of conversation. 'What sort of range do you get from it?'

'It's got different settings for whether you want to race or cruise or drive in town, but for normal driving about two hundred kilometres.'

'And is it fast?'

'Very.'

'How do you find the Range Rover?'

'It's okay around here. I prefer the Porsche Cayenne, it gives better traction in the desert.'

'Is that what you were driving in that race you won? I remember Sylvestre telling us about it.'

'I've won several, but the one he was talking about was a rally through the desert when I came in second. If there's nothing else . . .' His voice trailed off and he looked across the courtyard where Sylvestre was coming out of the main house.

'There he is, and now excuse me,' said Freddy as he stepped back inside and closed the door.

That went well, Bruno thought wryly as he strolled through the courtyard to greet Sylvestre. This time Balzac got a better welcome as Sylvestre bent down to pat him.

'Do you have a moment?' Bruno asked. 'It's about the problem you have with Oudinot. I notice that I can't hear the geese today.'

'They were there at dawn but he rang the bell about an hour ago for feeding time. He'll probably drive them back here later. Can I offer you a coffee?'

'Thanks, that would be good, and maybe some water for the dog.'

Sylvestre led the way back to the main house, saying, 'I made the family what I thought was a very decent offer. I just want to buy three hectares that would give me the land up to the top of the ridge. Then Oudinot and I need never have anything to do with one another again.'

'There's a saying that good fences make for good neighbours,' said Bruno. He paused in admiration as he entered the main hall, paved in chequered black and white stone with a handsome wooden staircase curving up to the next floor. A door to the left led to a sitting room and Bruno saw a couple of chrome and leather armchairs. Sylvestre turned right, through a dining room with a long, heavy table that looked antique and into a very modern kitchen where an iPad mounted on a speaker system was quietly playing classical music. Bruno sat on a high-backed stool at the raised counter overlooking the cooking area where Sylvestre filled an electric kettle and began loading coffee into a cafetière. He put a jug of milk and some sugar on a tray with two cups, and filled a stainless steel bowl with water for Balzac, who lapped at it eagerly.

Bruno turned to look out of the French windows that led onto the courtyard. Between him and the windows was a sofa facing a giant TV screen and flanked by two armchairs. There was a second dining table in bleached pine on which stood an open laptop and notebook and a mobile phone that had a headset attached. The table was large enough for eight chairs and for a very futuristic chair in black mesh and chrome that faced the open laptop.

'That looks like a very pleasant place to work. You've done a great job with the remodelling,' Bruno said. 'I can see how frustrating the situation with your cousins must be for you.'

'I'll win in the end,' said Sylvestre casually, pouring the hot water into the coffee. 'I can afford lawsuits and he can't.'

'Oudinot is aware of that, and I understand he's considering the offer you made to Martine, but he's worried about losing out on the sale of the timber.'

'That's a new one. I hadn't heard of any concern about timber, and anyway, I've got no plans to cut these woods down.' He poured Bruno some coffee. 'In fact I'd rather keep them. They add to the rural atmosphere.'

'He's also got some good cards to play,' Bruno said. 'You may know that all the communes are supposed to provide a certain proportion of social housing for low-income families, the disabled, and so on. We're desperately short of such places and if Oudinot applies to build some cheap social housing all around your buildings, he'll get instant approval. The Mayor would have no choice. It's Fernand's land and it's already zoned for residential use. You'd find that just as much of a problem as the geese, maybe more so.'

'I see.' Sylvestre stared at Bruno for a long moment. 'I presume you have a solution to put to me.'

'He'll want a high price per hectare, plus the fifty thousand you suggested to Martine and a half-share of any eventual timber sale, for a total sum of a hundred thousand euros. You get your peace and quiet, no geese and a good access road. And I'll propose to the Mayor to put the road leading here on the list for upgrading. I think he'll do it because he wants this business settled and your tourists to start coming here and spending money. Of course, he would also like to have the social housing.'

'A hundred thousand is a lot more than the land is worth.'

'I know that, but it buys you the certainty of the access and the calm you need to make this place a profitable business. Otherwise all the money you put into it could be wasted.'

'A hundred thousand also buys a lot of lawyers,' said Sylvestre.

'And not one of them would be able to stop Oudinot surrounding you with social housing.'

Sylvestre nodded, looking beyond Bruno to the French windows and the garden. He seemed to reach a decision and glanced back at Bruno.

'Fine, you can tell him I'll go with that.' He stretched out his hand and Bruno shook it, saying, 'You won't regret this.'

'And I want the transfer done fast, with a contract of sale signed before I have to leave for China in two weeks. More coffee?'

'Just a quick cup, I've got to get back for a meeting with the Police Nationale,' Bruno said, wondering how far to push Sylvestre. 'They're investigating what looks like a suspicious death, maybe a murder.'

Sylvestre raised his eyebrows. 'Really? You don't expect a murder here in the sleepy Périgord.'

'It was the day of the vintage car parade, the day before the rally,' Bruno said. 'You might remember I had to leave to go and register the death of a man named Hugon. He was a retired archivist who still did some freelance researching on the side, mainly for local lawyers. It looked like natural causes and the local doctor said it was a heart attack, but one of Hugon's lawyer clients was trying to find some research Hugon was supposed to have finished and found his recent files had all disappeared. So he called the Préfecture and they sent detectives. Hugon should have been buried today but it looks like they're doing an autopsy. His wife is very upset. She was the one who found his body.'

'That's understandable.' Sylvestre had shown no reaction that Bruno could discern.

'As soon as I've seen the Police Nationale, I'll talk to the Mayor and get him to talk to Oudinot and recommend the deal,' Bruno said. 'We'll try to get this wrapped up quickly. Have you a number where I can reach you?'

Sylvestre pulled out his wallet and gave Bruno a business card with his email address and various phone numbers.

'By the way,' Bruno said as he turned to leave. 'How's your search for that Bugatti going, the one you and Martine were talking about?'

Sylvestre shrugged. 'Nothing new to report, but thanks for coming by and for bringing your basset hound. He's the kind of dog that makes me smile.'

17

Bruno checked his watch and headed for Pamela's riding stables. He'd have to take Hector out early if he were to be back in time to prepare dinner, but he also wanted to have a word with Félix, who seemed to be settling in. After he pulled in, Balzac went off to paw at Hector's stable door, while Bruno went in search of Pamela. She was in the office, looking tired but going through her accounts.

'The good news is that we're no longer operating at a loss,' she said, looking up at him cheerfully. 'The bad news is that it's only because Miranda and I aren't taking any wages out of the school yet. But in terms of utility bills, taxes, fodder and running costs, our heads are above water. One bad vet's bill, however, and we drown.'

'You've only just started and you haven't begun letting out the *gîtes* yet,' Bruno replied. 'They'll provide a good income next summer.'

'Yes, but in the meantime we have to pay money to get them repainted, repaired and have the plumbing fixed. Sometimes I wonder why I ever let myself in for this.'

'You enjoy the challenge and you're good at it,' Bruno said. 'How's Félix doing? Is he still turning up on time?'

'Every day, and he's doing well. I think it's the first time in his life the boy has felt useful and he clearly enjoys what he's doing. He's out with Miranda now helping her escort the pony trekkers. I thought it was time to put him on horseback and they're only walking along. He's on the Andalusian; she seems to like him. She also seems to like your Hector, pity he's a gelding. That might have saved me the stud fees we'll have to pay to get her with foal.'

'If Félix isn't back soon, can I ask you to give him this with my compliments?' He handed her the printout he'd made of the photo of the lost Bugatti that Young had sent him. 'Tell him it's a gift for his wall collection.'

'You might find it fighting for space. He found a set of very out-of-date *Cheval* magazines in a stable loft and asked if he could take some home to put the pictures up in his room. I got the impression that the cars were now taking second place. It's a bit like you, Bruno. Once you got close to horses and began to enjoy them, you wondered where they'd been all your life.'

'Thanks to you,' he said. 'I hope the boy gets as much pleasure from horses as they've given me.'

'I know he's been in trouble, but fundamentally he's a sweet boy, Bruno. The horses like having him around and so do Miranda and I. He's even started having an afternoon cup of tea with us when he gets here from school.'

Ah, the British, thought Bruno, smiling to himself. It's just as we were taught in school. They believe everything can be resolved with a nice cup of tea.

'I'm grateful you've taken him on,' he said. 'I understand you can't pay him yet, but could he be useful in the long term?

Maybe you could get him to paint the *gîtes* and do some mainten-ance? I think his dad might be ready to do some odd jobs like that and it would be good for them to work together.'

'Let's wait and see. In the meantime, I've had a couple of phone calls about your new romantic interest. I'm told she's called Martine, is that right? Daughter of a local family who's briefly back from a high-powered career in the big city?'

'I only had an after-dinner drink with her at Ivan's last night,' he said. 'You know how people talk.'

'Passionate embraces in the rain is what I heard,' she said, arching an eyebrow and giving him one of those cool smiles that she did so well. 'That sounds rather serious. And now you're blushing.'

'A goodnight kiss in the rain is hardly a passionate embrace,' he said, irritated as so often before that he could never control his blushes. 'I'm a bit pressed for time so I'd better take Hector out before I have to go and see J-J about a case. Fabiola probably told you there's an investigation into Hugon's death.'

'She said there would be an autopsy, but you know how dis-creet she is. But if you're pressed for time, I'll take Hector out with the others when Miranda gets back. I always enjoy riding him.'

'Thanks so much for that. See you tomorrow.' He blew her a kiss and was about to drive back to town when her mobile rang. Her face went grave as she listened and she put out a hand to keep him close.

'Bruno's standing right here beside me.' She spoke in English. 'Hold on while I brief him.'

'It's Miranda,' she said, reverting to French for Bruno's sake.

'One of the girls has fallen off her horse and been injured. It could be serious. Some boys were throwing stones at the horses and one of them hit Denise in the eye. There's a lot of blood and the other girls are panicking. Miranda fears the girl could lose her eye.'

'Find out where Miranda is exactly and tell her I'll get there as soon as I can,' he replied. 'In the meantime I'll call the *urgences*.' He pulled out his phone and punched in his speed-dial number for the *pompiers*.

When Pamela gave Miranda's location, Bruno knew the *pompiers* could never get there in a vehicle. It was at a ford across a small stream, deep in the woods behind Audrix. He told Albert, the chief fireman, to get to a hunter's cabin known as La Mique, after a local specialty, a dumpling that one of the hunters always made there. From there the *pompiers* would have to proceed on foot with a stretcher, following the trail to St Chamassy.

'I'll take a horse, it will be faster,' he told Pamela. 'Is Hector saddled?'

'No, but my Primrose is, I was about to take her out. I can exercise Hector for you later.'

'You stay here and start phoning,' he said as they strode towards Primrose's stall. 'Alert Fabiola and then call the injured girl's parents and tell them to meet us at the clinic. Then you'd better call the other girls' parents and reassure them. Does Miranda know who these boys were?'

'I didn't ask.'

'No matter,' he said, swinging himself into the saddle. 'I'll find out. I'll leave Balzac with you.'

Bruno set off at a trot and then into a canter. Both he and

the horse knew these trails and they were mostly too narrow and tangled for any faster pace. He picked up speed when they came to a firebreak in the woods, Primrose seeming to understand the need for urgency, but then they had to slow again as he descended the narrow trail that led to the stream and then walked the horse upstream to the ford where he found the girls. La Mique was another three or four hundred metres down the path.

'Thank God you're here.' Miranda was sitting on the bank, the injured girl on her lap. Someone had tied a rough and now blood-stained bandage around the girl's head, but the rest of her face was as white as snow and she was shivering.

The other girls were huddled together on the bank, watching and silent. One of them was crying and Félix was trying to comfort her. He was wearing an old shirt which was missing a sleeve. It must have been the source of the makeshift bandage, Bruno thought. Someone, probably the boy, had sensibly looped the horses' reins together and tied them to a branch.

'Bruno's here,' one of the girls shouted and the injured one moved her head when she heard it. Bruno went across and knelt beside her, recognizing her from his tennis classes. She was ten years old, the daughter of one of the bank managers in St Denis.

'Hello, Denise, everything is going to be fine,' he said, taking her hand and leaning down to kiss the part of her brow that wasn't covered by the bandage. Her clothes were soaked from the stream and from her own blood. Head wounds always bled badly, he knew. He took off his jacket to cover her and give her some warmth, noting that Félix's old denim jacket was already covering her chest. 'And you're being very brave, Denise. The *pompiers* are on their way and Dr Stern is waiting at the clinic to fix you up and your parents will be there, too. Just lie still in Miranda's arms and you'll be fine. I need to learn what happened, but if you want me, just call, okay?' He felt her hand squeeze his by way of answer.

'It was a big boy, a young man, waiting in the trees until we were mostly across the stream, and then he came out and started throwing stones,' Miranda said. 'Denise was last in line, just ahead of Félix. He's been great, taking care of the horses and calming the other girls down and then tearing his shirt for the bandage. And he tied up the horses without being told. I don't know what I'd have done without him.'

'Would you know the young man again?' Bruno asked.

'Certainly, I'd know him anywhere.'

'How many stones did he throw?'

'Three,' came Félix's voice. 'The first one missed, the second hit me and the third one hit Denise. I know who it was and I think he was aiming at me.'

'Tristan?' Bruno asked and Félix nodded. Some of the other girls confirmed it. Tristan was well known among the school-children.

'Where were you hit?' Bruno asked the boy.

'Here.' He pointed to his thigh. 'It was lucky, really. If it had hit the horse, she'd have shied and I'd have come off into the stream like Denise. She screamed as she hit the water. Besides that wound on her head I think she hurt her shoulder badly when she fell.'

'You've done well, Félix,' Bruno said, clapping him on the shoulder. 'I'm proud of you and I'll make sure Pamela and your parents know what a fine job you did. Do you know the way back to the riding school from here?'

'Sure, I know the way.'

'And do you think you could lead the rest of the girls back to the riding school while I wait here with Denise for the *pompiers*? We've asked the parents of these other girls to meet them there.'

'If you take over Denise, I can lead them back,' said Miranda before Félix could answer. 'We really need Félix to bring up the rear just in case any of the girls fall behind. But I need to get the rest of these girls home. Their parents will be frantic. I doubt if they'll want their daughters to come out riding again and we've got that damn mortgage to pay. Oh God, why did this have to happen?'

Bruno put his hand on her shoulder to calm her. 'Denise is what's important now.' He kneeled down to talk to the girl.

'Will you be okay waiting here with me while Miranda takes the other girls home?' he asked, and heard a faint 'Yes.' Gently he took her from Miranda, and as he did so he noticed that one shoulder was hanging low. It looked like she'd broken her collarbone in the fall. Bruno's face set hard as he thought of what this meant. Tristan was sixteen, old enough to be judged as an adult.

When Miranda and Félix had got the remaining girls in their saddles, Bruno asked her to take Primrose back on a leading rein. He'd travel with Denise to the clinic. Shortly after the others had gone, Bruno heard noises from the undergrowth at the far side of the stream and Ahmed and Alain appeared carrying a folded stretcher. Ahmed had done the paramedic course required for the *urgences* service and after splashing and stumbling through the ford he quickly examined Denise.

'The bleeding's stopped,' he said. 'Whoever applied that bandage did a good job. But her collarbone is broken.' He took off his shoulder bag and found a sling and long bandage which he used to secure Denise's arm in place. They strapped her onto the stretcher for the hike back to the ambulance and the fast drive to the clinic. Bruno was able to put his jacket back on, still slightly damp and with smears of blood on the collar. From inside the vehicle, Bruno could hear the siren howling and he had to brace himself as Alain made fast turns. It reminded him of driving with Annette. Then they were at the clinic, Alain pushing his way through a small crowd gathered on the steps so that Bruno and Ahmed could get the girl inside and into Fabiola's examining room. She was waiting there with Denise's parents. She had changed from her usual white coat into scrubs and operating gloves, her hair tucked into a skull cap and a surgical mask hanging round her neck. Bruno had been aware of a camera flashing as they carried Denise in. That meant Philippe Delaron was taking pictures for the paper. This was getting more and more serious for Tristan.

'Don't go yet,' Fabiola said to Ahmed as they put Denise down, 'you may have to drive her to the hospital in Périgueux. But let's get her out of those wet clothes and take a look.'

Denise's mother fought back tears as she bent down to kiss her child and take her hand. Her father wrung Ahmed and Bruno by the hand with a muttered 'Thanks,' and Bruno told him the one to thank would be young Félix.

Fabiola cut the girl's clothes off with scissors, strapped her arm back into place and wrapped her in blankets. Then she removed the bandage and wiped Denise's face, neck and shoulder clean of blood, though more of it had clotted in her hair.

'I don't think it's as bad as it looks,' Fabiola said, for the parents' benefit as much as for Denise's. 'The main cut seems to be in the eyebrow and there's a tough bone there that took some of the force. The cheekbone is also cut but not as deeply. It's strange that there's no mark on the brow.'

'She was wearing a riding helmet,' said Bruno, remembering seeing it on the bank beside Miranda. 'They must have taken it off to apply the bandage.'

Fabiola took a small torch from the cabinet at her side, gently opened the swollen eye and shone the light inside.

'The flesh around the eye is bruised and scratched but the cuts aren't too deep,' she said after a careful examination. 'The pupil is reacting to the light, but not as normally as I would like and I think she's got a concussion. Do you know if she blacked out?'

'No, but we can ask Miranda or Félix,' Bruno said.

'Do you remember everything that happened, Denise?' Fabiola asked.

'I remember a pain and falling and being in Miranda's arms and then Bruno came,' the girl said, sounding sleepy.

'Good girl,' Fabiola said and continued her examination. Finally she looked up at Denise's parents. 'I can't be sure and I'm hoping there's no damage to the eyeball, but I'm worried about a possible detached retina. I don't think her sight will be affected but I'd like to be sure, so the ambulance will take her to Périgueux and I'll arrange for an eye specialist to be waiting. Depending on what he says we may have to send her on to Bordeaux. In the meantime I'd better give Denise a local anaesthetic and stitch that cut on the eyebrow and then make sure the collarbone is properly set.'

Bruno excused himself, and seeing that the hall outside was full, he let himself into Fabiola's surgery to make some calls. The first was to Yveline, to brief her and ask her to meet him at the supermarket where Tristan's father worked. Then he alerted Annette, as the magistrate in charge of prosecuting juveniles. Bruno was determined to leave nothing to chance. He rang social services in Périgueux, but as soon as they heard Tristan was over sixteen they said it was no longer a matter for them. Then he went outside to find Philippe, who was on the phone to one of the parents of another girl at Pamela's riding school, just having been reunited with his daughter.

'You're sure the youngster throwing the stones was Tristan, the son of the guy at the supermarket?' Philippe was saying into the phone, his eyes on Bruno. 'Your daughter is certain of it, and the other girls say the same? Can I quote you on that?' He listened for a moment, nodded and then closed the phone and asked Bruno, 'You going to arrest the little bastard?'

Bruno nodded, and said, 'But there's also a good part to this nasty story. Félix did well. Apparently the stones were aimed at him and one of them hit him. Tristan has been bullying him for years. But when Denise was hit and fell into the stream Félix took charge.' He described what Félix had done and told Philippe he could find the boy at the riding school. 'St Denis should be proud of a youngster like that, who kept his head, bandaged Denise and did all the right things. You can quote me on it.'

Philippe raised an eyebrow. 'Doesn't sound like him. But he's not the story. Problem is, I can't use Tristan's name if he's a juvenile.'

'Not any more, he isn't,' said Bruno, walking away. 'He's turned sixteen.'

By the time Bruno reached the supermarket, Yveline was pulling into the parking lot in a Gendarmerie van. As they mounted the stairs to Simon's office, Bruno told her Denise was being taken to an eye specialist in Périgueux. He wanted Yveline to make the arrest – Bruno was not under the same pressure as the gendarmes to meet arrest quotas. They strode together into Simon's office without knocking.

'I'm here only as a courtesy to you, Simon, since your son is now officially old enough to be arrested as an adult,' Bruno began. 'His bullying has got out of hand. Félix was out on horse-back this afternoon with some girls from the riding school and Tristan aimed a stone at Félix that hit a ten-year-old girl in the eye. She may lose it.'

Startled and rising to his feet, Simon began to interrupt.

'Shut your mouth and just listen,' Bruno snapped. 'The girl's on her way to an eye specialist in Périgueux right now. And I'm going to your house with the gendarmes to arrest your boy on a serious charge of aggravated bodily harm. It's aggravated because that's what the law says if a weapon or a missile is used. And I think I should warn you that Tristan very probably faces a custodial sentence in a youth detention centre. You may follow us to your home if you wish and arrange for a lawyer.'

'But don't use your phone to do so while driving or I'll arrest you for that,' said Yveline. 'And on no account call your home or your son or try borrowing anybody else's phone to do so. I'll be checking your phone records to make sure of that.'

They turned and marched out, leaving Simon to scramble from behind his desk to follow them, firing off questions. Were they absolutely certain it was Tristan? Who were the witnesses? Wasn't the boy still a juvenile? Had he not been provoked by Félix? Was it not some form of accident, perhaps a silly prank that had gone wrong?

Bruno and Yveline ignored the questions. As they got to her van, Bruno saw Simon fishing his own car keys from a pocket and heading for his car. Bruno suddenly became angry, thinking that there was one question Simon had not bothered to ask.

'You haven't asked the name of the little girl who was the victim,' he shouted. 'She's Denise, the daughter of Paul-Michel, the bank manager. I imagine that as soon as he stops sitting vigil outside the operating theatre he'll call his lawyer. You might want to prepare for a lawsuit, and also for some questions from the press. Philippe Delaron was at the clinic when I brought Denise in, her face covered in her own blood.'

As Yveline drove onto the Limeuil road, where Simon owned one of the expensive houses overlooking the valley, Bruno adjusted the rearview mirror to see him following behind in his Mercedes, both hands on the wheel but his mouth opening as if he were talking. Of course he'd have a hands-free phone in his car! He should have thought of that. Bruno told Yveline to be sure to check who Simon had been calling.

Simon lived in a modern house designed to look like a traditional Périgord building, but the tiles and the colour of the stone were wrong. The garden contained some unusual decorations, including a fountain disguised as a miniature stone windmill and an old bicycle that had been deliberately overgrown with plants. The shutters were painted a bright blue that would have been more suitable in St Tropez, and the flower beds looked as if they had been planted by a drill sergeant with an obsession for symmetry. Yveline rolled her eyes at Bruno as they rang the doorbell and heard it chime the opening notes of the Marseillaise.

'*Bonjour*, Bruno,' said Amandine, Simon's wife, looking surprised to see him with Yveline. She was holding up her hands in a way that Bruno knew meant she was letting her nail polish dry. Then she saw her husband's car drawing up behind the Gendarmes' van. 'What's this about?'

'We need to see Tristan. Is he in?' Bruno asked.

'Yes, he's upstairs in his room. Why?'

'We need to question him about an assault on a little girl this afternoon,' said Yveline. She attempted to move past Amandine, who had taken a startled step backwards, blocking the way.

'It's Denise, the bank manager's daughter, and she might lose an eye,' said Bruno, trying to distract Amandine long enough for Yveline to get past her bulk. 'Several witnesses have identified Tristan as the boy who threw the stone that hurt her.'

Amandine's mouth opened and closed, but she stayed immobile, then shouted, 'Simon, stop them.'

'Madame,' said Yveline coldly, 'either you let me past, or as well as your son I'll have no choice but to arrest you for obstructing the police in the course of their duty.'

'It's not true, Tristan was with me here all afternoon,' Amandine said, grudgingly allowing Yveline to pass. 'He's not well, he's delicate.'

'That's fine, Amandine,' said Bruno. 'If you say he was with you all afternoon and hasn't left the house, we'll take your statement to that effect. Why not show me where I can sit down to take your statement?'

'Don't say a word, Amandine,' Simon called from over Bruno's shoulder. 'I've got a lawyer coming and he said none of us should say a word until he arrives.'

'Don't be a fool, spending good money on lawyers when I can clear this up right now,' she told her husband, throwing him a contemptuous look. 'Follow me into the kitchen, Bruno.'

By the time he heard footsteps coming down the stairs, Bruno had Amandine's brief statement, signed and made official by the stamp Bruno kept in his shoulder case. Her statement included the key phrase that it had been made 'Freely and voluntarily and under pain of perjury.'

Yveline pushed Tristan into the room, stunned and silent as he stared down at his hands cuffed before him. A pair of headphones that looked familiar to Bruno were still hanging from the mobile phone tucked into the breast pocket of his shirt. Some tinny music was still playing. Bruno donned a pair of evidence gloves, plucked out the phone and put it in an evidence bag with the headphones.

'Madame Vaudon has just given me a statement asserting that her son was with her in the house all afternoon,' he told Yveline, keeping a straight face. 'Tristan's phone should therefore bear out what she says. If not, she's in trouble for making a false statement.'

'He's under arrest anyway, even without the assault charge,' said Yveline, holding up an evidence bag with a half-filled plastic bag inside it. 'Almost half a kilo of marijuana. Were you aware, Madame, that your son used illegal drugs?'

Amandine rose to move to her son and Yveline said firmly, 'Stand back,' and then, 'Stand aside, *Monsieur*,' as Simon hovered helplessly in the doorway. She pushed the boy out, Bruno following behind, and heard Amandine berating her husband as 'an utterly useless apology for a man'.

At the front door, Bruno turned and said, 'Your son will be at the Gendarmerie until the magistrate comes to press charges. Your lawyer is free to join us there but it would be a good idea to telephone the Gendarmerie first and see when the magistrate will be available. Thank you for your cooperation, and Simon, you might want to make your peace with Denise's parents while you can.'

Sitting in the back seat with a white-faced Tristan while Yveline drove, Bruno pulled out his phone to call Pamela. He needed his van and Balzac and he still had to collect the *écrevisses* from the Baron before Martine arrived for dinner.

18

As he left the Baron's place with his bag of crayfish, Balzac sitting up beside him, Bruno pulled off the road to answer his phone. He always did that now, ever since being called to a fatal road accident that had been caused by a woman texting as she drove. The screen named the caller as J-J.

'Forensics have everything they need from the house, but Yves is still trying to get into Hugon's computer,' J-J said. 'And there's no word yet from the autopsy lab so we're heading home. By the way, one of my detectives who was watching the rally on Sunday and saw Freddy win swears it was Freddy he saw on the station platform in Le Buisson yesterday evening boarding the train for Agen. But you said you'd heard from Isabelle that he was having dinner in Sarlat.'

'Not quite,' Bruno replied. 'She said his phone was at a fixed location in Sarlat.'

'Maybe he's playing games with his phones, leaving the one we know about in one place while he goes off to do business elsewhere, probably with a phone we don't know about. I've assigned someone to check the surveillance cameras at the station in Agen, but if he's wise to surveillance they aren't difficult to avoid.'

'Have you heard anything from Isabelle about when we should expect her?' Bruno asked.

'No, she must still be held up by paperwork. You wouldn't believe the number of forms I've had to fill in, defining the limits of the surveillance we're supposed to mount. I've still got to get a magistrate to countersign them and witness my guarantee to destroy any film or tapes not needed in court.'

Bruno felt a twinge of alarm as J-J ended the call. He'd filled out no forms and asked no permission for his own amateurish attempts to keep watch on the two targets. Perhaps he'd better keep that knowledge to himself, or even dismantle his cameras. He'd have to change the batteries by the next evening, he told himself, even if he took the risk of leaving them in place. But perhaps Isabelle and her team would be here by then.

He raced home, stopping only to buy bread just before the bakery closed, congratulating himself for letting Yveline make the arrest and sparing him the paperwork and witness statements that the magistrate would require. He had thirty minutes at the most before Martine was supposed to arrive. That left him no time to shower if he was going to pick some fresh lettuce and feed Balzac and his chickens.

He dealt with the animals first, then picked the lettuce and put another log into the woodstove. He checked that he'd put the vodka into the freezer. He always kept a couple of bottles of white wine and champagne in the fridge. He knew that he didn't have the two hours he needed for the dough to rise to make proper blinis to go with the caviar, so he'd have to offer toast instead. But then he remembered how Pascal at the food show had made what he'd called his 'instant blinis' using egg whites.

It was not the best time for an experiment with a new dish, he thought, but what the hell? Bruno washed his hands and face, ran his fingers through his hair and then gargled quickly with mouthwash to rinse away the taste of the day.

In the kitchen, he began making the *court bouillon* for the crayfish, pouring into a large saucepan half a bottle of Thomas's Riesling with the same amount of water. He peeled four shallots and sliced them thinly, and did the same with two carrots. He diced three stalks of celery and a thin leek and put all the vegetables into the saucepan with a couple of chopped cloves of garlic, one whole clove and some coriander and fennel seeds. He ground in some salt and pepper and then took a small *piment d'espalette*, the red peppers grown in the Basque country, from the bunch that hung from the beam in his kitchen, and added it to the broth as it heated. He looked at his vegetable basket, where he kept apples mixed with the potatoes to stop them from sprouting. No, potatoes would make the meal too heavy. Perhaps rice? No, he'd serve it just with the vegetables in the *bouillon*.

He opened the jar of caviar and put it on the table with a tiny silver coffee spoon for each of them. He'd found them in a *vide-grenier*, one of the town's regular jumble sales where people emptied their attics of stuff they no longer needed. Now for the blinis. He measured a hundred grams of buckwheat flour into a bowl, mixed in a little salt and pepper and made a well in the centre of the flour. He took an egg from the bowl by the stove, and was about to crack it and separate the white from the yolk when he heard the sound of a car coming up the road and turning into his drive. Balzac was already at the door, bounding out as soon as Bruno opened it to investigate the new arrival.

Balzac liked new people and he liked women, so he was squeaking with excitement when he reached Martine's car as she opened the door. Bruno thought for a moment Balzac was going to leap into the car, but instead the dog put his front paws onto the sill of the car door and gave her a happy bark of greeting and an amiable sniff at her black jeans as she swung her long legs from the car and stood up. Bruno came forward to give her the *bise* on each cheek, but she kissed him on the lips and then bent to caress Balzac. She was wearing a T-shirt of black silk beneath a short tweed jacket of dark blue, white and black checks that had been nipped in tightly at the waist. It had been beautifully cut to work as casual clothing or something more formal. It was somehow businesslike and playful at the same time, and made Bruno regret that with the pressure of time he had decided against changing.

'Horses, basset hounds, country dinners and a man in uniform – are there no limits to the props you use to seduce a woman, Bruno?'

He looked down at his uniform, suddenly realizing he had not cleaned Denise's blood from his collar.

'I'm sorry, I just got back. It was one of those days, dramas, injuries, arrests . . .'

'Not that awful attack on the little girl that was on the radio just now?'

'Yes, that was part of it. But when I had to choose between starting the dinner and having a shower and changing my clothes, the dinner won.'

'A true Périgordin in your priorities, and quite right, too.' As they went indoors, her eyes widened in surprise. 'Is that blood on the collar of your jacket? You should soak it in cold water at once.' She put a bottle of wine on the table and said, 'Come on, take it off . . . Through here?'

She marched into the bathroom with his jacket, still talking. 'I asked Natalie at the *cave* what wine you liked and she said your favourite was Château de Tiregand. But that's what my dad usually serves when I come home, so I thought I'd bring you something different that I came across when I was skiing in Gstaad. I was amazed to see a Bergerac wine, this one, Château Monestier La Tour. I loved it.'

From the way she was speaking quickly Bruno realized that Martine was probably just as nervous as he about the evening ahead and where it might lead. Standing in his shirtsleeves and watching her run the cold water, he knew he had entered that enticing but dangerous moment when both he and Martine recognized that a great deal was possible between them. But a single false step could send the edifice of fantasy they were hesitantly constructing tumbling down into embarrassment and disappointment.

'What a generous and inventive thought,' he said. It was a wine he recalled drinking some years in the past and not being overly impressed by, but he'd heard that the vineyard had come under new ownership and its wines were now spoken of with deep respect by people whose judgement he trusted. 'I always think a wine is better when it comes with a little story attached like that. So now I'll always think of you in the Alps, swooping downhill and dancing with the mountain, whenever I see this wine.'

She left his jacket to soak, took his arm companionably and asked him to show her his garden. He pointed out the white oaks where his truffles were growing underground, introduced her to Napoléon and Joséphine, his two geese, and to Blanco the cockerel.

'Named for the rugby player,' she said, rising even higher in his esteem when she recognized the name. She cast the experienced eye of a country girl over his vegetable garden, noting the well and nodding in approval at the three compost heaps, each at a different stage of fermentation.

'Are those woods yours?' she asked.

'All the way up to the ridge. That's where I get my mushrooms and there are a couple of spots where I can usually count on truffles. The meadow down below is mine as far as that lower hedge. The stream on the right is the boundary.'

'Does your well work?'

'Yes, I used to depend on it for water and still use it in summer for the garden. It's good to drink, somehow it tastes better than the stuff from the water tower. We'll be drinking it tonight with our meal.'

'Where do you keep your horse? Is there a barn behind the house?'

'Hector stays at a friend's house to keep her horse company and so that she can take him out for exercise when I'm tied up with police work. I do the same for her when she's busy. It's Fabiola, Dr Stern at the clinic.' After a moment he thought it politic to add, 'She and her boyfriend Gilles are good friends of mine.'

'Now tell me what you're planning for us to eat.'

'*Écrevisses à la nage,* the crayfish caught by a friend this morning about three kilometres from here,' he said. 'So we're drinking white wine.'

'Lovely, I haven't had those for ages.' Martine squeezed his arm in glee. 'Mandy says you're known in St Denis as a good cook.'

'I wish I could cook Asian food like she does,' he said. 'Before the *écrevisses* there's champagne and then some vodka to go with the caviar and the blinis that I'm making, and as soon as Balzac comes back from his security patrol of the chicken run we'll go into the kitchen and I'll cook. Meanwhile, I hope you appreciate this sunset I've arranged for you.'

'It will last another few minutes. Why not go and put another jacket on and come back with the champagne. Meanwhile I'll enjoy your view.'

'It's hardly as good as the view from your folks' house, with the valley and the river.'

'That's why I like it, all these ridges, one after the other and not another house in sight,' she said, almost dreamily, as Bruno left. He donned a black leather jacket over his uniform shirt. Fetching the glasses of champagne, he cast an eye on the *court bouillon*, which was just about to start simmering. He turned down the gas and added another splash of Riesling. Back on the terrace he and Martine toasted one another and then Balzac returned, perhaps at hearing the familiar sound of glasses being clinked. She took Bruno's hand as they strolled back into the house and he showed her the sitting room with its dining table set for two and the wood crackling warmly in the stove. He took off his jacket and draped it over the back of a chair.

She did the same, looking briefly around and noticing the absence of a TV before glancing at his collection of CDs. She picked out Francis Cabrel's *Hors Saison* and said, 'I haven't heard that album since I was twenty. I'm in a mood to hear it again, but softly.'

In the kitchen, she perched on a high stool at the counter, topped up their champagne glasses from the half-bottle he'd opened, and then poured herself a glass of his water from the well. She sipped at it, considering, and then said she liked it. She watched as he washed his hands again before going back to the blinis. He cracked the egg he'd put aside when she arrived and poured the contents back and forth between each half of the shell over a little bowl to separate the white from the yolk. He put the yolk into the flour, added a wine glass of milk and began whisking, pausing only to add, little by little, a second wine glass of milk, some chives and then a tablespoon of melted butter. When the mixture was well mixed, he began to whisk the egg white until it was stiff, then folded it into the batter and put the gas on high under a frying pan he greased lightly with butter.

'One of the few times I don't use duck fat,' he said. 'This isn't the proper way to make blinis but I didn't have time for the yeast to rise. I hope this works well enough.'

He put a tablespoon into the batter, filled it and poured the mixture onto the pan. He did this four times. As the batter spread out and began to sizzle he reached into the fridge, pulled out a bottle of the Cuvée Quercus and opened it. After a couple of minutes, he used a spatula to turn the blinis, and took the vodka from the freezer.

'How hungry are you?' he asked.

'Two blinis will do for me. Are you serving them with crème fraîche or do you have some other devious recipe?'

He flipped the blinis one more time, took the bowl of crème fraîche from the fridge and showed it to her and then put the blinis onto a warmed plate with a knob of butter. He then poured the *écrevisses* into the simmering bouillon and invited Martine to the dining room. She brought the vodka, so frozen that it poured sluggishly into their small glasses, and then she divided the caviar into two portions. She spread some cream onto her first blini, covered it thickly with caviar, ate, and her eyes widened.

'That's good,' she said, and finished the blini before raising her vodka glass and draining half of it. '*Naz dorovya,*' she said, or that was how it sounded to Bruno. 'I think that's what Russians say. There were a lot of them in Gstaad this year and they seemed to say it all the time when they drank. Another blini for you, too?'

'Yes, please. I can make more if you change your mind,' he said, thinking a fashionable ski resort like Gstaad was way out of his financial league. Martine's business probably made her a wealthy young woman. He remembered the amount of money she'd assumed was customary for the work she did.

'Where did you get the caviar? Is it Russian?'

'No, it's French, from around here. Now that we have sturgeon in the river again a friend of mine has started a business. We used to get Russian caviar sometimes when I was stationed in Bosnia with the UN, though I can't imagine how the quarter-masters got hold of it. Our Dordogne caviar tastes very much like that.'

'This is as good as any I've eaten. If our electric car rally comes off, we can proudly serve our home-grown caviar to the winners. *Vive la France*!' She finished her second blini and downed the rest of her vodka. 'And now do we go back to the kitchen to watch the master at work again?'

'No, we go back to watch me fumble to peel the *écrevisses* and get the veins out. Then we wait for them to cool a little as we enjoy the white wine and toss the salad.'

'You don't peel them before you put them in the *bouillon*?'

'I find it easier this way, and it helps me get the tails out without tearing the flesh. Getting my fingers a bit burned seems a modest price to pay.'

'Somebody once said that laziness is the origin of genius because smart people look for easier ways of doing things.'

He smiled. 'I don't think I'm that smart to begin with.' And then stopped as he heard the opening notes of the title song on the album. 'Here's the song you liked.'

'There was a guy at the time, but I recall the song better than I remember him,' she said. 'I had a lot of growing up to do.'

'We always do,' he said. 'Malraux in his *Antimémoires* says he asked an old priest what he'd learned after a lifetime of hearing confessions. The priest thought for a moment and said, "There are no grown-ups".'

'Thank heavens for that,' she said, taking his hand and giving Bruno that dangerous feeling that their eyes were saying much more than their mouths. 'Time for the *écrevisses*?'

He nodded, took the empty plates and returned to the kitchen, picked up the white wine and poured each of them a glass before taking out the crayfish. He filled a bowl with iced water from the fridge and took a set of evidence gloves from his bag. He put them on before twisting off the heads, squeezing out the flesh from the tails and taking out the long veins. Between each one, he dipped his fingers into the iced water to cool them.

'The ice water is a clever trick; the laziness of genius again,' she said. 'This wine is terrific.'

'Glad you like it,' he said, putting the crayfish back into the bouillon and turning off the gas before turning to look at her. 'I'm happy you're here.'

'What now?' she asked, her eyes teasing.

'Now we wait until the bouillon cools to the point at which we want to eat,' he said, peeling off the gloves and taking a sip from his wine.

'In that case . . .' She eased herself from the stool and came around to stand close to him and began to unbutton his shirt. She dipped a finger into the bowl of iced water and left it there while looking into his eyes. Then she brought up her chilled finger, rested it lightly against his bared nipple and leaned forward to kiss him as he shivered from the sensation. Her tongue teased at his lips and she murmured, 'You haven't yet shown me your bedroom.'

Later, in front of the stove in the sitting room, Balzac was dozing with his head on Bruno's thigh as Martine caressed the dog's long silky ears. She was wearing Bruno's white terrycloth robe and he had pulled on a rugby shirt and some tracksuit bottoms. The emptied bowls of crayfish and salad plates were beside them on the floor. She had declined the zabaglione, insisting she'd eaten too much already. Now she put down her wine glass, looked at him fondly and said, 'I'd like to stay, but my mother will be wondering where I am.'

'I'd like you to stay, too, but I understand. Can we meet again tomorrow?'

'Will you let me do the cooking this time?'

He laughed. 'Was the meal as bad as that?'

She gave him a gentle slap on the thigh. 'No, don't be silly. It was perfect. But I'd like to cook for you and you seem to have everything I might need in your kitchen. Can you get away a bit earlier tomorrow to give us some more time together?'

'I'll try. Coffee before you go?'

'That would be great. You can make it while I dress.'

Bruno put the kettle on as she went to his bathroom. He spooned coffee grounds into the cafetière, readied the cups and sugar and then glanced at his phone, which was giving the gentle beep that said he had text messages waiting. The first one was from Fabiola, to say that the specialist had diagnosed Denise with a slightly torn retina, relatively easy to repair, and she would stay in the hospital in Périgueux.

The second was from Yveline, telling him that Tristan had been released into the custody of his parents but would be charged with aggravated assault and illegal possession of cannabis tomorrow at the Procureur's office in Sarlat.

The third was from Isabelle, and read: 'Paperwork fixed. Arrive this evening. Propose to drop by for briefing unless inconvenient.'

He typed back, 'Not tonight. Breakfast at Fauquet's café at 8 tomorrow,' and was just hitting 'Send' when he heard a car coming up the road and saw the glare of headlights turning as it headed for his driveway.

The car stopped, its headlights illuminating Martine's vehicle. Then it reversed down the driveway and turned to head to the road back to town. It must have been Isabelle, realizing when she saw the other car that he was not alone. She had no right to expect that he would be, he told himself, but felt awkward just the same. She would probably tease him tomorrow about having a new friend, but there would be an edge to it.

The kettle was boiling. He closed the phone and made the coffee, letting it rest before he pushed down the plunger. He went into the living room to clear away the bowls, plates and glasses, and then Martine was back fully dressed and looking terrific, eyes shining, skin glowing.

'Did I hear a car?' she asked.

'Probably someone who took a wrong turn. But there's good news from the hospital. That girl, Denise, her sight will be fine, though they'll keep her in for a few more days. I'll try to get to Périgueux to visit her. Maybe you'd like to come, too, and we can have dinner there.'

'Sure, but not tomorrow, that's my evening to cook for you.' She leaned forward and kissed him. 'The cold water has got the blood out of your jacket. I hung it up to dry but it will still need cleaning.'

She looked at her watch, drank her coffee quickly and said, 'Do you think I'll pass my mother's inspection or will she detect that I've been disporting myself with a louche bachelor all evening?'

I don't know, he thought, since I never had a mother. But he said, 'You can complain about the boring local official you had to dine with while persuading him to support your plan for the rally.'

'The one who told me that his wife didn't understand him just before he made a clumsy pass at me over the dessert,' she countered. 'Bad breath, overweight and with hairs growing out of his nose.'

'That's the one, but don't pile it on too thick.'

She came into his arms and kissed him goodnight, then bent to stroke Balzac. At the door she stopped, turned towards him and said, 'I'm glad about that little girl, Bruno, and thank you for a wonderful evening. I'll look forward to tomorrow, at about six, unless you call me.'

'About six should be fine,' he said. 'We can walk Balzac together before dinner.'

He stood at the doorway to watch the tail lights of her car disappear, knowing himself to be a very lucky man but wondering how long it would last and how much time they might have to deepen the relationship before her work took her away again. Independent and wealthy, with her own business to run in London, he could see her coming back to the Périgord only for visits even if the rally project worked out. Even then she'd feel obliged to stay with her parents. He sighed, thinking that his love life seemed to run in a predictable but ultimately unsatisfying pattern, driven by his attraction for women who were determined to forge their own lives without the conventional constraints of a family and children. He shook his head and went back indoors to slip on some shoes and a jacket and take Balzac out for the last stroll of the night.

19

Refreshed by his morning ride on Hector and still glowing from the evening with Martine, Bruno entered the café a few minutes before eight. He glanced at the café's copy of *Sud Ouest* as Fauquet put a still-warm croissant on Bruno's plate and set about making his espresso. Bruno shook hands with the regulars, explained that he was meeting someone and took his croissant and the paper to a table by the window. Some new horror in the Middle East took up most of the front page, but there was a small headline saying 'Horseback girl blinded in St Denis?'. Below it was a passport-sized photo of Denise's bloodstained and bandaged face that steered him to an inside page where he found a much bigger photo of Tristan in rugby clothes, probably blown up from a team photo, with the caption 'Teen vandal arrested'. A smaller photo of Félix carried the caption, 'Young hero saves the day – Police.'

'Specialist eye doctors in Périgueux were battling last night to save the sight of a ten-year-old girl from St Denis while a local schoolboy rugby star was arrested for throwing the stone that may blind her,' the story began. It must have been printed before the good news came from the hospital. Further down the page was Bruno's official police photo. He was quoted as saying the town should be proud of Félix. Tristan's lawyer was quoted as saying he would appeal to the public prosecutor for his client, just a few weeks beyond his sixteenth birthday, to be treated as a juvenile for 'a foolish schoolboy prank that had ended in tragedy'.

Fauquet brought Bruno's coffee, muttering, 'Terrible business, that poor girl. You won't catch me using Simon's supermarket anytime soon. You know there's talk of a boycott?'

'It wasn't Simon's fault,' Bruno said. 'His son's sixteen, old enough to be responsible for his own behaviour. A lot of local people work at the supermarket so I hope that idea goes nowhere.' He handed the paper back to Fauquet as he saw Isabelle heading across the town square towards the café with that unmistakable stride of hers, a long black coat floating out behind her. 'Would you bring an extra croissant and some more coffee for my guest.'

Fauquet turned, looked through the window at Isabelle and back at Bruno. 'It's her again, is it? The one who broke your heart.'

'Just get the croissant,' Bruno replied, shaking his head in mock despair. The one disadvantage of the close-knit community of St Denis was that his love life seemed to be everybody's business.

'I hope you know what you're doing, just when you've started seeing Oudinot's daughter,' Fauquet went on.

Bruno rolled his eyes and then stood as Isabelle came into the café, eyed him coolly and presented her cheeks for the usual *bise* in a way that signalled she wished courtesy did not require such a greeting.

'*Bonjour*, Bruno, I'm sorry you weren't able to brief me yesterday,' she said. 'It means we have all the more work to do today. I see you're in the local paper again.'

'Never a dull moment in St Denis,' he said.

'That's not quite how I recall it,' she shot back, and then flashed a smile at Fauquet as he served her breakfast and said how pleased he was to see her in his café again. She murmured a polite reply about how much she missed his croissants and turned back to Bruno.

'You can't brief me here,' she went on. 'I've arranged a room at the Gendarmerie. We'll go there as soon as we've finished our coffee. So tell me, how is that poor young girl?'

'Doing better, she won't lose an eye. But it won't do the riding school any good, and it's a tough enough business venture in times like these without pupils having stones thrown at them.'

'J-J told me the place is now being run by your mad English-woman in partnership with that spy's daughter. I can see why you're concerned.'

'That's really not worthy of you,' he said mildly. 'You know perfectly well that her name is Pamela and that she's Scottish and that Crimson is not just retired but a good friend to the Brigadier as well as to me. You'll have me thinking you're getting prejudiced against our friends across the Channel.'

Isabelle was the only one who still referred to Pamela as 'the mad Englishwoman', the nickname she'd been given by the locals when she first arrived in St Denis. Pamela had long since been affectionately absorbed into the community, but it was one of Isabelle's few unpleasant traits that she would never accept any woman she saw as a rival, even though she had long since ditched Bruno to focus on her career. He'd have to make sure he steered Martine out of Isabelle's way.

'Are you and Pamela still an item?' Isabelle asked casually, sitting back in her chair as if she couldn't care less either way. 'J-J wasn't sure. I'd have thought she was a little old for you. Or did that car in your driveway last night belong to someone new?'

'I hope J-J said it wasn't any business of yours,' he said, and instantly regretted letting Isabelle see how easily she could provoke him. She'd always known how to get under his skin. He took the final mouthful of croissant, washed it down with coffee and then smiled at her, knowing that most of his memories of her were still precious and fond.

'Shall we start again, without any point-scoring?' he asked, leaning forward. 'You're looking great. From that forceful way you strode across the square it seems your leg has fully recovered, which is even better, and congratulations on your new job. I'm sorry I wasn't available at short notice yesterday but as you know from the newspaper it was a difficult day.'

'Very well,' she said, as if acknowledging a brief truce rather than a peace treaty. Then she smiled, with what seemed like a trace of an old affection. Perhaps she was mollified that he had made the peaceable gesture. 'I hope I'll get to see Balzac.'

'You can come with me to pick him up. He's having a regular check-up at the vet and getting his nails clipped. I'm always worried of hurting him if I clip them myself. He can come with us to the Gendarmerie, they know him well.'

As he paid for their breakfasts, Fauquet came across and handed him an envelope.

'I almost forgot,' he said. 'That little devil you called a hero in the paper came in about seven thirty and asked me to give you this. He said he didn't have a phone. Then he rode off on a bike he'd probably pinched.'

Bruno quickly scanned the note, neatly handwritten, noting that the individual letters were not joined up. In his day, teachers had made them practise writing cursive script every day. Félix thanked him for the photo of the car and said he'd seen another one just like it, and if Bruno was interested, could they meet at the retirement home at 12.30?

Bruno put the note away, wondering what Félix meant. He thanked Fauquet and he and Isabelle took his van to the vet's office, where Balzac was declared to be in excellent shape. As the vet brought the dog out, Balzac saw Isabelle and galloped towards her, ears flapping like the wings of some mythical creature, half-dog and half-bird, before he leaped into Isabelle's arms, licking passionately at her throat.

'That's what I call a welcome,' said the vet, staring admiringly at Isabelle as much as at the dog. 'I wish I got them like that.'

At the Gendarmerie, Sergeant Jules gave Isabelle a welcome just as warm and took her into an embrace where she was almost hidden by his vast bulk. She was delighted to see he was still passing his annual fitness tests, she told him.

'Oh, we don't bother about those around here,' he said cheerfully. 'How long are you with us for?'

'Not sure yet,' she said, and went in to pay her courtesy call on Yveline as post commandant and to thank her for offering a workspace.

'She hasn't changed a bit,' said Sergeant Jules, fondly. 'You should never have let that one get away, Bruno.'

'If only it had been up to me,' he replied.

Isabelle came out with Yveline, who greeted Bruno formally and showed them into the room set aside for Isabelle's team.

'We'll need a statement from you on what you found at the scene of Denise's injury, Bruno,' Yveline said. 'Can we do that sometime this morning before the Procureur's meeting this afternoon?'

'As soon as I've briefed Commissaire Perrault,' he said, and followed Isabelle into the modest room with two desks, two chairs, one phone and an empty bookcase.

'I see the facilities here haven't changed, but it's certainly a warmer welcome than we used to get with Capitaine Duroc,' Isabelle said, putting her computer case on a desk and handing Bruno her coat as she took a chair. He found a hook on the back of the door. 'So what can you tell me?'

He described what he had learned of Sylvestre and Freddy since meeting them at the Concours d'Elégance, from the family row with Oudinot to Sylvestre's hunt for the lost Bugatti.

'I mentioned that the Police Nationale were planning an autopsy of Hugon, but he showed no reaction,' Bruno went on. 'I also talked to the local policeman back in Alsace, a friend of mine, who said there was a rumour that Sylvestre came close to bankruptcy back in 2008 with the financial crisis and was bailed out by Arab contacts. Certainly his operation in the Gulf seems to be very lucrative, and he's planning a new showroom in Shanghai.'

'What's your impression of him?'

'Very smart and determined, probably ruthless when he has to be, but also ready to cut his losses and strike a deal, which is what he's doing with the family feud.'

'You mean you think he might be open to working with us if he knew the alternative was a prison term?'

'I think it's very likely, unless he was a lot more frightened of his Arab friends than of going into a French prison.' He paused and added, 'There's a complication. J-J and I think Sylvestre and Freddy might be involved in a murder. They were working with a local researcher, a retired archivist who died in suspicious circumstances. There's an autopsy under way in Bordeaux and we're waiting for the report.'

'How was this man killed?'

'We suspect cyanide poisoning, though we're not sure how. That's what the lab is testing for. The dead man had recently sent off some papers to Freddy at a *poste restante* in Strasbourg.'

'Researching what?' she asked and Bruno explained about the lost Bugatti, its history and the fact that one just like it had sold for thirty-seven million dollars.

She shook her head in disbelief. 'That much money may well be worth killing for. But let's wait and see if the lab confirms murder before I discuss the implications with J-J. I'm sure he'll agree to wait until my operation is complete.' She paused and then added, 'He'd better.'

'J-J and I already talked about it,' said Bruno. 'I think you'll find him sympathetic, but as soon as the lab confirms it he'll have to bring in the Proc, who might not be so ready to cooperate.'

'We'll see. What can you tell me about Farid, the one you call Freddy?' she asked. 'Have you met him?'

'He's not at all forthcoming and I've only met him briefly. I tried to start a conversation but was politely rebuffed. He's a fitness freak and a very good driver, that's all I know. And he seems to be living in a separate house from Sylvestre, so I don't think they're gay. Can you tell me where you're going with this operation?'

'We're trying to draw a map of what we think is a very sophisticated financial network,' she said. 'Sylvestre and Farid are the middle men, taking the money at auctions from the buyers and then distributing it to the supposed sellers. And from what we can see, Farid is the one in charge, the one making the connections. Sylvestre is just the facilitator. Some of the business is legitimate; we're trying to identify the parts that aren't. So far we've found five sellers in different European countries, each of them with known terrorist connections. We're also tracking the bank accounts, the routes and companies through which the money is moved. Once we've mapped the whole network, we'll pounce.'

'How close are you?'

'Pretty close, but we might not have mapped the whole thing.'

'You know Sylvestre is heading for China in a couple of weeks? That's the deadline he's set for the deal with Oudinot to go through.'

'Thanks, I didn't know that. It means we too might be facing a deadline when he'll be out of our jurisdiction.' She made a note to herself on a pad and then looked up. 'Anything else?'

'Yes, when you asked me to conduct discreet surveillance I installed a couple of cameras left over from a previous case, the one your American friend Nancy was involved in. I'll need to change the batteries tonight but I imagine you have much better equipment.'

'You know that's illegal.' She raised an eyebrow.

'No it's not. I'm a licensed hunter and known to be a wild-life enthusiast. Monitoring wildlife movements on a friend's land with cameras is perfectly legal. And I'm not responsible if the wildlife has moved them so they unfortunately cover the entrance to a house rather than the undergrowth.'

'You might just get away with that here in the Périgord,' she said. 'What's the recording system? I hope it's not transmitting on wi-fi. If their computers are good enough they might pick that up.'

'No wi-fi. It's on a small data card and Sylvestre was working on what looked like a top-end Apple laptop. I don't know what Freddy was using, or rather Farid, as you call him.'

'How friendly are you with Oudinot, the man whose land borders Sylvestre's house?'

'Very friendly, and he often asks after you. We met him a couple of times at *marchés nocturnes* that summer when we were together.'

'I can't say I recall him but I suppose I might if I saw him again. Would he let us use his property for proper surveillance?'

'He'd be delighted. He hates Sylvestre, or at least he did, but who knows, now they're getting close to a deal. The problem is that I don't know how discreet Oudinot would be. The advantage is that there's a small hut on his land less than ten metres from Sylvestre's house that would be good for surveillance except for the noise of the geese. I told you about them.'

'Could you arrange for the geese to be withdrawn once we're installed?'

'Probably. We could say it's a goodwill gesture to help the

deal go through. I can do that today. What about Freddy's trip to Agen when his phone was in Sarlat? J-J was worried that he might know his phone's being monitored.'

'We're cool on that. We got him on the security camera at Agen station, meeting someone of interest to us from Toulouse. It helped that you sent us the photos with the licence plates.'

'I'm glad. Other than Oudinot, how else can I help?'

'Get me those data cards from your cameras tonight.'

'Do you want me to remove the cameras at the same time?'

'Why would I want to interfere in the perfectly legal wildlife-monitoring techniques of a law-abiding citizen?' She smiled, a twinkle in her eye that touched Bruno's heart. He sighed and rose to go.

'Just one more thing,' she said, a little hesitantly. 'Would you mind leaving Balzac here with me for the day?'

'Of course not,' he said. The dog had been her gift to him. 'Balzac would like that.'

He left, walked back to his van and then took the long way around so he could stop at the wine *cave* of Hubert de Montignac, whose extraordinary collection of vintages of Château Petrus and Château Angélus going back fifty years and more had made it one of the great tourist attractions of St Denis. For the locals, it was also the place to take their *bidons* of glass or plastic to the huge vats at the back of the shop and fill them from the tap with good Bergerac white and red for a couple of euros a litre. Bruno was looking for something between those two extremes of wine for Martine's dinner this evening. He spent a pleasant twenty minutes gossiping with Natalie, the saleswoman, and tasting a couple of wines he did not know before leaving with a bottle of one of their own wines, a Cuvée Lisa, made in honour of a local artist. Then he set off to see Oudinot at his farm, wondering if he might be fortunate enough to catch Martine before she set off again to woo the local mayors and councillors into supporting her plan.

20

Bruno was waiting on the bench in the pleasant garden of the *maison de retraite*, a grandiose modern building that the *département* architects thought suitable as a retirement home. He was texting Isabelle that Oudinot would be delighted to allow her team to use his hut for a police operation. Bruno had been evasive about the purpose when he'd gone to Oudinot's farm to seek permission. Oudinot had at once assumed that it was to investigate Sylvestre for tax evasion. When Bruno had shrugged his shoulders and refused to deny it, Oudinot had rubbed his hands together gleefully and pronounced himself eager to cooperate. He would withdraw his geese that very day and call on Sylvestre to shake hands on the deal and announce that the geese were gone as a gesture of good will. With any luck, Oudinot had added, he'd get Sylvestre's signature on a contract and a cheque before the taxman took all the money away.

'*Bonjour*, Bruno,' said Félix, suddenly appearing, slightly out of breath after running all the way from school, and holding out his hand to be shaken. 'The science teacher showed me what you'd said about me in the paper and read it out in class. And then the headmaster called in my mum to show it to her. It made her cry and she said I had to be sure to thank you.'

Of course, Bruno thought, his parents wouldn't get *Sud Ouest* at home. 'It was no more than the truth, Félix. And did you hear the good news that Denise will be fine?'

'Yes, Madame Pantowsky told me she heard it on the radio.'

That was the science teacher Bruno knew as Florence. 'So, what is this mysterious photo that made you write me that note?'

'I've seen a photo of the same car. It belongs to my grand-father. I could take you to see him and he'll tell you the story about my great-uncle.'

'Do you visit your grandpa often?'

'Two or three times a week. I like him. They eat early here so he brings out a sandwich for me from the dining room when he knows I'm coming. He's very old, over eighty.'

The St Denis retirement home stood close by the town cemetery, which Bruno had considered unfortunate until he'd learned that most of the inhabitants enjoyed the convenience of being able to attend funerals without having to walk too far. Some even claimed to take comfort from being able to gaze out over their eventual resting place. The home was a curious mixture, a few rows of single-storey buildings which contained one-room apartments all surrounding an aggressively modern structure that housed the offices, recreation and dining rooms and wards for those too enfeebled to continue living in their private rooms surrounded by their own furniture and belong-ings. The gardens were a pleasant mix of ornamental flower beds and small allotments where the residents were encour-aged to grow vegetables for their families or for the communal kitchen.

Gaspard Boulier, Félix's grandfather, lived in one of the studios, as the rooms were called, and was mobile enough to come to the door and welcome his visitors, kissing his grandson on both cheeks. Shaking the old man's hand, Bruno recognized him as one of the group of old cronies who sat around a table in the cheapest of the town's cafés, drinking their glasses of *petit blanc* and watching the horse racing as they grumbled that St Denis and the whole country were not what they used to be.

'I didn't expect you so I didn't bring a sandwich,' the old man fretted, then ruffled Félix's hair. 'How's my little nut-brown grandson?' he glanced up at Bruno. 'That's what I call him because he's the colour of a walnut. I was very proud when I saw what you said about Félix in the paper.'

'I brought Bruno to look at your photo album, Grandpa,' Félix said. 'He's interested in the photo with this car in it.' He showed him the printout of the Bugatti that Bruno had given him.

'You know that album by heart,' the old man said affectionately as he shuffled to the bedside table, sat down on the neatly made bed and gestured the others to join him. He began leafing through to a familiar page that displayed four small photos in black and white, each one about twice the size of a passport photo. The images of young Resistance fighters from the Second World War with rifles and Sten guns and armbands that carried the letters FFI for *Forces Françaises de l'Intérieur* were instantly recognizable.

He put a wavering finger on a snapshot of two men standing by a car that looked to be the very image of the Bugatti on the printout. One was wearing flying gear, the fur-lined jacket open to reveal a uniform. He was hatless, his hair smoothed back glossily. He was standing beside a young man in farming clothes whom Félix's grandfather identified as his older brother, Henri, a member of the Resistance who had been killed later in the war. Beside this photo was another of the same young man in farming clothes carrying a Sten gun with his hand on the shoulder of a young boy who looked to be about twelve.

'That's me with Henri, the family hero,' the old man said. 'That was in the summer of forty-four, just before he went off to fight. He went from the Resistance straight into the French army and was killed that winter in the fighting around Stras-bourg. I never saw him again after the photo was taken. It broke my mother's heart. She died not long after the war and my dad followed soon after, when I was away doing military service.'

He asked Félix to pass him the magnifying glass and the boy darted across to snatch it from the windowsill beside the room's sole easy chair, clearly its usual location.

'You can see the family resemblance – me, my brother and young Félix here,' the old man said, his voice quavering and his hand trembling as he held the glass over the little photo.

'What's that ruin in the background?' Bruno asked.

'Rastignac, after the Nazis burned it. It was springtime and I remember watching it burn for days.'

'The one that was supposed to have all those paintings that disappeared?'

'That's it, just the other side of Thénon. They were nice people, the owners, even the English ones in the family. My dad worked for them in a way, he was a *métayer*, but every Christmas they'd have all of us *métayer* families up to the château for a party and give the children presents. Not all the landlords were like that, I can tell you.'

The *métayer* system was a form of sharecropping that had been common in the region until it was finally regulated almost out of existence by President François Mitterrand's' socialist government in 1983. The tenant farmed the land and in return the landowner took a half-share of everything that was produced – crops, livestock and wine, everything except the family's chickens and their eggs. In the reforms after the war, the landlord's share was reduced to a third, but it was still widely blamed for rural poverty and the system's existence helped explain the remarkable number of Communist party members among the rural population.

'How near was your farm to the château?'

'You can see from the photo, which was taken in our farmyard; it's about a kilometre away. The land we farmed stretched out the other way, towards Laboret, all the way down to the river Cern. We had cattle, wheat and tobacco, an apple orchard and woods full of walnuts. We spent every winter's night around the stove, shelling them.'

'Did you ever see the car that's in the photo?'

'Only from a distance. The driver wanted to hide it, I don't know why. He was supposed to be a famous racing driver but I forget the name, maybe never knew it. My brother said he'd hidden the car in one of the old tobacco-drying barns that belonged to a friend of his. The government didn't trust us to dry the tobacco ourselves because it was rationed, so a lot of the old barns were disused.'

'Was this friend also a *métayer* for the château?' Bruno asked.

'No, I think the barn belonged to the family of a girl Henri was sweet on. They'd been at school together in La Bachellerie, where I went to school.'

'Do you remember the name of the family?'

'No, but her name was Marie-France. She got married to somebody else after my brother was killed and they moved away. One thing I do know is that they didn't just hide the car, they dismantled it. My brother said he helped take the body off and the seats out and they put it in with some other old farm equipment, broken ploughs and the like. I don't know what they did with the bodywork.'

'Did you come back home when your father died?'

'Yes, they gave me a week's leave from the army. I was stationed at Montauban, down near Toulouse, so it wasn't too far to come back for the funeral. It was lucky, in a way; the rest of my unit was sent off to Indo-China. A lot of Henri's old Resistance mates turned up for the funeral and one of them said he'd give me a job when I got out. I'd been a driver in the army and that was what I did when I came out, drove a truck for the logistics firm in Le Buisson. That's why I settled here.'

'You never went back to look for the barn or the car?'

The old man shook his head. 'Nothing to go back for, not for me. After my dad died, I still had a year to go in the army, so the landlord found a new tenant. I hadn't really thought about that car until today.' He picked up the magnifying glass to examine the photo more closely. 'Fine-looking vehicle, isn't it? I bet it would go like the wind.'

'What about that pilot in the photo, did you ever meet him?'

'No, but Henri told me he was English, from the RAF.

Somebody in the château had connections to another Resistance group that organized escape routes across the Pyrenees into Spain. Henri said he often wondered what had happened to that fur-lined flying jacket. He'd have liked to have it for himself.'

He moved the magnifying glass to a photo of half a dozen young men, all armed and wearing FFI armbands, standing around an old Citroën. 'That's my brother and there beside him is Jean-Pierre, the one that gave me the job. He's dead now, of course.' He looked up at Bruno. 'Why are you interested in all this?'

'That car, it's famous, and probably pretty valuable if anybody could find it. I know some people who are looking for it and there may even be a murder involved. That's why I'm investigating. Is there anything else you remember about it?'

'Can't say I do.' The old man put down the magnifying glass and stared at Bruno. 'Murder? Who was it got killed?'

'Sorry, I'd better not say anything until we get the results from an autopsy. It's still a matter of suspicion at this stage. When the investigation is over I'll come back and tell you all about it. Can you tell me if anyone else has asked you any questions about this car recently, or has the topic come up in any way?'

'No, the only one who's ever asked me about it is Félix, when we look through the album together. It's mainly his great-uncle Henri who interests him, but he's always liked cars. I'm only sorry the photo is so small.'

'If you like, I could get it blown up for you and also the one of you and Henri,' Bruno said, thinking that Philippe Delaron could easily do it, and he owed Bruno several favours.

'I'd like that. Do I have to take them out?'

232

'I'll do it, Grandpa.' Félix took the album and gently prised the two photos out of the little triangular pouches at each corner and handed them to Bruno. He carefully put them inside his notebook, shook the old man's hand and thanked him. At the door he asked if Félix was going back to school.

'In a few minutes, then I'm going to the riding school again.'

'Thanks for this, Félix. Take care.'

Félix didn't move but looked up shyly at Bruno. 'I'd like to give Grandpa a photo of me on a horse. Could you take one for me, please?'

'No problem, we'll do it next time I see you at the stables.'

Bruno went back to his office and texted Philippe, asking him to come and meet him in the Mairie. Then he called Florence, knowing that she'd be at home with her children during lunch-time. Rollo the headmaster had excused her from the usual roster of supervising the school lunches because her children were still little.

'I'm calling to thank you for letting Félix know about the story in the paper today,' he said when she answered. 'I gather his mother was very touched.'

'It was good of you to say what you did,' she replied. 'I've been worried about that boy and the way Tristan bullies him. He usually makes sure to do it where we can't catch him at it. What happens to him now?'

'It's up to the magistrate, who in this case is probably Annette, and as you know she always tries to avoid putting anyone into a detention centre. It depends if the Procureur decides to inter-vene. Given the publicity and the prospect of some political pressure I suspect he will. He may take it out of Annette's hands and give the case to a more experienced magistrate.'

Even as he spoke, Bruno realized that he hadn't followed up on this case as he should have. If he hadn't been in such a rush to get back to Martine he'd have gone to the Mayor and asked his advice. The Mayor would probably have called the sub-prefect in Sarlat, who in turn would have had a quiet word with the Procureur about this being the kind of assault that stirred public opinion. But was juvenile detention really the right treatment for Tristan?

'What do you think should happen to Tristan?' Florence asked. 'I know the boy deserves to get punished and he probably needs a real shock. But I'm with Annette, I never like the idea of putting young people behind bars. If the girl had been blinded I might think differently, but since they saved her eyesight . . .'

'I was so angry with him at the time,' said Bruno. 'All I could think of was making Tristan pay. He's been a bully for years, spoiled rotten by his parents and so cocksure that he could get away with anything. And now there's the drugs charge as well. The Proc can't ignore that after all the fuss he's made about drugs in the past.'

'You know possessing drugs triggers automatic suspension from the *collège*, so that means Tristan won't be going to the *lycée* as he expected.'

'What sort of student is he?'

'Lazy and arrogant, doing just enough to get by and he's intelligent enough to get away with it. He's from a good home with educated parents, books in the house, his own laptop at home.

I've caught him plagiarizing his homework a couple of times, just copying stuff straight from some website or other, usually Wikipedia. His parents have been warned that it could mean holding him back a year but they said they'd hire a private tutor to make sure he caught up. They want him in a good *lycée* and then in a good university. Juvenile detention would probably wreck his life.'

'He very nearly wrecked Denise's life and did his best to do the same to Félix. So how do we treat him?'

'We get you and me and his parents together and try to hammer out some agreed course of action,' Florence said. 'If Tristan doesn't go to prison, what's likely to happen to him?'

'Two years of community service, probably with a hefty fine that his parents can easily afford to pay. Part of the problem is with them. The husband is henpecked by Tristan's mother, who thinks her little darling is perfect. She swore out a false statement saying Tristan was with her when we know from witnesses and from his phone that he was throwing rocks at Denise at the time.'

'Can't you use that to make her see some sense?'

'I don't think the Procureur would want to charge her with perjury, not for a mother trying to protect her child. She'd get no more than a slap on the wrist.'

'She doesn't know that.'

'They've already hired a good lawyer for Tristan who'll probably tell the mother she's unlikely to face any trouble. But maybe you're right. Let me discuss this with Yveline. We can't let this drop here.'

'I've got to get the children back to school before my next lesson. I'll have a word with Rollo and see what he thinks.'

Bruno called Claire to ask if the Mayor was free, to be told he was in a meeting. She would let him know when it ended. He used the time to call the Mairie at La Bachellerie to ask if they had any school attendance records for the late 1930s and 1940s. No, he was told, they would all be somewhere in the *département* archives in Périgueux. He looked up the number, called and asked for Madame Tronquet, the helpful person he'd spoken to about Hugon's searches. Yes, she told him, they kept their school registers, organized by commune.

'Could someone look up the records of La Bachellerie for 1935 and 1938? I'm looking for any information about a girl called Marie-France who was in the same class as a boy named Henri Boulier. It's urgent and important, part of what we think is turning out to be a murder investigation. If you want to check with Commissaire Jalipeau of the Police Nationale . . .'

'No, no, it's all right, Monsieur. I was reading about you in the paper today, about that poor little girl who got hit in the eye. I'll do it myself and call you back.'

Bruno began going through his emails, deleting or acknowledging as he went, when his mobile phone rang. It was J-J, to say that the Bordeaux lab had confirmed Fabiola's theory. Hugon had been murdered with cyanide, sprayed into his face. J-J had a meeting scheduled with Isabelle at the St Denis Gendarmerie in an hour's time to discuss the implications of the murder for her operation. The Procureur would send someone and could Bruno attend? He checked his watch and said yes, telling J-J that he'd already briefed Isabelle on the matter.

There came a knock on his door and the Mayor came in, sat down, and said, 'I presume you want to know about Tristan? I already had Simon calling me last night, asking if I could use my influence with the Proc to go easy on his son. As you know, that supermarket is the biggest taxpayer in the commune.'

Bruno said nothing.

'I know you're not a great fan of putting teenage kids in prison. Nor am I. But you understand the politics of this, particularly with the drugs as a second charge. Rollo tells me that Tristan had so much cannabis he suspects the boy may have been dealing. Have you heard anything about that?'

'No, which makes me feel guilty. I had no idea that amount of stuff was available around here and I ought to have known, or at least kept more of an eye on the *collège*.'

The Mayor nodded. 'Rollo also said Tristan will now be suspended, but I can't see how that will help. Is there anything we can do that would keep the boy out of jail and also get him back on track? Isn't there some early engagement system for the army?'

'There used to be,' said Bruno. 'That's what I did. But seventeen is the minimum age now and the army probably wouldn't have him after this. We'll need to find him a useful and preferably tough job for the rest of the school year, then if he stays out of trouble and Rollo agrees, Tristan can retake his final year and go on to the *lycée* a year late.'

'Any ideas? We can't give him a job that someone unemployed could fill, which rules out most community service work.'

'That means an internship, and it would have to be with someone he could look up to, someone to set an example.'

'You mean the way you seem to have taken Félix in hand,' the Mayor said, smiling for the first time since he'd come in.

'No, I couldn't give Tristan full-time attention,' Bruno said. 'You're on the Conseil Régional and we've got the state forests. Do you know any foresters who might fit the bill? Get him doing something like that and the Procureur might give him conditional probation.'

'You mean if he doesn't shape up he goes straight to jail?'

'Exactly.'

'I'll talk to the chief forester.' The Mayor rose.

A few minutes after he'd gone, Madame Tronquet called Bruno back and asked for his fax number. She would send him a copy of the school register. Henri Boulier had been a classmate of Marie-France Perdigat, whose address was listed as Perdigat; the coincidence of names suggested a farm that had been in the same family for generations. Bruno thanked Madame Tronquet profusely and hung up just as his fax machine began to whir. Then came a knock on the door and Philippe Delaron arrived.

'I was doing some shopping at the supermarket when I got your text,' he said. 'What's up?'

Bruno gave Philippe the two photos and asked him to blow them up and give him two copies. He suggested Philippe keep copies for himself, since it could well turn into a story.

'You know Gilles, the guy who used to be at *Paris Match*?'

'Yes, Fabiola's boyfriend, the lucky guy.'

'He's been working on the background to this and I'm sure he'll do the usual deal with you – he gets the story nationally and you break it in *Sud Ouest* at the same time. One look at that photo of the car and Gilles will know what it's all about. These were taken in wartime. The kid in the second photo is now a sweet old guy called Boulier who's in the *maison de retraite*.

The guy with him holding the gun is his big brother Henri, a Resistance fighter who was killed later in the war, and the man in uniform is a downed RAF pilot whom Henri helped to escape over the Pyrenees.'

'That's a pretty nice story as it stands, but what about the car?' Philippe asked. 'It's a beauty.'

'Gilles can tell you all about it,' Bruno said. 'I'll call him now if you can start working on those blow-ups. I've got a meeting at the Gendarmerie on a separate matter that will also be a big story and I'll make sure you get it first.'

He called Gilles to brief him and told him to expect a visit from Philippe with photographic evidence that the Bugatti had been in the region at the time of its disappearance. He briefly related what Boulier had said and added that the car had been dismantled and hidden in a barn somewhere on a farm called Perdigat, near La Bachellerie.

'Jesus,' said Gilles. 'This is starting to get real. As soon as Philippe gets here we can go over to La Bachellerie and take a look.'

'That's what I hoped you'd say,' said Bruno. 'If you're still at the house at about four I may see you. I want to pick up Hector for an early ride.'

He ended the call, put on his *képi*, checked his appearance in the mirror and strolled down the Rue de Paris to the Gendarmerie, thinking it was convenient to have a couple of inquisitive and friendly journalists around. They could save him a great deal of legwork.

21

As he passed the office of Brosseil, the *notaire*, the door opened
and Oudinot emerged looking extremely pleased with himself.

'Ah, Bruno,' Oudinot greeted him. 'The deed is done, the
land sold and the feud settled. Sylvestre has signed the contract
pledging the sale and paid a fat deposit to ensure that the deal
goes through as quickly as possible. You must come to dinner
at the farm so I can thank you for all your help, and I still want
you to meet my daughter, Martine, properly, over one of Odette's
good dinners.'

'Congratulations,' Bruno said, startled, but thinking quickly.
'You know, I met your daughter when she came to the Mairie
to explain her proposals for the electric car rally, and at your
famr when we first discussed the deal with Sylvestre. She's a
charming woman and obviously very good at business. You must
be very proud of her.'

'Very much so, I just wish her business let us see a little more
of her. And it's time she got started on making me a grandpa.
My wife tells me she suspects there may be some new romantic
interest in Martine's life.'

A blush starting, Bruno looked away at the door of the *notaire*'s
office.

'Wasn't Sylvestre in there with you to sign the deal?'

'Yes, he's still there. Apparently he has some other property deal he's arranging, so he stayed behind to discuss it. I have to get back to the farm. So you'll come to dinner, shall we say Sunday evening at seven?'

'I'll be delighted to come and I'll look forward to it, but now you must excuse me, I have to get to a meeting at the Gendarmerie.'

'Of course. I'm so pleased it all worked out with Sylvestre. I really made him pay through the nose for the land.' Oudinot looked around with a conspiratorial air and whispered, 'When should I expect those colleagues of yours to come, about Sylvestre's taxes?'

'As soon as they get here. I'll let you know, and not a word to a soul. I know I can count on you, Fernand.'

'Indeed you can. *Au revoir*, Bruno.'

Oudinot headed to his car, parked immediately behind a Range Rover that Bruno recognized as Sylvestre's. With a glance at the still-closed door of the *notaire*, Bruno walked on, wondering if the sale to Sylvestre would still go through if he were arrested before the final contract was signed. If not, he'd forfeit his deposit, so Oudinot would not lose out by it. As he trotted up the Gendarmerie steps, noting J-J's official car parked down the street with Annette's blue Peugeot behind it, Bruno wondered what other deal Sylvestre might be negotiating.

The meeting was being held in Isabelle's temporary office. J-J was in the visitor's chair, beaming paternally at Isabelle, who rose with a smile to greet Bruno. Balzac jumped out from under her desk to welcome his master.

'Thank you for letting me have some time with him,' she said, bending to stroke the dog. 'Maybe you could bring him again tomorrow? I'd like to keep him with me but I don't think my hotel would welcome his staying in my room tonight.'

'Of course,' said Bruno, picking up Balzac's leash from her desk. 'I'll buy you croissants again at Fauquet's if you like. I'll be there at eight.'

'If you two dog-lovers have finished,' said J-J, 'Isabelle and I have agreed that you and I can continue our investigation into Hugon's murder as far as we can without alerting the two suspects, but once Isabelle's operation is complete, we move in.'

'If Isabelle succeeds in turning Sylvestre into an informant, her operation could last for some time,' Bruno said, his tone deliberately neutral. J-J looked surprised and Isabelle gave Bruno a sour look. 'Or didn't she explain that?'

'She didn't have to,' said J-J. 'Prunier got a call from the Minister's office saying that this Eurojust operation was to be given my complete cooperation and top priority.' Prunier was J-J's boss, the police commissioner for the *département*.

'I understand,' said Bruno. 'You'd better make sure nobody from the Bordeaux lab says anything about the autopsy. Murder by cyanide spray is unusual enough for people to start talking. If Sylvestre hears about that, he'll know the game is up.'

'I'll make sure nobody talks,' J-J said. 'I have to go to Bordeaux anyway. One of the two targets is there today, the Indian fellow, and I have a meeting with the Bordeaux detectives who've been handling the surveillance there.'

'I'm told you have another meeting in the post commandant's office over the case with the girl who was almost blinded,'

Isabelle interrupted. 'That young magistrate from Sarlat is going to be there, so you mustn't let us keep you. And don't forget those data cards you promised me.'

'I won't,' Bruno said. 'By the way, if your surveillance picks up anything about a property deal that Sylvestre is arranging, not the one with Oudinot himself, I'd be grateful to know what it might be.'

'So long as it doesn't compromise my operation, of course,' she said and fell silent, pointedly waiting for him to leave.

In Yveline's office next door, the mood was grim and even from the corridor he'd heard their raised voices. Yveline sat stony-faced and Annette's cheeks were flushed and she looked flustered. As if grateful for the distraction, Annette looked at her watch when Bruno entered. He apologized to them both for being late, explaining he'd been called in to see J-J about another matter.

'I was expecting him to be at this meeting as well,' Annette said. 'The Procureur said to be sure to get his views on the cannabis aspect of this case.'

'I'm sure he'll be here as soon as he can,' said Bruno. 'Are you both agreed on how to proceed against Tristan?'

'No,' said Yveline firmly, while at the same moment Annette was saying, 'Not exactly.'

'The young man has been told he'll be charged with aggravated bodily harm and possession of cannabis in quantities suggesting he's a dealer. It's open and shut,' said Yveline. 'Annette is trying to get me to recommend a non-custodial sentence and I won't. Tristan needs locking up. If he just had a couple of joints, maybe, but he had half a kilo and I don't want that being peddled around the kids in this town.'

'You know as well as I do that juvenile detention centres are like a high school for criminals,' said Annette. 'They're understaffed, underfunded and probably do more harm than good. This is an intelligent youngster from a stable and comfortable home who made a bad mistake, two bad mistakes. But there's a chance we can set him right. If he goes inside we're likely to have a very smart criminal on our hands when he gets out.'

'I don't think a stable and comfortable home entitles him to escape the penalties the law requires. It doesn't seem to have done him much good so far.'

The two women, usually good friends, glared at one another and then they both looked at Bruno, each of them obviously expecting him to agree with her. He could lose two friends here if he couldn't find a way to move them beyond their immediate argument.

'I don't know what to say,' Bruno began. 'I think you're both right. Tristan is a nasty piece of work who deserves to be punished. At the same time, if he goes into a detention centre he's probably going to come out more of a menace than when he went in. We all know that.'

He paused. 'As I understand it, we're not taking a decision here. We're simply expected to come up with a recommendation for the Procureur, and if we can't agree, we send him separate recommendations and he makes the choice.'

Yveline nodded agreement and Annette said, 'He specifically asked us to come up with an agreed recommendation.'

'Well, it looks like he's not going to get one from you two but he will be getting one from the Mayor, and since the Mayor has been a Senator and sits on the Conseil Régional, I think he'd take that one very seriously.'

'Where does the Mayor come into this?' Yveline asked, suspiciously.

'Tristan is one of his constituents and Tristan's father is the very competent manager of the supermarket which is the biggest employer and leading taxpayer in St Denis.' Bruno opened his arms and gave an exaggerated shrug, as if to say matters were now out of his hands.

'You can't have one law for the rich and another for the poor,' Annette began, and this time she looked in appeal to Yveline, who was nodding vigorously.

'That's shameful,' Yveline said. Ah, thought Bruno. It worked.

'Shameful, probably, but it's the reality, it's politics,' he said. 'The Mayor is planning to find Tristan some tightly supervised physical labour with the forestry department. But what if we three agree to insist on putting some real teeth into that? Tristan is prosecuted and found guilty, sentenced to two or three years, but then the sentence is suspended on the strict condition that the court get a satisfactory weekly report from the forester. One false move, one day playing truant, and he goes straight to jail.'

Yveline and Annette exchanged glances. Yveline shrugged. Annette said, 'If that's the best you think we can do.'

'I think it's important that we come up with a joint recommendation,' he said. 'Let me draft something, and then leave you two to tidy it up and put it into the right terminology.' Bruno, disguising his relief, took a notepad from Yveline's desk and began to write.

Ten minutes later, escorting Annette to her car, he asked, 'How's George Young? Still looking for that famous Bugatti?'

'Don't talk to me about that damn Bugatti. I get enough of that from George. I don't think he's making much progress and it's getting him down,' she said, in a tone that suggested she no longer felt she was being swept off her feet by the man of her dreams.

'I went to a lot of trouble to get him something I thought was bound to cheer him up,' she went on, sounding aggrieved. 'I planned it as a kind of consolation present, and he barely even thanked me before setting off again on this wild goose chase of his.'

'It sounds like he's a bit obsessed by it,' said Bruno sympathetically. 'But he's been interested for a long time, through his family connection with the English racing driver.'

'I suppose so. I just wish he'd talk about something else once in a while.' They reached her car and she stopped, looking appealingly at him. 'Am I being unreasonable?'

'No, not at all,' he said. 'But I suppose you could say that in a way it's flattering that he wants to share with you something that's so important to him.'

'It's not just the car, it's also this rivalry he has with Sylvestre about the Bugatti. It gets on my nerves, and I went to such a lot of trouble to get him that damn radiator.'

'Radiator?'

'A real Bugatti radiator, they're very distinctive with a kind of horseshoe shape. You remember Marcel, whose car we drove in the rally? He has one on the wall of his garage, along with ones from a Rolls-Royce and I don't know the names of the other cars. But this one had Bugatti written on it, and I wheedled and fluttered my eyelashes and finally Marcel let me buy it from him.'

'Young must have been delighted.'

'He was, for about thirty seconds, then he asked where I'd found it and when I told him he said he had to run.'

'And that surprised you? You hand him a piece of solid evidence that a Bugatti has been right here in the Périgord and you don't expect him to go hunting to see which car it might have come from?'

She looked down at her feet, a little abashed. 'I suppose so. But he didn't have to rush off right away, did he?'

'No, of course not. And I suppose you never have to rush away in the mornings to be on time for work? Perhaps he sees this as his work. By the way, did Marcel say where he got the radiator?'

'Years and years ago, he said, when he first opened the garage. He found it in some local junk shop in Sarlat that closed down years ago.'

'So as soon as Young realizes the trail has gone cold, he'll come back to you,' said Bruno. 'And you are young and lovely and alive and loving, all the things that a Bugatti radiator is not. I suspect he's the kind of man to appreciate that. So cheer up, Annette.'

'Thanks, Bruno.' She rose on tiptoe to her full height to kiss him on the cheek before getting into her car.

Balzac at his heels, Bruno walked back to pick up his van, noting that Sylvestre's Range Rover was still parked outside the *notaire*'s office. And Freddy was in Bordeaux. That meant the coast was clear. He could pick up the data cards from his cameras, put in new ones and change the batteries before taking Hector out. He headed out to the *chartreuse*.

Half an hour later, leaning forward in the saddle as Hector plodded up the slope, Bruno was wondering how difficult it would be to track down all the closed junk shops in Sarlat. He'd have to find out when Marcel had first launched his garage and restrict the search to those that had been open at the time. It would mean looking through old business directories, and then trying to track down members of the family who had owned the shop and see if anybody remembered where the Bugatti radiator had come from. The prospect dismayed him, until he remembered that he could ask Gilles to do it. And then he thought, as he topped the rise onto the ridge that looked down on St Denis, he had the evening with Martine to look forward to. He looked back to see that Balzac was still following along behind, running as fast as his short legs would allow. Bruno leaned forward and loosened the reins to let Hector know it was time to run.

For a time, at least, the ride drove all the other thoughts and concerns from his head. There was nothing but this moment, this speed, this wind in his face and this powerful, galloping creature that seemed almost to be a part of him. More than that, on horseback he felt himself to be much more a part of the physical world around him even as its trees flashed by, sensed rather than seen.

As he slowed at the end of the ridge, the thought stayed with him; this feeling of being connected to nature was at its most immediate and dramatic when he was riding, but it was also something he felt with his dog and even with his geese and chickens. Humans were meant to live with animals, he concluded, to know that humankind was not alone on this planet but shared it with other species in a state of mutual interdependence. People who lived in cities might know that intellectually, but could they ever truly feel it in the way he did in the woods with his horse and his dog? He turned in the saddle to watch Balzac catch up, and then unbidden Hector set off at a walk down the familiar bridle path for the long canter back to the stables.

As Bruno finished rubbing down his horse, Gilles drove into the courtyard in Fabiola's old car, the Twingo that he'd started to use now that she had her new electric vehicle. They shook hands and Gilles said, 'The Perdigat farm is now a housing estate, a filling station and a couple of warehouses for supermarkets. It's right by the extension to the new autoroute. There's no trace of any old barns and the farm and its contents were auctioned off fifty years ago. The next step is to check old newspapers and try to find the auctioneers.'

'There might be a shortcut.' Bruno pulled out his phone to call his counterpart, the municipal policeman of Terrasson, the nearest town to La Bachellerie. Grégoire was a pillar of the *département*'s tennis federation and Bruno had met him often; his father had been the town policeman before him. They exchanged greetings and Bruno explained he was trying to find out which company had auctioned the farm of Perdigat.

'Probably the Melvilles from Périgueux, they've always done most of the auctions around here,' Grégoire replied. 'But I'll ask my father, he might even remember it. The farm's partly built over now, of course. I'll call you back.'

Gilles grinned. 'You and your local knowledge, Bruno. I should have thought of that.'

'I didn't know Grégoire's father was still alive or I'd have gone straight to him,' Bruno said, thinking that Grégoire was nearing sixty, close to retirement, so his father would be getting on for ninety. He'd certainly have been around at the time of the auction. He might even have known Félix's grandfather.

'I have to go, Gilles, but there could be another clue,' he said, and recounted how Annette had found the radiator at Marcel's garage and given it to Young.

'I'm disappointed that Young didn't tell me that himself,' said Gilles. 'We're supposed to be cooperating.'

'Maybe he feels he's getting close to the car and the money it could bring him.'

'We went through all that, remember? I'd better give him a call, and I'll count on you to call me back when you hear from Grégoire. Do you mind if I follow up with Marcel at the garage? His place is the big Citroën dealership, is that right?'

Bruno stopped at the Gendarmerie to give Isabelle the data cards from his cameras and got home not long after five. He fed his geese and chickens, got the fire going in the wood stove and set the table for two. He was about to climb into the shower when Grégoire called him back to say his father remembered the sale. The auctioneer had indeed been Melville. The farm had been broken up into lots and all the old farm equipment, mostly out of date, had been bought by a scrap-metal merchant and junk dealer in Sarlat called Bérégovoy.

'I don't think they're still in business, Bruno,' Grégoire added.

'Thanks anyway,' Bruno said. 'You might also ask your dad

if he remembers people called Boulier, they were *métayers* at Rastignac. One of them is in our *maison de retraite* and he told me that he remembers seeing the château of Rastignac burning during the war. Your dad will certainly remember that. He's about your dad's age so they were probably at school together. He had a big brother, Henri, a Resistance fighter who died in the war. If your dad remembers the family, it might be nice to bring the two of them together to reminisce about old times.'

'Good idea,' said Grégoire. 'I'll ask him. My father's always been interested in what happened at Rastignac, spent years talking to everyone in the area to try to establish whether the paintings had been stolen or burned in the fire. I'm sure he'd love to get together with someone who could talk about it with him. Old folks like to reminisce about their young days. Maybe one day someone will do the same for the two of us. Keep well, Bruno.'

Bruno called Gilles to tell him about the Bérégovoy scrap-metal merchants and to commiserate. If the old tobacco barn at Perdigat had indeed been the last resting place of the chassis and engine of the legendary Bugatti, it had probably long since been melted down for scrap.

'It's not bad news as far as I'm concerned,' Gilles replied. 'Quite the opposite – it makes a good, haunting ending to my story. The most valuable car in the world, melted down and recycled, and some of its molecules are probably now speeding around in some of the family cars in France.'

Bruno put his phone down, stripped, hung up his uniform and tossed the other clothes he'd worn into the laundry basket. He climbed into the shower that he'd built and tiled himself, thinking that someday he might invest in one of those grand multi-jet showers his friend Horst had installed. He shampooed his hair and was soaping himself down when he was suddenly aware of a shadow against the frosted glass of the sliding door. Then he heard a tap on the door and a woman's voice said, 'Bruno?'

Was that Martine, arriving early, or another voice? With the shower running, he couldn't tell. Heaven forbid it was Isabelle making an unexpected visit. He slid open the door a crack and with relief saw it was Martine, smiling cheekily at him and swiftly unbuttoning her blouse to reveal a black bra. She began unzipping her jeans.

'I just showered at home before I came,' she said. 'But I think I'm in the mood for another.' She reached behind her back to undo her bra. 'I've brought the food but I'm not hungry yet – at least, not for the food.'

She climbed in to join him in the running water and put her arms around his neck. 'You're already soapy,' she said. 'Why don't you soap me?'

22

Bruno awoke feeling refreshed and aware that he was smiling, with the scent of Martine still lingering on his pillow. The smile lasted through most of his morning run. It was not until he began the final sprint through the woods back to his cottage and his shower that he remembered that he was having breakfast with Isabelle and that it was a work day. How was it, he asked himself in the shower, that while steeped in the rapture of a new affair he found himself still thinking of Isabelle? She was a woman who had scarred him more deeply than any other; perhaps that was the reason. Her determination and her ambition had left little room for tenderness. Passion, yes, and fire; a fierceness in her pride that still awed him, even as he felt it marked her for grief and perhaps spelled tragedy for those like him who had been caught in her flame. But that was the question: were there others like him? Even as he told himself he doubted it, he thrust the thought away. However often she might erupt once again in his life, Isabelle was history. He never wanted to go through that sense of loss again. And, as he told himself as he drove into town, he had work to do.

Saturday was the second, smaller market day of the week, but it still required his presence. A few minutes before eight most of the stalls were already erected, with early customers moving purposefully from one to the next. Bruno had noticed that most of them shopped in the order in which they ate: first the olives stall and the organic bread, then the fish or the duck, then the fruit and vegetables and finally Stéphane's cheeses. Even those he knew to be apartment dwellers paused at the flower stall, the last one before the bridge, picking up seedlings of herbs for their balconies and window boxes. Bruno moved through the stalls, shaking hands and kissing cheeks, tasting a ripe fig and then a fat black olive.

'Nems not hot yet, come back later,' Madame Vinh called to him from the glass-fronted stand where she kept the samosas and the lumpia, the prawn curries and beef rendang, for all of which the people of St Denis had developed a taste. Take-out containers were stacked beside the vast cauldron of pho soup heating on the portable gas stove. It would be empty by noon. In the decade that Bruno had been the town policeman, the usual radishes and cucumbers had been joined by mangoes and papaya, heirloom tomatoes and pomelos. Sausage rolls and Cornish pasties now stood beside the quiche Lorraine. But the cheese and the charcuterie stalls were still the most thronged. The people of St Denis were prepared to experiment and the stallholders were ready to adapt, but all of them always returned faithfully to the foie gras and smoked duck sausage, to the Brie de Meaux and Vacherin Mont d'Or, emblems of a nation that still liked to define itself by the way it ate.

Fauquet's café was crowded and the windows steamed up, people standing three deep at the bar and all the tables filled. This was no place for his dog. He tied Balzac's leash to a railing and then moved through the crowd, shaking hands until he caught Fauquet's eye and asked for coffee and croissants on the terrace. The café did not usually have the chairs and tables out into the open this late in the season, but Fauquet nodded and Bruno leaned across the counter to pick up a dishrag and the key that hung by the cash desk. He went outside to open the padlock to a discreet door into the storage area, pulled out two chairs and a small table and put them at the far corner of the terrace, by the stone balustrade that overlooked the river, where he and Isabelle would be out of earshot of any other arrivals. He wiped the furniture clean with the rag, collected Balzac and took his seat. By the time Isabelle arrived, the coffee and croissants had been served, while other regulars had liberated another half-dozen tables and lifted their faces to enjoy the gentle early morning sun.

'In Paris the cafés have installed heaters on the terraces,' she said as he rose to greet her.

'It being Paris, they will probably be denouncing the perils of global warming while they cluster beneath the artificial heat,' he said, and pointed up to the clear blue sky of autumn. 'Here in the Périgord, we prefer solar power.'

'My team have finally arrived and been issued their warrants from the Prefect, so at last we can get started,' she said, sitting down to pet Balzac and tell him what a fine dog he was and how much she missed him.

'I hope you had a more interesting evening than I did,' she said, looking up at Bruno. 'I was staring at those images from your data cards until my brain flagged. It was always the same two Range Rovers coming and going, and so the high point was when a new vehicle turned up, until I realized it was you. The postman didn't even get out of his car, just pushed the supermarket flyers and catalogues into the box. And there was one courier delivery.'

'Any result from the Bordeaux surveillance?'

'Freddy had lunch with a junior professor of sociology whom we're now checking out, French but a Muslim convert and wearing her headscarf as if it were a veil. The guy from Toulouse whom he met at the station in Agen was interesting, a trade union rep at Airbus, already on the Brigadier's watch list. They went to a kebab house to eat.'

'These legalistic delays must be very frustrating for you,' he said.

'They are, but that's the price Europe pays for human rights,' she said wryly. 'And since we French invented them, we've only ourselves to blame. But the surveillance is only part of the operation. Mostly it's about tracking bank accounts and money trails, which is why we need the Americans, and that's going well.'

'How much money are they moving through the vintage car system?'

'They're being discreet, mostly cars in the very low six-figure range, nothing above three hundred thousand. But we think they're doing three or four at every auction, so the total is already close to five million.'

'Do you know where the money is going?'

She shrugged. 'Some of it, not all by any means. But we're building the map of local paymasters, giving the Brigadier and his counterparts in other countries the names of people to watch. It's slow but as the Brigadier says, this is going to be a very long war.'

'Do you want me to take your surveillance guys up to meet the farmer whose hut they'll be using?'

'That's the plan. We meet at the Gendarmerie at eight thirty and you can take them. The sooner they get started the better. Do you need me to come along and show our Eurojust credentials?'

'No, the farmer thinks it's a tax investigation. Eurojust will simply confuse him. His feud with Sylvestre is nominally over – they signed a deal for Oudinot to sell the land. But he still enjoys the thought of Sylvestre in tax trouble.'

They made their way to Isabelle's temporary office in the Gendarmerie, just as two men in hunters' garb came into the building wearing rucksacks.

'Bruno, this is the team, Hanno and Friedrich. They've just been taking a preliminary look at the target building. And guys, this is an old friend of mine, Chef de Police Bruno Courrèges, who runs this town. If you're very good and very lucky, you might get him to cook for you some evening.'

'Are you the one who warned us about the geese?' Hanno asked, in serviceable French with a heavy Dutch accent. 'Christ, I've never heard anything like it.'

'There seemed to be two tribes of them, white geese and grey ones,' said Friedrich, who was German. 'They didn't seem to mix much. Is there any difference?'

'A lot,' said Bruno, smiling as he explained. 'The white ones get roasted to eat at wintertime, usually at Christmas, and the grey ones have the best livers so we use them for foie gras.'

'In Germany we eat them on the eve of St Martin's Day, November eleventh,' said Friedrich.

'Any excuse will do,' Bruno replied, grinning. 'How do you stuff them?'

'Pork sausage and apples.'

'Guys,' Isabelle chided, 'if we can get back to business. Did you see a small hut near the target house? Bruno thinks he can get you installed there. Would that help?'

'Perfect, we should be able to get full audio there,' said Hanno. 'And we may be able to get into his computer.'

'How would you do that?' Bruno asked.

'A pinhole camera to get the keystrokes for his password.'

Isabelle rapped the table. 'OK, let's get started.'

Well before nine, Bruno and the two technicians arrived at Oudinot's farm and declined the offer of coffee, only to learn that they had missed Martine. She had a few minutes earlier walked across to the *chartreuse* to thank Sylvestre for agreeing to the deal that would end the feud.

'Good,' said Bruno. 'That will provide a distraction while these men install their equipment in your hut.'

Hanno and Friedrich, their surveillance gear in their rucksacks, followed in Bruno's footsteps as he crept through the woodland towards the hut. The area was littered with geese droppings and the ammoniac stench inside the hut was daunting, even with the door open. The two technicians wrinkled their noses and glared their dismay at Bruno. He left them to it, heading back to Oudinot's farm where his van waited, when the phone at his waist began to vibrate. He pulled it out to look at the screen and smiled when he saw Martine was calling.

'*Bonjour, ma belle*,' he said. 'I'm missing you already.'

'Bruno, stop. This is serious. It's Sylvestre. He's dead. I couldn't find him anywhere although all the doors were open, and then I looked in the pool. He was face down.'

'*Merde*,' he gasped. 'I'll be right there. Don't touch anything.'

'I already pulled him out and tried to revive him.'

'That's fine. I'm at your dad's place and I'm on the way.'

He turned and crashed through the woods, skirting Oudinot's fence, and along the road to follow the dirt path as he had on his first visit. Martine, her clothes drenched, was on her knees by the pool. The sliding glass arches that covered it had been partially opened. As he approached, Bruno saw a male body stretched out beside Martine. Wearing just bathing shorts, its eyes were open and glassy. He could detect no sign of injury. Draped on the rim of the pool lay a dark, sodden bathrobe.

Bruno kneeled down and put the back of his fingers on Sylvestre's neck. He was cold and had no pulse. The body was white except for the chest, which seemed bruised and red.

'You tried pumping his chest?' he asked.

'I came looking for him, found him in the pool, climbed in to haul him out and began pumping him. I was hopeful at first because a lot of water gushed from his mouth and nose, but that was all. Then I called you and started again.'

'He's dead, sure enough.' He helped her to her feet and hugged her. 'It must have been a terrible shock to find him this way. I'm sorry you had to see it.'

'I'm fine, just sorry I came too late to be of any use. He must have drowned. Maybe he was drunk.'

'Was the bathrobe there when you arrived?'

'No, he was wearing it, or rather, half wearing it, on one arm and shoulder. It came off when I was trying to get him out of the pool.'

'You did well to get him out.'

Bruno looked around. On the table were two tall glass vases, each with a burned-out candle inside. Beside them was a book, an ashtray, cigarettes and lighter, two empty brandy glasses and an empty bottle of Drambuie, a Scottish liqueur that Bruno had drunk once after one of Pamela's dinners. He rose to look more closely. A bath towel was draped over one of the chairs. At each end of the table was what looked like a metallic umbrella, an outdoor heater with a gas bottle in its base, designed for the heat to come out at the top and be reflected back down by the metal parasol. Each of the heaters was switched to 'On'. He slipped on some evidence gloves and rocked the gas cylinders. Each one was empty as if they had burned all night until the gas ran out.

The book was square, glossy and in English, with the photograph of a silver-blue Type 57 Atlantic on the cover, the one that he recalled was now in a California museum. The title was *Bugatti, Yesterday and Today*. Beside the cigarettes on the table lay a small leather pouch of the kind used for pipe tobacco. Bruno opened it and smelled marijuana. There were several stubbed-out joints in the ashtray alongside the cigarette butts. He put the ashtray, the glasses and bottle, the lighter and cigarette pack into separate evidence bags and called Fabiola to ask her to come up to certify a death. Then he called Isabelle.

'Bad news,' he said. 'One of your targets, Sylvestre, is dead.'

'*Putain*,' she said. 'What happened?'

'He drowned in his pool sometime in the night. There are no

visible injuries and nothing immediately suspicious. It looks like he was drunk and stoned.'

'Maybe it was meant to look that way,' she said. 'Was it you who found him?'

'No, he was found by a neighbour, his cousin, less than half an hour ago. She got him out of the pool and tried to resuscitate him, but no luck. Then she called me and I got here maybe five minutes ago, no more.'

'Is Freddy there?' she asked immediately.

'No obvious sign of him but I'm about to take a good look around. Shall I bring Hanno and Friedrich here?'

'No, I'll do that when I arrive. I'll leave now.'

'I already called a doctor.'

'*Merde*,' she said. 'I wish you hadn't done that yet.'

'No choice,' he replied. 'It's the law.'

'See if you can find his phone or laptop anywhere and secure it, that's the priority now. And if you do find Freddy, hold him.'

'What about J-J? Should I call him?'

'Not until I get there and see for myself. I'll probably want a full autopsy and forensic check. I'll ask the Gendarmes here to send a team up to secure the grounds.'

She sounded as if she were about to hang up and he said quickly, 'Don't forget your own laptop – the data cards, remember.'

'Of course, thanks for reminding me,' she said. 'I remember that one of them covered part of the pool area, so it's a pity they're not infrared.' She hung up.

'Sorry,' he said to Martine. 'Police commissioner.'

She looked at him sceptically. 'And who are Hanno and Friedrich?'

'Did your dad tell you about the surveillance operation?' She nodded. 'They're the ones in the hut, installing the surveillance gear which now won't be needed. Did you look in the lodge by the gate?'

'Yes, the door is open there, too.'

'Do you mind staying here while I look around?'

'I'd rather come with you and I need to get out of these wet clothes. Sylvestre isn't going anywhere.'

'Call your mother and ask her to bring you a towel and some fresh clothes. You can tell her what happened but that she is not to tell anyone else, okay? I'm sorry about this but there's a lot more involved than I'm able to say.'

'All this for a tax inspection?' she said, raising an eyebrow. 'I find that hard to believe.'

Bruno shrugged. 'When I can, I'll tell you the whole story, but it's likely that I don't know all of it.'

'That was a woman's voice on the phone,' she said. 'All the police commissioners around here are men. I know that because I went to see them to talk about the plans for the rally.'

'You're right. But she is a police commissioner, a French-woman who used to work for the Police Nationale in Périgueux. Right now she's attached to Eurojust and the surveillance is her operation. Now, excuse me, but I need to look around.'

Martine looked at him curiously, then picked up her phone and began dialling. Bruno smiled apologetically and turned to head for the lodge where he had found Freddy on his last visit.

Then he remembered something. He called the Gendarmerie in St Denis and Sergeant Jules answered.

'Something very urgent, Jules,' he said. 'You know the truck park in Le Buisson? I need you or someone to go there right away and secure the big van belonging to the guy from Alsace who had that old car at the parade. His name is Sylvestre Wémy and there should be two cars inside, the one he showed off and a new electric car. Don't let anybody touch it until I get there or some of J-J's forensics people arrive.'

'There's only me and Yveline here,' Jules replied. 'Just as Isabelle ran out of the door she asked for the others to head up to Sylvestre's place to meet her there and be prepared to stay guarding it all day, but she didn't say why.'

'You can tell Yveline that we found Sylvestre dead, drowned, and I'm trying to track down that Indian guy who was with him. But I really need that truck of theirs to be secured if you have to do it yourself.'

At the lodge where Freddy had stayed, the door was open, leading into a sparsely furnished sitting room with an armchair, a TV set and a rowing machine. He called out but heard no reply. Car magazines were scattered around the floor and a driver's helmet was perched on top of the TV. The kitchen was dominated by a machine to make espresso that looked complicated and expensive. The fridge held bottles of mineral water, milk, apple juice and some yogurts and the freezer compartment revealed ice cubes and two frozen pizzas. Upstairs were two bedrooms and a bathroom, soap and toothpaste on the sink, a towel on the floor by the shower that was still wet. Freddy had not been gone long. One bedroom was empty, the other had an unmade bed, more car magazines and a handsome antique armoire that was empty. An adapter was still in the plug in the wall beside the bed but whatever it had recharged was gone.

Sylvestre's house was also deserted, but the bed in the main bedroom was made and the wardrobe was full of clothes. On top of the bed was a shirt, sweater and trousers and on the floor beside it a pair of underpants, socks and shoes, as if he'd undressed in a hurry, perhaps before getting his bathrobe and going out to the pool. Bruno saw a wire snaking from an electric plug in the wall and disappearing beneath the underpants. He pushed them aside with his foot to reveal the charger for an iPhone, but the phone had gone. He put an evidence bag on top of it.

The bedside table was piled with books. The top one was titled *Bugatti Type 57, the Last French Bugatti*. It seemed to have more photos than text. Beneath it was a paperback that looked like a novel or a history book in English, *The Grand Prix Saboteurs* by Joe Saward. On the cover was a photo of a Bugatti like the one Sylvestre had brought to the vintage car parade with a swastika atop it. The long subtitle heralded the unknown story of the Grand Prix drivers who became wartime intelligence agents. At the bottom of the pile was a hardback, also in English, *A Different Danger, Three Champions at War*, by Richard Armstrong.

Down in the kitchen everything was as he'd remembered it, except that the laptop had gone and there was a single glass and an empty bottle of Chablis on the counter. He looked in the other rooms but failed to find the laptop. In the sitting room with its armchairs of leather and chrome was a large bookcase, almost filled with books on cars and issues of classic car magazines, auction catalogues and invitations to more Concours d'Elégance. Bruno marvelled at the scale of the subculture all this represented. Between the leather and chrome armchairs stood a glass and chrome coffee table with several magazines on top, all of them from the Club Bugatti of France. The one on top was dated November 1996, and a bookmark had been inserted into its pages.

Bruno looked inside and skimmed an article by a woman named Stella Tayssedre who had been Ettore Bugatti's secretary in Paris and a member of Benoist and Grover-Williams's Resistance network. She had been arrested by the Gestapo the same day as Benoist along with her husband, and had been five months pregnant at the time. She was taken to the railway station at Compiègne along with Benoist and the others to board what she called 'the death train' to Germany. At the station, someone from the International Red Cross noticed her pregnancy and took her off the train. The Swedish consul subsequently managed to get her released but her husband never returned.

Bruno closed the magazine, shaking his head at the thought of those grim times, but struck also by the breadth and depth of Sylvestre's research. Annette might have been irritated by her English boyfriend's fixation on the lost Bugatti but Sylvestre seemed just as obsessed.

The other two houses, one in each of the wings around the courtyard, were locked and the shutters closed. He walked back to the pool where Martine and her mother, Odette, were standing by Sylvestre's body, Martine now clad in dry clothes, jeans and a cotton sweater.

'Such a young man, it's so sad,' said Odette. 'What a terrible accident and such a shame that Martine had to be the one who found him.'

He heard the sound of a car being driven fast, too fast for the road, and it went rushing past the entrance. It braked hard, reversed, and then Isabelle climbed out, walking across and leaving the car door open and the engine running.

'*Bonjour, mesdames*,' she said briskly. 'I understand you live next door. You may return home. Thank you for your help and we'll contact you as soon as we're done here. Just one question: Did either of you see or hear anything in the course of last night?'

Martine and her mother shook their heads and left for Odette's car, parked in the driveway. Isabelle had to move her own car to let them out. When she got back Bruno said, 'Sylvestre's phone and laptop are both gone.'

'What about cars?'

'That's Sylvestre's rented Range Rover in the courtyard. The one Freddy was using isn't here.'

'Right.' She pulled out her phone, dialled, introduced herself and said she wanted an emergency 'Watch and Detain' order to go out to all airports, airlines and traffic police. She gave Freddy's name, two aliases that were new to Bruno, and the licence plate number of his Range Rover.

'That was the Brigadier,' she said. 'Now I have to try to get Europol to move as fast.' She dialled again and then said to him as she waited, 'Could you bring Hanno and Friedrich here, please?' Then she turned back to her phone.

Bruno headed for the rear of the *chartreuse*, called out to identify himself, and Hanno poked his head around the door.

'Operation's over,' Bruno said. 'The target's dead and Isabelle is here and sent me to get you.'

'You're kidding,' said Hanno, rolling his eyes. 'At least we'll be out of this smell of duck shit.'

'They're geese,' said Bruno, and the two men started to repack their gear. Bruno pushed down the fence to let them come across and told them to follow when they were ready and join him and Isabelle at the pool.

By the time Bruno got there, Fabiola had already arrived and was examining the body. Isabelle was still on her phone.

'Scratches on the back of his shoulders and some of his hair is pulled out at the back,' said Fabiola.

'Could that have happened when Martine got him out of the pool?' he asked. 'He's a lot heavier than her, so she'd have had a hard time.'

'I doubt it, looks more like a struggle to me, as though some-body might have been holding his head underwater. We'll need to examine his fingernails, see if he scratched anybody. Could you bag his hands? And I'll want to know how much of that alcohol he had.'

'That might not be all he had,' said Bruno. 'There's an empty bottle of wine in the kitchen as well as that empty bottle of Drambuie out here. It's inside one of those evidence bags. And he'd been smoking joints.'

'Drunk and stoned, it wouldn't have been difficult to drown him.' Fabiola turned to look at the surface of the pool. 'Is that a bit of hair floating there?'

'There was a second glass with the Drambuie bottle. He may not have been drinking alone.'

Isabelle joined them. 'Are you saying it looks like murder by drowning?'

'I'm saying it could be, maybe even probably. There are signs of some kind of struggle. But if he was extremely drunk, he might have passed out in the pool and drowned that way.'

'We're going to need J-J and the forensics team,' Bruno said to Isabelle. 'By the way, Sylvestre has a big van in a truck park near here, containing a vintage car and a fancy electric one. It looks like a travelling workshop inside. I've asked Sergeant Jules to secure it.'

Isabelle nodded, dully. 'Check on that, if you would. And see if there are any keys around here that might open it.' She looked across at him, shaking her head. 'If it hadn't been for those delays in getting the warrants – ah, there's no point crying over spilt milk. I'll call J-J now.'

'I trust this means that J-J can now make public the murder inquiry into Monsieur Hugon,' Bruno said.

'I suppose so,' said Isabelle, as though it didn't much matter to her.

'In that case, do you mind if I look round for anything that might establish a link that connects Hugon with Sylvestre and Freddy, perhaps papers or letters?' He wondered if he should tell her to pull herself together and act like the efficient, purposeful Isabelle he knew.

'Be my guest,' she said. 'You'll wear gloves, of course. Anything to do with finance or Dubai, put it to one side.'

She sighed deeply and looked at him. 'This was the operation that was going to make my name and really put Eurojust on the màp, penetrating the finance network, turning Sylvestre so he worked for me.'

'I understand,' he said. 'I'm sorry it didn't work out as you hoped. But then you never want things to be too easy. And it's not as though you failed. You've mapped the network, traced some of the payment routes in Europe and the paymasters in the Gulf. And you've still got a shot at picking up Freddy.'

'Dear Bruno, always looking for the positive in every disaster.' She gave him a fond look and then braced herself. 'And you're right. Time to gather what we can from the wreckage and start all over again.'

23

The whole panoply of a murder investigation began to build around Bruno – forensics teams and photographers, uniformed police searching the grounds, detectives combing Sylvestre's Range Rover and sifting through the contents of the houses. Bruno sat by the pool with his notebook, skimming through it as he tried to work out what motive Freddy might have had to kill his partner and flee. Did he suspect that they were under surveillance and that Sylvestre might agree to work for the authorities to gain immunity from prosecution? Had Freddy learned that Sylvestre was taking money meant for the cause? Had he simply become too much of a risk? Or might it have been personal, Freddy trying to take over Sylvestre's business? But in that case, would he not have prepared matters better? From the look of Freddy's place, he'd left in a hurry if not in a panic. And how could he take over Sylvestre's business ventures, unless he was certain he could thumb his nose at a French extradition request?

Bruno could see no explanation that satisfied him. And Freddy had left all the books and journals behind that dealt with the lost Bugatti. Perhaps he had no interest in it, but it had been to Freddy that Hugon had mailed his research report or whatever it was. That reminded Bruno: he should ask J-J if his team had been able to break into Hugon's computer. The research report should be in there. And had Freddy and Sylvestre together killed Hugon, or just one of them? There had been three coffee cups, Bruno remembered. And what was Sylvestre's second deal with the *notaire*? At least he could check that. He was about to ring Brosseil's office when he remembered there was someone who would need to know about the death. He called his friend Thomas in Alsace instead.

'I've got bad news. Sylvestre was found dead this morning in his swimming pool.'

'*Mon Dieu*. Was it an accident?' asked Thomas.

'We're not sure yet.' Bruno explained the circumstances, said that the family feud had been settled and that two of Sylvestre's land deals had been almost completed. 'There's an autopsy later today. I'll keep you informed.'

'Thanks, I'd better tell the Mayor. That's our richest citizen gone and the last of his line.'

'Can you let me have the name of his lawyer, and find out if there's a will?' Bruno said, and then stopped. 'I remember you saying before that he was the last of his line?'

'He was an only child and had no direct heirs. His father and grandfather were only sons.'

'So who are the nearest relatives?' Bruno asked.

'None around here. I imagine it will be your lot, the ones he was having the feud with. They'll inherit a fortune.'

'*Mon Dieu*,' said Bruno. 'That's quite a motive. And it was his cousin, Oudinot's daughter, who found the body.'

Martine had left him not long before eleven, he recalled. Fabiola was putting Sylvestre's death at somewhere between midnight and four in the morning; Sylvestre's immersion in the heated pool had made the usual body temperature tests meaningless. But did she and her father know there were no other heirs to Sylvestre's estate?

'I'll call the lawyer and find out about a will, just as soon as I've seen the Mayor. He'll probably want the body brought back here for a big funeral. It's quite an event in a town like this.'

'I understand, and thanks, Thomas, and my love to Ingrid.'

Rocked by the prospect that the woman he was sleeping with might be a murder suspect, Bruno tried to remember every meeting he'd had with Martine and Sylvestre, including that first time when the two cousins had been together at this very spot by the pool. There was nothing to suggest that Martine was anything but what she said, keen to help resolve the family feud, and a bit embarrassed by her father's hostility. Surely he now knew her well enough . . .

No, he didn't, he told himself. There had been only a few meetings, a lunch, some meals, two glorious evenings making love, a sense of mounting excitement that went beyond his attraction to her looks and brains and talent, the enjoyment he took in her presence, the pleasure he felt at the prospect of seeing her again. He liked her a lot. No, he more than liked her, and Bruno knew himself well enough to suspect that he was falling for her. And that would skew his judgement. Duty as well as decency required that he hand this over to J-J to investigate.

In the meantime, he had work to do. He called the *notaire*'s office and after a short pause Brosseil came on the line.

'Bad news,' Bruno began. 'Your new client, Sylvestre from Alsace, is dead. Drowned in his pool last night. I'm at his place now. Those deals of his won't go through now and I need to find out what they are. I know about Oudinot, it's the other one.'

Brosseil stuttered something, dropped the phone and then said, 'Sorry, it's a bit of a shock. At least the deposits are paid. He did bank transfers for each of them from my office, so I'll get my fee, or some of it. The second deal was with Jérôme at the amusement park. Monsieur Wémy was planning to buy it, enlarge it and build it up. He said something about adding a car museum.'

'The Mayor will be sorry to hear that's fallen through,' Bruno replied, recovering quickly from the surprise. 'How much of a deposit did he put down? The usual ten per cent?'

'No, fifty thousand to Oudinot, half the final price, and a hundred thousand to Jérôme, ten per cent. He paid extra because he wanted the deals wrapped up fast before he went to China. I'd better get on to Oudinot and Jérôme.'

'Oudinot already knows,' Bruno said. 'His daughter found the body, but don't pass that news around yet.'

As he closed his phone, he wondered if someone other than Freddy had been involved in Sylvestre's death. The Oudinot family had had a motive to loathe him in the past, but surely not once the land deal was agreed. Oudinot had been very pleased with the sale when Bruno had seen him. But then, he might expect to inherit. And Jérôme was looking at a million-euro payday if the sale of the amusement park had been completed. Could the lost Bugatti have been sufficient motive, perhaps for someone equally obsessed like George Young? Certainly with all his books and hiring a researcher, Sylvestre's search had been far better organized than Young's dependence on some old family memoir that hadn't taken him far. But that was hardly a motive for murder. And Young was aware of the legal complications of the vehicle's ownership, if it was ever found. However much it might be worth, the finder would get only a fraction of an eventual sale price.

'I wish I could sit around a pool all day while others slave away,' came J-J's booming voice.

'I'm thinking,' said Bruno. 'I'm trying to work out if anyone but Freddy might have had a motive.'

'Start by asking yourself who else has fled the scene. That van you mentioned with Sylvestre's cars in it, did you find the key?'

'I found a key case in the kitchen with a lot of keys in it. I left it there in an evidence bag to be fingerprinted.'

'That's done. Can you go down to wherever the van is parked with a forensics team, let them in and give them a hand? They've just arrived from Bergerac with Inspector Jofflin. You've worked with him before and you've at least seen inside the van and know the cars.'

'Okay. Any interesting papers turned up yet?'

'Isabelle's handling that with her two guys, and she knows to keep a special eye out for anything that might have come from Hugon.'

'What about Hugon's computer?'

'Yves can't get into it. We may have to send it to Bordeaux, maybe to Paris; they have machines that can run through millions of possible passwords in a few minutes. Given time they'll break it.'

'There's something you need to know,' said Bruno. 'The young woman who found the body, his cousin Martine. I'm involved with her so I can't follow this up myself. But my friend Thomas in Alsace has just reminded me that Sylvestre has no other heirs. That means his estate will go to Martine and her parents and there's been a long-standing and bitter family feud that I thought had been settled. Given Sylvestre's wealth, that's quite a motive, and I think you ought to pursue it, even though I've known the family for years. I really don't think they are killers, least of all Martine. It would break my heart if I'm wrong.'

J-J studied him in silence for a long moment. 'Okay, Bruno, I'll look into it myself.' His voice was quiet and sympathetic. 'And thanks for telling me.'

Bruno went to get the keys, joined the team from Bergerac and headed for the truck park at Le Buisson. He didn't know the security man on duty, but at the sight of Bruno's uniform and the police van that carried the forensic specialists, the guard opened the electronic gates to let them in. One of the keys opened the door. They pulled out the ramps and Inspector Jofflin and Bruno donned their snowman suits and booties and climbed in. From their van, two members of Jofflin's crew unloaded a portable generator, fired it up and connected two floodlamps to illuminate the two cars, ancient and modern, that dominated the van's interior. But that was not where Jofflin began his search. He looked at the racks of oils, lubricants and chemicals that lined one side of the van, each of them secured for travel with bungee cords. Then he looked at the workbench and the tools above it on their sturdy hooks. Beneath the workbench were several pieces of equipment. One by one, Jofflin pointed to a welding kit, a generator and something else that Bruno did not recognize.

'Three-dimensional printer, industrial size,' said Jofflin. 'All the race-car teams use them these days. They can design a new component or piece of bodywork over dinner, print it overnight and have it ready to test the next day. This one has DMLS, direct metal laser sintering.'

'You mean they can print metal, not just plastics?' Bruno asked, thinking how much Jofflin relished showing off his knowledge.

'Absolutely, that's the point. But this system can print both. Whoever designed this van really knew what they were doing. It's better equipped than most garages.' He pointed to the van roof, where six steel girders, each anchored to the floor, rose up the walls and then curved in to meet at a fixture that held a hook and chain. 'That's a heavy-duty engine-hoist. They can lift out engines, print new parts and even electroplate them. Let me see . . .'

He looked along the cans of chemicals, muttering something about permits. On a shelf above the workbench, Bruno saw a book-sized file marked 'Permits', and asked Jofflin, 'Is this what you're looking for?'

'That's it,' said Jofflin and began leafing through. 'Acids, hydroxides, metallic oxides, halogens, di-isocyanates, it looks like all the approvals are here, even cyanide. That's for the electroplating.'

Bruno's eyes widened. 'You know J-J already has a cyanide poisoning case, another murder. Could a specialist lab tell us whether the cyanide that was used in that killing came from the stuff they have here?'

'I don't know, but if the guys who drove this truck are possible suspects you'd better tell J-J right away,' Jofflin replied. 'Meanwhile we'll inventory all this and check for fingerprints.'

When Bruno called J-J to inform him of what had been found, J-J suggested that Jofflin call the Bordeaux lab directly to see if the batch of cyanide could be identified.

'In the meantime, Isabelle has come up with some papers from Sylvestre's house that look as if they're related to Hugon,' J-J told Bruno, adding that it seemed to be a research report on the Bugatti. Even more interesting was a handwritten note of a phone conversation with Hugon, attached to it with a paperclip.

'I think Hugon was trying to blackmail Sylvestre,' J-J said.

'How do you mean? What could he have on Sylvestre?'

'Information,' said J-J. 'At least, that's how I interpret the note.'

It contained just a handful of words and figures: 'Hugon', 'Bugatti', 'new lead', and then 'Bonus'. Finally came the figure five followed by four zeros. After the figures had been scrawled an exclamation mark made with such force that the pen had ripped the paper.

'Whoever wrote it was angry or maybe just excited,' said J-J. 'Maybe you should come back here and take a look.'

'Sylvestre was rich,' said Bruno. 'Fifty thousand was small change to him, but I suppose it could be a motive for murder. And we found no trace of fifty grand in Hugon's bank accounts.'

'It certainly meant Sylvestre could no longer trust Hugon, and maybe Sylvestre wanted him silenced anyway,' J-J replied. 'Isabelle has people looking at Sylvestre's bank accounts as we speak. By the way, I went to the farm and talked to the Oudinots, and while they only have each other as alibis, they seemed genuinely stunned by his death. I think they're in the clear. Of course, I may be biased by the brioches Oudinot's wife served with the coffee. And that daughter of theirs is really something, you're a lucky man.'

'Let's hope I'm still lucky after she's been grilled by you. I'll leave Jofflin and his guys to go over the truck and I'll head back.'

'One more thing – Isabelle has started to track Freddy. He took an early morning flight to Amsterdam from Bordeaux. It left just after six, so he must have set off from the house by four this morning at the latest. They're trying all the outbound flights from Amsterdam now but suspect he's using other ID.'

'How did he buy the ticket?'

'At the airport with a platinum credit card, but he paid for a business-class return so was waved right through. He must have known they do extra checks on one-way tickets bought at the last minute.'

When Bruno returned to the *chartreuse* he found Philippe Delaron in the driveway, trying to take pictures of the house despite the two gendarmes standing stolidly in the way. Bruno brushed aside Philippe's questions and went looking for J-J. He was out of reach, closeted in Sylvestre's kitchen with Isabelle and the Procureur, who had driven down from Périgueux to take charge of the inquiry. While Bruno had been at the truck park, the forensic pathologist had confirmed Fabiola's suspicion that Sylvestre had been held under water until he drowned. That meant they were now dealing with two related murders. As he waited for J-J to be free, Bruno called Fabiola to tell her she'd been right.

'Gilles texted me to say he'd be late back. He's out at Rastignac again, seeing some local policeman who's a friend of yours,'

Fabiola told him. 'He's gone with George Young in the E-type. They seem to be interested in junkyards all of a sudden.'

'Have you told him about Sylvestre's death?' Bruno asked.

'Yes, I texted him back. Why, is it a secret? I assume he told Young, since they seem to be working together.'

'Not a secret, it's just that we may need to talk to Young about his whereabouts last night. Since he knew Sylvestre and they were rivals for the Bugatti, he's on the list of potential suspects.'

'Annette won't like that.'

'It's just routine, he's not a serious suspect. Anyway, since I assume they're sleeping together she's his alibi.'

'I'm not sure they are. She called me last night to complain about him being so obsessed with that old car he's hunting for,' Fabiola said. 'I told her I sympathized, since Gilles was also getting caught up in the thrill of the chase.' Her voice dripped sarcasm, then became matter-of-fact. 'I have a waiting room full of patients, so I may see you later with the horses. Bye, Bruno.'

As Bruno put his phone away, Isabelle, J-J and the Procureur came out of Sylvestre's house and J-J waved him across to join them.

'It's me who wants to speak with you,' said the Procureur. 'It's about this young man who nearly blinded a little girl. I've seen your recommendation and I spoke to your Mayor this morning on the drive down. I'll go along with the plan, but only on condition that the parents sign a guarantee to enforce it. After all the fuss in the media about the case I'm going to be criticized for being too soft, so the regime is going to have to be really strict. And I don't want this kid to think he's getting away with something, so that means no phone for him and no computer.

I'll email you the text to print out and I want it signed by both parents.'

The Procureur left, Isabelle had disappeared and J-J led him into the kitchen and showed him the research report and the attached note. Bruno glanced at it and agreed; it was hard to put any other interpretation on it. Hugon was demanding more money for his new lead.

'Take a look at that document underneath,' J-J said. 'You'll know more about this business than I do. Let me know what you think and then you'd better take care of whatever the Proc has asked you to do. We've got more than enough manpower here.'

The report was mainly a list of negatives. No Bugatti had been registered in the Dordogne or any neighbouring *département* between 1939 and 1946, except for the Gironde, where most of the stock in the Alsace factory at Molsheim, which the German military had requisitioned, had been moved to a replacement factory on Rue Alfred Danat in Bordeaux. There was nothing in the Vichy archives that suggested the car had been authorized to enter the Vichy zone. And there was no indication of any insurance policy being taken out on the car with the relevant chassis number after 1940.

Hugon had researched the history of the four Bugatti Atlantics and Bruno was surprised to learn that until little more than ten years ago it had been assumed there were only three. The two bought by the English customers Lord Rothschild and R. B. Pope and now in the possession of Ralph Lauren and the museaum in California were silver-blue and sapphire blue. All the known photos of the black Atlantic were assumed to feature the car bought by the Holzschuch family, the car that was wrecked by a train at a level crossing in 1955.

Then a sharp-eyed French historian, Jean-Pierre Cornu, realized that the photos of the black Atlantic were of two different cars with different headlamps and different bumpers. In the spring of 1937 there had been a Concours d'Elégance in Juan-les-Pins on 31 March, and another at Nice the next week. Each featured a black Atlantic, but they were different cars. In the first photograph, from Juan-les-Pins, Madame Holzschuch stood next to the car. The second, at Nice, featured Yvonne Williams, the wife of William Grover-Williams, and this was the photo that appeared in the Bugatti catalogue for 1938. This was also the car that Williams had taken to 121 miles per hour on the outskirts of London in a road test during the British automobile show in 1937 and it had even become the first road car to reach 200 kilometres per hour, 125 mph, at the Montlhéry circuit south of Paris.

Then came the crux of the report. The researcher confirmed that Grover-Williams and his wife had been guests at the Château Rastignac, the first real connection between the car and the Périgord. He had found evidence that a black Bugatti Atlantic had been seen at the château in 1941 and had then been dismantled and hidden in a disused tobacco barn just a few miles away. And he was now close to learning what had happened to it.

The researcher had to be Hugon, although no name was listed on the title page. The report, which included copies of the photos described in the text, was dated the day before the date on the post office receipt that had been in Hugon's pocket. That in turn was five days before Hugon's death. Bruno began to scribble down in his notebook the timeline of events.

The report was bound to have excited Sylvestre and Freddy. Presumably it was a day or two later that they had received Hugon's phone call, demanding another fifty thousand euros. At that point they must have decided to take up the invitation to the St Denis vintage car show. They could then have visited Hugon, and either forced him to tell them what he knew or given him a cheque and learned the Atlantic's fate. Then, to ensure he could never pass the information on to anyone else, they killed him in a way that looked like a heart attack, and tore up the cheque.

That made sense, but it left two big questions. The first was Freddy's role. Sylvestre was the one obsessed by the car. Why had the report been sent to Freddy? Possibly, Bruno thought, because Sylvestre wanted to cover his own trail, probably because he was so well known in Alsace that collecting a parcel of documents from a *poste restante* would provoke unwelcome curiosity. And why use a *poste restante* rather than Sylvestre's home address, unless Sylvestre had wanted to conceal his interest? The far bigger question was, if Sylvestre had learned of the car's fate and its hiding place just before killing Hugon, why had he not gone to find it and reap all the fame and fortune that would go with the dramatic discovery?

Perhaps Hugon had not finally established the car's whereabouts. Maybe the car's location was known but it had been cached somewhere Sylvestre could not obtain physical possession. Or perhaps he could not even see it to confirm its presence; somewhere like a junkyard, mused Bruno, buried under tons of scrap metal.

He went to share his thoughts with J-J, and found him with

Isabelle, who was looking exhausted and elated at the same time.

'We're onto him, your Freddy,' she said, looking at Bruno. 'You've got us all calling him that now. It was Sylvestre's iPhone that did it. Freddy forgot to turn it off. We picked it up in the Bordeaux airport, and then in Schiphol in Amsterdam, where he landed not long after seven. We then lost the signal when he took off on another plane at eight thirty. That gave us five flights to choose from and we monitored each destination. He arrived in Athens just before noon. He's still there and we're trying to get the Greek police to pick him up. We also think we have the name and passport number he's now using.'

'Unless he spent the flight downloading everything on Sylvestre's iPhone onto his own,' said J-J. 'Then he could have emptied the memory and tossed the phone into an Athens waste bin where it's still transmitting. Meanwhile Freddy's on a new flight to Dubai or somewhere.'

'Thanks,' she said, tiredly. 'Just what I needed. But that's not all. Sylvestre's bank accounts have all been emptied. Freddy must have used Sylvestre's laptop to do it, programming it to order the transfers while he was on the plane to Amsterdam. He hit the "Send" button just after eight, but at least we have all the details of the accounts to which he sent the money and now we're able to monitor them.'

'How much did he get?' J-J asked.

'Just over a million. Sylvestre had loaded up one account to finance the new Shanghai venture.'

'So your operation has been a success,' said Bruno. 'You've mapped their finance network.'

She nodded and said, 'It's like that old medical joke. You know the one, where the doctor comes out of the operating theatre wearing his scrubs and mask and tells the patient's family that the operation was a success, but unfortunately the patient died.'

Isabelle walked out with Bruno when he left. At first she said nothing, but once they were out of earshot of the others, she turned to him. 'I just did you a favour. I took down your two cameras before the forensics team turned up because I didn't want them found. For both our sakes, I didn't want the Procureur realizing that we'd started the surveillance before we were legally authorized to do so. I'll get them back to you but I want to review the data cards first.'

'You won't be able to use them as evidence.'

'Agreed, but it might help me know what happened. I'll keep you posted.'

24

Bruno went first to Oudinot's farm to offer his condolences and to ask Martine if she might be free that evening. In the house he found only Odette, rolling pastry and listening to a call-in show about gardening on Périgord Bleu. He said he was sorry about the family's loss and hoped J-J's questions had not been a strain. Odette continued her rolling, cocked her head at the radio and said, 'Idiots.'

'They're saying it's a good weekend to plant *mâche*, which shows how little they know,' she said, looking at Bruno. 'You use the lunar calendar, don't you? Have you seen what it says for today? No gardening of any kind.'

Bruno nodded, he had seen it and it had eased his guilt a little for neglecting his garden with all the extra work involved with Sylvestre and Félix, and the time he was spending with Martine.

'And have you seen the horoscope today? Read what it says about Virgo, that's Martine's sign. Read it out.'

Bruno picked up *Sud Ouest*, already turned to the horoscope page. It was something that always reminded him of that happy first summer with Isabelle; she would always read out both his and hers. He read aloud: 'This is not a good time for romance. Avoid any new amorous entanglements, they are doomed to fail

285

and make you miserable. Stick with old friends and family and take lots of exercise.'

He put the paper down and Odette looked him in the eye. 'I'm not a fool, Bruno. I know Martine is seeing you. She seems very happy about it but it's not going to last. She's never going to settle down here, whatever fantasies Fernand may have about his daughter coming home to breed grandchildren. She never will. She's a big-city girl now, able and ambitious, and that's fine by me. If you two go on with this affair, you'll both be unhappy. What's more, she's Virgo, you're a Libra; it can never work.'

'I think you're reading a lot into a newspaper horoscope, Odette,' he replied, embarrassed.

'I know my daughter. Anyway, you're coming to dinner tomorrow night and then she's off back to London next week, which is for the best.'

'Isn't she staying for the funeral? Do you know if it's going to be here or in Alsace?'

'I don't know. It would be a bit hypocritical of us to put on a great show of mourning. Still, family is family when all's said and done.'

'I'll see you tomorrow evening, and thank you for the invitation. I'll just go and have a word with Fernand and Martine.'

'You'll find them down with the new-born calf, but they'll probably be talking about Sylvestre's will and who's going to inherit. I hope it's not us. Fernand and I aren't the kind of people who know what to do with money. Martine's different.'

In the barn, the calf was being licked clean by its mother and trying to stand, rear legs first and tottering. Martine squeezed his hand as he greeted her with the *bise* on both cheeks and then he shook hands with Fernand.

'So the commissaire's interrogation wasn't too difficult for you?' Bruno asked.

'No, he was very polite, just wanted to know if we'd seen or heard anything and if we'd all been together in the house all night,' Fernand said. 'Do you know anything about Sylvestre's will?'

'I spoke to the police in Alsace who are contacting Sylvestre's family lawyer. We should know on Monday. And the mayor of his village in Alsace may want to have the funeral there.'

'It's quite a shock,' said Martine. 'We're all a bit depressed by it so I think the three of us will just have a quiet evening together here.'

Bruno understood her message; no love-making tonight. 'Well, I'll look forward to seeing you at dinner tomorrow.'

The calf had made it to its feet and the mother stood and nudged it with her head to get it under her belly and towards her teats. The calf licked around her udder but seemed unsure what to do next. Martine reached down and put a teat firmly into the calf's mouth and then began stroking its throat to start the sucking and swallowing reflex. Her father watched her proudly, and said, 'Still a country girl at heart, our Martine.'

Bruno went back to pick up his van and drove to the supermarket. Simon was in his office, leafing through what looked like sales figures, when Bruno came in, closing the door behind him. He sat down and handed across the printout of the Procureur's draft. Bruno had used his own official notepaper, with the seal of St Denis and the heading of the Police Municipale.

'If you want to keep your son out of jail, you and your wife need to sign this. Where is she?'

'She's taken Tristan to our cottage near Arcachon,' Simon replied. 'She thought he needed a break after the shock of the arrest and being handcuffed.'

Bruno shook his head. 'You never learn, do you? Here I am trying to save that son of yours from a juvenile detention centre and you send him off for a vacation at the beach. You're thinking of him as some kind of victim in all this, when in reality he's the perpetrator.'

'It wasn't my idea. In fact I was against it—'

'But you never argue with your wife,' Bruno interrupted. 'That's half the trouble. She spoils him, she lies for him, perjures herself for his sake. And you put up with it, Simon. I think you're rotten parents. You've certainly done a lousy job of raising your son.'

'One mistake—' Simon began.

'More than one. Let's not forget he's also facing a charge of possessing illegal drugs in commercial quantities. I doubt it will take me more than twenty minutes to get a few affidavits from his classmates saying he's been dealing drugs in the *collège*.'

'You say you can keep him out of detention?' Simon began to scan the document, frowning as he read it. 'You're going to make us responsible for his behaviour.'

'It's called being a parent.'

'And what's this forestry business?'

'It's part of the tough regime the Procureur requires as the price for keeping Tristan out of jail. You can guess what's likely to become of him in there and what kind of life lies ahead of him when he gets out. This way, he has a chance of finishing his education and maybe even going on to university. It's his last chance, and you and your wife have to sign up for it or it won't happen.'

'He won't like this – no phone, no computer, not to be out of our custody at any time when he's not working. It sounds like house arrest.'

'It's punishment; he's not supposed to like it. Maybe if you'd been enough of a father to punish him earlier he wouldn't be in this mess now.'

'They won't be back from Arcachon until next week.'

Bruno sighed heavily. 'You just don't get it, do you, Simon? If they're not back here tonight with that signed document on the Procureur's desk by Monday morning, the Arcachon police will go to your beach house and arrest your son. They will then hold him in a police cell until we get around to sending a prison van to take Tristan directly to the detention centre to await trial.'

'Will it be enough if I sign?'

'No, I've told the Procureur that your wife is more than half the trouble. And if she doesn't sign, then we still have the perjury charge hanging over her.'

'Our lawyer says—'

'Bullshit. Call your lawyer if you want and he'll tell you that charging her with perjury is a matter for the Procureur's discretion. I just spoke to him and he's decided to go with my recommendation to keep Tristan out of jail, even though he knows he's going to take a lot of flak for going soft on your son. If you spurn his offer, he'll throw the book at all of you, starting with your wife.'

'You say this plan for Tristan is your suggestion?'

'It's a joint recommendation to the Procureur from me, the head of the Gendarmes and the magistrate in charge of juvenile justice. It's been endorsed by our Mayor, who personally arranged this forestry work.'

Simon signed the document in small neat handwriting, and printed '*Lu et approuvé*' above it; read and approved, the legal requirement in France.

'I'll get them back tonight and somehow I'll get her to sign it.'

'And you will hand-deliver that document first thing Monday morning to the Procureur's office in Périgueux. And you'd better get a receipt from his office because the Mayor and I will need to see it.'

Bruno rose and left without another word. He headed to the Mairie, still fuming at the thought of Tristan being rewarded with a trip to the beach, to report to the Mayor on Sylvestre's death. It might be a Saturday afternoon, but the Mayor would be at work, on his endless project of writing the history of St Denis, if there were no official duties to be performed. Bruno also wanted to check his emails. As he scrolled through, his phone pinged with an incoming text. It was Gilles, asking for a meeting at the *maison de retraite* in twenty minutes' time. He texted back confirmation and went back to the emails. One was from Tristan's mother.

'I will never forgive you for that dirty trick you played on me, nor for what you have done to my boy. I'm one of the people who pays your salary and I begrudge every penny of it. You're a disgrace to your uniform,' he read. He sighed, and forwarded copies to the Procureur and to Annette. Then he printed it out twice, added one to his file on Tristan and took the other to the Mayor, who was at his desk, fountain pen in hand, his manuscript before him and several old books open around him. He looked up as Bruno entered and gave him a copy of the denunciation.

'One of your voters doesn't like me,' he said.

'What was the dirty trick?'

'She swore that Tristan was at home with her when he threw the stone that hit the girl. I got her to sign a formal statement to that effect. Yveline was present when it all happened.'

'I don't think the Procureur would bring a perjury charge against a mother lying to protect her son.'

'I think he will when he finds out that she's the one blocking the forestry job you arranged. She's taken him off to their weekend cottage in Arcachon so the poor boy can recover from his ordeal. She's the problem and her false statement is our leverage.'

The Mayor put down his pen, removed his spectacles and rubbed his eyes. 'What a foolish woman. Human folly never changes,' he said, sighing. 'I'm just working on the saddest moment in the history of our town. Do you know that St Denis and its convent were sacked and burned in 1577, during the Wars of Religion? The troops were Protestant, but they were having a private war between themselves, between Galiot de la Tour, the lord of Limeuil, and his brother Jacques. We have a square called La Place du Temple because they built a Protestant chapel after the town was burned. The chapel was itself demolished a hundred years later when Louis XIV revoked the rights given to Protestants under the Edict of Nantes.'

'I've sometimes wondered why the square was so named when there was no Temple there.'

'Now you know. What do you want me to do with this?' He waved his copy of the email from Tristan's mother.

'Nothing really. I just wanted you to know about it. I've told Simon to be sure that Tristan and his mother return from the beach today. I also wanted to tell you that we have the results of one autopsy that confirms Hugon was murdered with cyanide and another that says Sylvestre was deliberately drowned in his pool.'

When Bruno left the Mayor's office, he went to the retirement home and was there to greet Gilles when he arrived in Fabiola's old Twingo with a white-haired man in the passenger seat.

'*Bonjour*, Bruno,' said the passenger, grinning at him. 'Grégoire sends his regards.'

Bruno realized this must be Grégoire's father, Etienne, come to visit Félix's grandfather. He had white hair and a white moustache and was wearing dark glasses, a suit and tie. Bruno had always been struck by the formal way so many old people chose to dress.

'Am I right to think you're coming to visit an old schoolmate?' he asked, shaking the heavily veined hand through the open car window.

'That's right. Gilles called the *maison de retraite* and got him on the phone. I've brought an old school photo to see if he can pick me out. I'm pretty sure I recognized him but it's a lifetime since we were last together.'

Gilles let Etienne out and went off to park. Bruno matched his pace to the old man's shuffle and steered Etienne to the right door, already open, with their host rising to greet them. His photo album was under his arm. It was crowded in the small room but Bruno perched on the windowsill and Gilles was offered the easy chair when he arrived, but remained standing. The two old men sat side by side on the bed to look at the photos and reminisce.

'Can I bring you gentlemen some coffee or some tea, maybe a glass of wine?' Gilles asked.

They agreed that they would each like a *petit blanc*. Gesturing with his head for Bruno to follow, Gilles led the way out and across the road to pick up a bottle of chilled Bergerac Sec from the corner shop. They then borrowed some glasses from the kitchen of the *maison de retraite*.

'I'm sure that Etienne knows something about this junk shop, but he's not talking,' Gilles confided as they went. 'He just said he wanted to see his old friend and talk to him. He thought it might trigger some memories.'

'How much have you told him?' Bruno asked.

'Everything about the car, nothing about Sylvestre.'

'You know Sylvestre was found dead in his pool this morning.'

'Yes, Fabiola sent me a text. Naturally, I told Young. He made some joke about giving a medal to whoever did it. What was it, heart attack or something?'

'We won't be sure until the autopsy,' Bruno said quickly. If Fabiola had not told Gilles of her suspicions, that meant Young would also not know. 'I thought you and Young were going together to see Etienne in the E-type.'

'He called to ask if we could go separately. He wanted to get

293

back to Annette, feeling guilty about neglecting her, and it was a Saturday, one of her days off.'

They took in the wine and glasses, the two old men pausing in what had been animated conversation over the photo album. Bruno had the feeling they were up to something.

'Funny how the old photos bring it all back,' said Gilles, as Bruno opened the wine and poured out four glasses.

'Maybe with young memories like yours,' said Etienne, raising his glass. '*Santé.*'

'So were you two in the same class?'

'Same school, different class. Etienne's older, but we were in the same soccer team. And his big brother is in the photo with Henri.' Félix's grandfather pointed to another of the young men with an armband and Sten gun. 'They'd been at school together, too, chased the same girls.'

'So what happened to the scrap merchant, Bérégovoy?' Bruno asked.

'He died, sometime in the early Seventies, but he'd run down his stock by then,' Etienne replied. 'He had a place near the viaduct in Sarlat and when they started cleaning the town up they changed the zoning and he was told to move. I don't remember where he went, if I ever knew. He had a daughter but she moved away when she got married.'

'Her name was Céléstine,' said Gilles. 'I checked her out in Sarlat where she worked at the Mairie before getting married in 1961. I'm trying to trace her now, she might know what happened to the remaining stock.'

'Sounds like a dead end to me,' said Etienne, with a quick sideways glance at his old schoolmate.

Bruno's phone vibrated and he saw it was Thomas calling from Alsace. He went outside to answer it, to learn that Thomas had tracked down Sylvestre's lawyer, passed on the news of his death and asked about a will.

'He hadn't drawn one up, although the lawyer had advised him to do so,' Thomas went on. 'He said he might have used another lawyer, maybe in Paris because of the scale of the family holdings, but he'd check in the registry of wills and get back to me on Monday. Any more news?'

'The autopsy has been done and it was murder, but we're not releasing that news yet. Somebody held his head under water but he was very drunk and also stoned.'

'*Putain*, that's going to cause a stir. Any suspects?'

'That Indian partner of his took the first early morning flight from Bordeaux and cleared out Sylvestre's bank accounts. He's the obvious suspect and Europol is trying to track his movements after he landed in Amsterdam. If they lose his trail, the Proc will announce that it's a murder inquiry, but that probably won't be until Monday morning. I'll let you know. Keep this to yourself, don't even tell your Mayor or it's bound to leak.'

They hung up and Bruno turned on the 'record' function on his phone, held it up to his ear as if still talking and went back to join the others. He said some words of farewell as if to end a conversation and then asked if anyone wanted more wine. Etienne held up his glass, so Bruno poured out some more, in the process leaving his phone discreetly behind a potted plant on the windowsill.

'We'll leave the wine with you. Gilles and I have a couple of errands to take care of,' he said and turned to Gilles. 'Will you drive Etienne back?'

Gilles nodded, saying he'd be back in an hour or so. Once outside, Bruno asked his friend to collect the phone when he picked up Etienne, and say that Bruno had forgotten it.

'My phone is recording because now that they're alone, I think we might learn something,' he said. 'What are your plans for this evening?'

'Nothing particular. Fabiola wants to exercise Victoria, which reminds me: you know Pamela and Fabiola are going fifty–fifty on the Andalusian horse? They also want to move all the horses, your Hector included, to the riding school. Pamela reckons that Victoria will be placid enough for the children when they move on from ponies. That would mean leaving Hector alone in our stables, which doesn't seem like a good idea. And having Hector there would mean an extra adult horse for her customers.'

Bruno raised his eyebrows. He had once thought of stabling Hector on his own property but he hadn't liked the thought of leaving him alone. And police work meant he could not always be back in time to exercise the horse. Until now, he could count on Fabiola to take Hector out behind her on a long rein. It made sense to leave all the horses at Pamela's stables, but would it change his relationship with his horse if others were to ride Hector from time to time? He wouldn't even have owned a horse if Pamela had not organized all his friends to band together and buy Hector for his birthday. He owed her too much to refuse.

'It makes sense,' Bruno said. 'Fabiola and I could ride Victoria and Hector over to Pamela's place this evening while you drive Etienne back.'

'Pamela is coming back here for dinner afterwards,' Gilles added. 'Why not join us? I bought oysters in the market this morning and Fabiola is making her fondue. We all know how much you like it.'

'That sounds good and I'll bring some wine,' said Bruno. 'Just don't forget to pick up my phone when you collect Etienne.'

25

Sunday mornings in St Denis began with the church bell summoning the faithful to Mass and Father Sentout donning his vestments. Less religious citizens began heading to Fauquet's to buy a special gateau, fit to grace a Sunday lunch *en famille*. Bruno, wearing civilian clothes, was sitting in the café and feeding the heel of his croissant to Balzac. They had taken Bruno's morning run through the woods together and then, feeling the need for some more exercise, Bruno had cleaned out the ashes from his wood stove while Balzac sat patiently watching. The dog had followed to observe Bruno empty the ashes onto that part of his vegetable garden that still lay fallow. Then he had turned over the soil to dig the ashes in, thinking that did not count as the kind of gardening forbidden by the lunar calendar.

With nobody else at the nearby tables, Bruno switched on the playback feature of his phone and tried once again to make out the indistinct and mumbled words it had recorded between the two old men. The previous evening, over Fabiola's fondue, he and Gilles, along with Fabiola and Pamela, had all tried with only occasional success to follow the conversation. But some words had come over clearly. One of them had been 'Bugatti', a second had been 'millions', a third 'park', and the fourth had been 'Bérégovoy', the name of the junkyard owner who had bought the contents of the barn at Perdigat.

Bruno was almost sure of a few more phrases, but there were some loose ends to tie up first. He called Marcel, the owner of the garage where Annette had found the Bugatti radiator. Marcel remembered the name of the junk shop where he'd bought the radiator. It had been the closing-down sale of Bérégovoy's place when the old man died. Had anyone else enquired about that recently? Bruno asked. Yes, Marcel replied, two of them: that Englishman who was supposed to be driving with Annette and then, in a separate visit, a reporter from *Paris Match*.

Another word that Bruno had caught was 'Félix'. At that point on the previous evening, Pamela had put down her wine glass and said that there had been a phone call for Félix at the stables that afternoon. When he'd finished the call, the boy had asked to use the computer in her office when he'd finished work.

'I was checking emails before coming over here and there was a window that he must have left open. I remember it had a photo of an old car, which didn't interest me, so I closed it,' Pamela had said. She had promised to look up the 'history' function on her browser and Gilles had written down the steps she should take.

Bruno ordered a second cup of coffee and called her. Pamela reported that Félix had looked up websites about Bugatti, the Type 57 Atlantic, and the latest Concours d'Elégance at Villa d'Este in Italy, which had been won by Ralph Lauren's car. Félix had then looked at a YouTube video of that same Concours, which carried the headline in English, 'Ralph Lauren's $40 million Bugatti Atlantic'.

You didn't need fluency in English to understand that, thought Bruno, thanking Pamela and then listening once again to the voices of the two old men. But he only caught odd words or snatches of phrases. At one point Etienne had said 'Rome', which baffled Bruno. He listened to that section again and shortly before the reference to the Italian capital he was almost sure he heard the words, '. . . *naud qui l'a acheté.*' Who or what was 'Naud' and what had he bought? Bruno gave up and put the phone down. Perhaps if he gave it to J-J's forensics experts they could find a way to enhance the recording.

'*Bonjour*, Bruno,' came a voice, and Bruno looked up, surprised to see his colleague Grégoire, Etienne's son. He invited him to sit down and share a coffee and recommended the quality of the croissants. Then, as Grégoire made friends with Balzac, Bruno asked what had brought him to St Denis.

'My dad,' came the reply. 'He's always been religious and he said this morning he wanted to hear Mass in your church with his old school friend. He asked me to drive him over so here I am. I thought I'd just kill some time in the café.'

'Not religious yourself?'

'Not really, just marriages and funerals, but it's a nice day for a drive and it's not a day for gardening so I was happy to agree. My wife's with them in the church.'

'Lunar calendar,' said Bruno, smiling. 'We're gardening by the same rules.'

'They always worked for my dad and his garden's still a sight to behold,' Grégoire said. 'Dad told me he'd often wanted to visit your amusement park here in St Denis, so we'll go there after church. Then I thought we might make a day of it, go out for lunch and then drive home the long way up the Dordogne valley and back through Sarlat.'

As Grégoire's coffee came Balzac jumped to his feet and gave a little yelp before trotting out of the open door and into the square to welcome Isabelle. She dropped to one knee to greet the basset hound, struggling to manage her shoulder bag, a plastic bag and a large manila envelope as Balzac tried to clamber onto her lap. Bruno called to Fauquet for another croissant and coffee.

'*Bonjour*, Bruno,' said Isabelle, offering each cheek for his *bise*. He introduced Grégoire and told her that he was also a cop.

'I remember you,' said Grégoire. 'You used to work for J-J in Périgueux. I think you were Inspector Perrault back then.'

'And you were the municipal cop in Terrasson,' she declared. 'I remember you as well, that bank robbery that turned out to be an inside job. The guy went down for five years.'

'A good result,' said Grégoire. 'I haven't seen you for ages but J-J always said you'd be the one to succeed him.'

Isabelle shook her head. 'I transferred out. I'm with Eurojust these days, up in The Hague.'

'So you're here on holiday, visiting old haunts?'

Bruno was sure Grégoire was simply making conversation, but Isabelle clammed up, saying simply, 'Old haunts, old friends.' She fell silent and devoted her attention to her croissant. Grégoire took the hint and stood up, muttering something about the sermon being over by now.

'Mission complete?' Bruno asked Isabelle, once Grégoire had gone.

'Pretty much, but we have a lot of follow-up to do on the

301

banks they used,' she told him. 'And there's going to be a legal row over whether we can confiscate Wémy's cars and garage as proceeds of a criminal enterprise. That's pretty much all that's left. He was running out of money. Most of his Alsace properties were mortgaged to the hilt.'

'What about Freddy?'

'They lost him in Athens, found his phone dumped in a trash bin at the airport. The police showed his photo round the check-in desks and one of the attendants thought she checked him into a flight for Beirut, but she wasn't sure. We've got the numbers of the credit cards he used to buy tickets, so we're monitoring them and we're asking the Emirates police to seal off the Dubai showroom.

'We've sworn out a murder warrant for him, but I'm not altogether sure Freddy was Sylvestre's killer,' she went on. She finished the remainder of her coffee and handed Bruno the manila envelope and the plastic bag. 'Your two cameras are in there and I printed out some of the better stills from the data card.'

She led Bruno through the photos. There was no sign of Freddy until he drove off in the middle of the night in his Range Rover. The timer on the print said he left at ten to four. But another car had come to the *chartreuse* after midnight. The image was too vague for the driver to be identifiable, but then the next print showed two people sitting by the pool. One of them was Sylvestre in a dark dressing gown. The other one had his back to the cameras. The image wasn't helped by the flaring on the film from the open-air heaters that Bruno remembered. It could be Freddy, it could even be a woman with short hair and wearing slacks, or it could be someone else altogether.

'It's clear that this other person and Sylvestre were drinking and smoking for over two hours,' Isabelle said. She turned over the next still, which showed Sylvestre standing by the pool and the other figure rising from a chair, wearing what looked like jeans and a sweater. The next image showed Sylvestre being pushed into the pool, his unidentified companion following right behind.

'I've never watched a murder in process before,' said Bruno, shaken by what he was seeing but fascinated. 'Could we enhance some of the images?'

'I tried, and I've got good enhancement software on my computer. This is as good as you'll get.'

The cameras couldn't see into the pool and the next movement that was triggered was of the second person climbing out, still fully dressed, still with his or her back to the cameras.

'Here's your killer, standing right beneath one of the heaters and drying himself with a towel from the chair,' she said. 'Because of the flare we can't see the face and then he covers his head with the towel and disappears. I say "he" because his clothes are wet and the shape's male, no sign of breasts. The next thing we see is Freddy leaving in his car and that's all.'

'I couldn't identify anyone from that,' said Bruno.

'You may not need to. And if you take my advice, you won't use the prints in interrogation or when it comes to trial. Any decent lawyer would see through your little story about wildlife photography and argue the evidence was illegally obtained. If you have a suspect, don't let them know that you have the prints but use what the images tell you. You know when the killer arrived, what he did, when he left, and you have a car. It's a Peugeot but it wasn't driven far enough in for us to pick up a licence number. If you can't leverage all that into a confession you're in the wrong business. Above all you have the towel. I made sure it was bagged and the forensics guys should be able to get some of the murderer's DNA from it. J-J is taking care of it.

'Oh, and before I forget, J-J told me you didn't want to go rally-driving again, so I talked to the Brigadier. He'll keep you under military orders. That's your excuse to back out. Think of it as our way of saying thanks.'

She leaned forward and kissed him on the lips. 'Goodbye, Bruno, and good luck.' She headed back across the square to her rental car.

Bruno watched her go, called for the bill and began to look again through the prints, hoping against hope that something in the killer's stance or dress might trigger something. Bruno was almost certain it was a man, but could it be Martine? She was tall enough but there was no way she could ever have concealed her breasts. It could be Freddy, but the skin of the arms seemed too pale. Who else might it be? Bruno looked again at the photos, pondering.

After a moment wrestling with his conscience, he called Fabiola and said, 'I need you to do me a very big favour, but if you feel you can't do it, just tell me. I wouldn't ask if it wasn't really important.'

'Tell me what it is,' she said, and he explained. He could hear the reluctance in her voice when she replied that she'd think about it and call him back. Bruno put the photos back in their envelope and the envelope into the bag with the cameras and called J-J's mobile.

'Any word from forensics on that towel Isabelle gave you, the one by the swimming pool?' he asked.

'Hair and follicles from two different males, one dark, the other fair,' came the reply. 'They're checking the dark hair against Sylvestre's DNA. No match for the other male, but it certainly wasn't Freddy and it could be the killer. Any ideas before my wife takes me out to the golf course?'

'I'm checking out one theory and I'll let you know,' Bruno said and closed the phone. He glanced across the square where people were coming up the Rue de Paris from the church.

As the churchgoers reached the crossroads their numbers thinned and Bruno saw the two old men, Etienne and Gaspard. Félix was beside them, and an elderly woman following whom Bruno did not know. Grégoire appeared in his car and greeted them all. The old man and the woman, presumably Grégoire's wife, climbed into the car. Félix went to his bicycle, parked in the rack outside the Mairie, and unlocked a chain from around the rear wheel. He cycled off, following the car.

Then Bruno recognized three more people, dressed for church, coming across the square towards him. It was Simon, his wife and Tristan. They came onto the terrace of the café and stood awkwardly before him. He rose saying, '*Bonjour,* monsieur-dame.'

'As you can see, I got them back from the beach,' said Simon. 'And I heard from the Mayor, so my wife has something to say to you.'

She squared her shoulders, fixed her eyes at some point about twenty centimetres above Bruno's head, and said quickly, without drawing breath, 'I want to apologize for writing you that email. I was very upset and not myself. And now I know you are doing everything you can to prevent Tristan from being sent to prison I want to thank you.'

She stopped, dropped her eyes to look him in the face and nodded. Then she nudged her son, who kept his eyes on the ground. She nudged him again and in a strained voice Tristan said, 'Thank you, Bruno, for giving me this chance. I'll try not to let you down.'

Mother and son then turned to look challengingly at Simon, as if they'd been given some gruelling but unwelcome test and had managed, despite themselves, to pass it. Simon ignored them, and stepped forward to hold out his hand. Bruno shook it.

'Thanks, Bruno. That document will be in the Procureur's hands tomorrow morning.'

He led his family back to his Mercedes, opening the passenger door for his wife. Bruno watched them leave, wondering what art of persuasion or force of character Simon had deployed for the apologies to be delivered. Or perhaps it was something the Mayor might have said to Simon.

'It's a good job that family didn't try walking into my café,' said Fauquet, coming outside. 'I wouldn't have served them, not after what that boy did. I never liked his mother anyway, stuck-up old cow. Thinks she's the lady of the manor just because her old man manages a supermarket. It's just a big shop, when all's said and done.'

'You've never liked him since he opened the bakery department in the supermarket and took some of your business away,' said Bruno.

'You'd have to be pretty hard up to eat that frozen muck they reheat and sell as fresh bread, and don't even get me started about those mass-produced things they call cakes. They say it's not even his son,' Fauquet went on. 'Simon had just arrived in town as one of the under-managers and Amandine was working as a cashier. She'd been going out with a man from the butchery department who looked a lot like Tristan. He left town and before you could turn round she was going out with Simon and married him a couple of months later. It was all before your time, Bruno. And then Simon was promoted to manager and she started putting on airs. Arnaud, his name was, Arnaud Messager. I wonder what happened to him.'

Something clicked in Bruno's mind. That phrase on the recording that had eluded him, the 'Naud' who had bought something. It could have been Arnaud.

He reached for his wallet to pay Fauquet, who looked at him in surprise and said, 'Losing your head? You already paid me once.' Then he handed Bruno a brown paper bag, big enough to hold a dozen baguettes. 'Stale bread for your chickens,' he said. 'No charge, just give me a few eggs if you get any extra this week.'

'Thanks, Fauquet,' said Bruno. 'Do you know of anyone else around here called Arnaud, apart from the guy you were just talking about?'

'Nobody who's still alive,' said Fauquet. 'There was a man who used to sell cheese in the market before Stéphane, but he wasn't from St Denis. I think he was from Belvès. And there was Jérôme's dad, from the amusement park, but he's been dead for over thirty years.'

'Park', thought Bruno. And 'Rome', that could be Jérôme. And Grégoire had said the two old men wanted to visit the amusement park. Bruno slapped a fist into his other hand, and turned to kiss an astonished Fauquet on both cheeks.

'If I'm right, my friend, I'll get you a lot more than half a dozen eggs. You might just have solved the case!'

He used his key to get into the Mairie, closed on Sundays, and went to his office to drop off the bag of bread. He then went into the registry to check the *cadastre*, the giant map that listed each house and property lot in the commune. He looked up the section that included the amusement park and then compared that with the tax records. He called the Mayor and then Gilles.

'I think we're getting to the end game for your story on the Bugatti,' he told Gilles. 'Can you meet me at the amusement park, just as soon as you can? Call Young and see if he wants to join you. I finally worked out what the old boys were saying on my phone.'

'On my way,' Gilles replied. With Balzac at his heels, Bruno walked over the bridge and turned right at the bank to go down the Rue de la Paix. It led to the park where an asbestos Joan of Arc was burned at the stake twice a day and the guillotine's blade was raised and ready to fall on the bared neck of Marie Antoinette.

26

Bruno recognized Félix's bike, chained to the cycle rack outside the entrance to the park. He pulled out his wallet to buy a ticket, handed over a ten euro note and asked the cashier if Jérôme was available.

'He's in the back,' said the cashier, handing back a two euro coin and calling for his boss. 'But no dogs allowed.'

'Bruno's an exception,' said Jérôme, coming out to shake Bruno's hand. 'What can I do for you?'

'You know your sale has fallen through?' Bruno began. 'Sylvestre was found dead in his pool yesterday.'

'I know, it was on the radio. Still, I get to keep the deposit, the *notaire* says, even if his heirs don't want to go ahead with the sale. That will give me enough to get going with the expansion.'

'Remember you told me about your father's idea to expand the park with a museum of local life here in the nineteenth century? You said something about re-creating an old village and farm. How far did your dad get with the project?'

'I was still a boy at the time, but I have the plans he drew up and with just a few modifications, that's what I'll be using.'

'Did he buy anything that he planned to use, like old school desks, blackboards, farm equipment?'

'He bought a classroom full of those old double desks where two kids sat side by side. And he got some old farm gear, ploughs and reapers, all horse-drawn, a threshing drum, stuff like that. He bought a job lot from some junkyard that was going out of business. If the Mayor gives me the go-ahead I'll look through it properly and see what can be salvaged.'

'Where do you keep it?'

'In the old barn just beyond the windmill. Nothing's been moved since my dad put it there.'

'Do you mind if I take a look around with my dog? I paid the entrance fee.'

'You didn't have to do that, Bruno. And sure, take your dog. It's too late in the season for me to be busy.'

'When the Mayor turns up, tell him to look for me near the windmill.'

Bruno strolled past the carousel and skirted round the line of parents and children waiting to buy *barbe à papa*, the tendrils of spun sugar on a stick that would turn their faces pink and ruin their teeth. He could hear the pop of air rifles at the shooting range and glanced across to see Grégoire taking aim, his wife at his side. Bruno could smell the aroma of frying sausages, or it might have been Joan of Arc. He nodded and waved regretfully in return to a greeting and an invitation to join a group at the beer tent. Nobody was dancing on the stretch of bare ground but three musicians were dutifully playing *bal musette* songs from the years before the war, or maybe even before the Great War. The guillotine blade stood stark against the sky.

He strolled on, through the water garden with its copy of a Japanese bridge and the benches in discreet corners beneath the fronds of the willow trees where courting couples could go after a successful navigation of the Tunnel of Love, or when the young lady had been suitably terrified by the Ghost Train.

He saw the windmill ahead of him on its slight mound. Beside it stood the two old men, looking across the fence to the barn where Jérôme's father had stored his junk. Bruno ducked back into the willows and kneeled down to stroke Balzac into silence until he heard footsteps and a quiet, familiar voice saying his name. He beckoned the Mayor to join him and put his finger to his lips.

'Did you check the *cadastre* and the tax files?' Bruno whispered.

'It's definitely town land and no taxes have been paid for thirty years. I wasn't even Mayor then. It must have been forgotten.'

After a moment, a small figure emerged from the barn and began running across the open ground towards the windmill. As he neared the fence Bruno recognized Félix and heard him call out, 'Grandpa, I think we found it.' The boy had a flashlight in one hand and a small notebook in the other and then ducked beneath the fence and hugged his grandfather.

'I found the plate on the chassis and cleaned it. It's Bugatti, serial number 57453SC,' Félix said. 'But that's all there is, the chassis, the engine and the axles.'

Bruno pushed through the willow fronds, the Mayor behind him, watching the stunned faces of the two old men and returning a cheerful greeting from Félix.

'That's all you need,' Bruno said. 'Three out of five are enough for it to count as a restoration and you have four. Only the transmission is missing, and we might even find it with the rest of the junk. *Bonjour,* messieurs, and my congratulations.'

'On behalf of St Denis, my friends, let me thank you for your efforts,' said the Mayor. 'But since this land and barn belong to the town, and we are claiming the contents in lieu of thirty years of unpaid rent and taxes, I'll have to ask you not to trespass again, young man. This time, of course, we'll let it go.'

'*Merde,*' said Etienne, and then looked over Bruno's shoulder to where Gilles was pushing through the willows to join them.

'Success, sort of,' Bruno told Gilles. 'What's left of the Bugatti is in the barn over there. Shall we go and see? And don't look too crestfallen, Messieurs. St Denis is a generous town and I'm sure there'll be some suitable finder's fee for you to share.'

They set off across the field, Bruno and Félix holding up the wire fence to let the old men through before helping them across the uneven ground. The wooden doors of the barn were closed with a rusted chain and padlock that hadn't seen a key for decades.

'Come round here,' said Félix, and led them to the far side of the barn where a plank had been pulled away and then clumsily replaced. He pushed the plank aside and squeezed inside.

'I'll never get through there, pull another plank away,' said the Mayor, and Bruno heaved the rotten wood aside.

'Careful,' said Félix, shining the torch at Bruno's feet to illuminate a tangled maze of rusted machinery, ploughs, desks and rotted wooden shafts of farm carts. 'I had to pick my way through and some of it's still pretty sharp.'

The Mayor and the two old men stood at the gap, peering

inside as Bruno and Gilles stepped cautiously inside. Each of them pulled out his phone and started taking photos of the tangle, and finally of the plate on the long chassis with that magic name Bugatti.

'Lost for seventy years,' said Gilles. 'I never believed we could find it.' And at that point, two phones began to ring, one immediately after the other. The Mayor pulled out his phone and Gilles followed suit.

Bruno heard the Mayor say, 'Yveline, yes, we'll need gendarmes right away,' while Gilles had a finger in one ear to cut the background noise and was loudly telling someone, probably George Young, where to find the barn.

Bruno picked his way out to the open air and his phone began to vibrate at his waist. He saw that Fabiola was calling him back and hit the button to accept the call. It could be one of the final pieces of the puzzle.

'I did as you asked, but it wasn't easy and I feel bad about it. I don't even know if we'll still be talking after this, so I hope it's worth it,' she said, her voice cold. 'And the answer is no, not last night and not for the last three nights.' Before he could thank her, the phone was closed at her end.

It was all falling into place, his suspicions hardening, almost confirmed. The Mayor interrupted his thoughts to suggest that Bruno try to break the padlock. 'It's town property and I authorize you to open it.'

'Shall we call in Delaron to take some photos?' Bruno asked. 'We can tell him to hold the story until we have the car secured, and it would be good to have everything properly recorded.'

The Mayor nodded and pulled out his phone. Bruno sent Félix

trotting back to ask Jérôme for a crowbar or a heavy screwdriver and invite him to join them.

'But don't tell him what you found,' he called after the boy's disappearing back.

Félix crossed another figure on the way, ducking through the fence and approaching them. 'So you finally found it, here in this barn,' said Young, once he arrived. He shook hands with Gilles and Bruno and then looked curiously at the two old men. 'Congratulations,' he added, his tone sounding forced. 'Was it kept here all along?'

'For about thirty years,' said Bruno. 'It was the former owner of the amusement park who bought Bérégovoy's junk and stored it here, planning to open some kind of old farm museum. He died before he could look through it and the plan was shelved. So here it all stayed.'

'So in the end Sylvestre never knew where it was?' Young asked.

'I think he did,' said Bruno. 'He'd signed a contract with Jérôme, the current owner, to buy the whole park. Sylvestre assumed that would include this field and barn and all the contents. He was wrong. It belongs to the town. Jérôme's father was apparently a good friend of a former mayor who said he could use the barn for a nominal rent and taxes. They signed an agreement to that effect which is still in the town files, but the taxes were never paid so it all reverts to the people of St Denis.'

Félix returned with Jérôme, carrying a crowbar. The Mayor explained everything all over again, as Jérôme's face first lit up with hope and excitement and then lapsed into gloom.

'Cheer up, Jérôme,' the Mayor went on. 'I'm going to

support your plan to enlarge the park and build the nineteenth-century village you told Bruno about. I think it will be a splendid addition to the town and bring in lots more tourists than your falling guillotine ever did. We'll even let you have this land and the barn and almost all the contents, once we've removed the Bugatti.'

The siren of a gendarme van could be heard, coming closer, and then they saw it at the far side of the field, on an unmade road that skirted a campsite. Not seeing a way through, the van stopped, disgorged four gendarmes and then Yveline climbed down from the driver's seat. They all ducked through the fence and headed for the barn.

'Good,' said the Mayor. 'They'll help us move some of this junk so we can see the Bugatti properly and then secure the barn. Bruno, break that padlock.'

Bruno took the crowbar and levered free one of the clasps holding the chain and Gilles helped him swing open the tall wooden doors, the rusted hinges groaning in protest. With daylight streaming in, the contents of the barn seemed less of a jumble even through the haze of ancient dust their entry had stirred up. Most of the school desks were piled, quite neatly, by the entrance. Behind them were three ancient farm carts.

Bruno left the Mayor to deal with the gendarmes and he and Jérôme squeezed past the desks and clambered onto a cart. Reapers were stacked against the rear wall, and ploughs had been piled against the side of the barn where Félix had first made his entry.

'Is that an oil drum?' Bruno asked, pointing to a large cylindrical object that was resting on the Bugatti's chassis.

'No, it's an old threshing drum,' Jérôme replied. 'And I think it's a twine bailer beside it. They stopped using wire to hold the bales when they found animals swallowing strips of it with the hay.'

Gilles and Young clambered up onto the next cart to look down in silence at the object of their search. Young moved gingerly forward, lowered himself down and picked his way to the chassis, bending low to examine the vital plate.

'Five, seven, four, five, three followed by an S for *Surbaissée*, the lowered chassis, and a C for the supercharger,' he said very quietly, as though to himself. 'The most beautiful car in the world.'

A gendarme's face appeared in the gap in the side of the barn and Yveline was clambering up onto the third cart.

'I'm glad you're here,' said Bruno, and then turned to look down at Young, who was still kneeling in reverence beside the chassis.

'While you're down there, would you mind telling me where you were the night before last, Friday night?'

Young looked up at him, startled. 'What? Friday night, I was having dinner with Annette.'

'And after dinner?'

'None of your business.'

'I'm afraid it is. This is important. Where were you from midnight until four in the morning?'

'I was with Annette.'

'That's not true. You haven't slept with her for the past three nights.'

Young's eyes flickered towards Yveline and he swallowed. 'It's true that we weren't together last night, we had a bit of a row over dinner.'

'I'm not asking about last night. It's the night before that interests me, the night Sylvestre was murdered.'

'Murdered? The radio said he drowned in his pool.'

'He did. You pushed him in when he was drunk, jumped in after him and held him under. Then you woke Freddy, told him the police were already after him and they'd be sure to blame him for Sylvestre's death.'

Young gave a mocking laugh. 'This is all a fantasy. You're making it up.'

'No, I'm not,' said Bruno. 'You got to the *chartreuse* around midnight and you sat beside the pool with Sylvestre, under those outdoor heaters. You were drinking Drambuie, him a lot more than you. And he was smoking joints. He was celebrating because he'd beaten you. He knew where the Bugatti was and he'd just signed a contract with the owner of this amusement park to buy the place along with all its contents. He had one of his Bugatti books there on the table with him, and knowing Sylvestre, he probably started to gloat about how smart and rich he was and to mock you for having failed. You sat there, taking his taunts, getting angrier and angrier, trying to hold it in. When he went to the pool something inside you snapped. You pushed him, jumped in after him and held his head underwater until he drowned.'

'You have no evidence for this tall story,' Young said.

'Yes, we do. And now we'll take you to the Gendarmerie to test your DNA, and I'm pretty sure we'll match it to the traces on the Drambuie glass.'

'Not possible,' Young retorted, shaking his head.

'So you cleaned it before you left. And I doubt whether we'll find any traces of you on the joints. That was Sylvestre's little vice, not yours. You don't even smoke. But you forgot one important thing.'

'What do you mean? I admit nothing.'

'You forgot the towel you used to dry your hair when you came out of the pool after killing him. That's what will convict you. Too bad, while you're in prison the Bugatti will be restored and looking magnificent.'

Epilogue

For dinner with the Oudinots, Bruno had thought of taking a bottle of champagne to celebrate the finding of the Bugatti and the closing of both cases, the murder of Hugon by Sylvestre and Freddy, and Young's killing of Sylvestre. But since the family was supposed to be in mourning, he decided against it and instead took a bottle of Château de Tiregand from his cellar. It went perfectly with the veal escalopes that Odette had prepared with *morilles* mushrooms she and her daughter had picked in the woods that day. The first course had been *œufs mimosa* from goose eggs. Martine had made the mayonnaise.

'You didn't garden today, did you?' Odette had asked by way of greeting. He confessed to digging in some ashes, which she said might bend the lunar rules but probably wouldn't break them.

'I wouldn't get your hopes up,' he had replied when Fernand had asked if there was any news yet about Sylvestre's will. He told them about the mortgaged properties in Alsace and the state's determination to seize the cars and what was left as criminal proceeds. 'Hard to say what's going to happen to the *chartreuse*, but you'll keep your deposit money.'

Young was in a police cell in Périgueux and the British consul in Bordeaux was arranging a lawyer. After Fabiola's phone call,

Annette had arrived at Fabiola's house in tears. Gilles was writing up his story for the *Paris Match* website, and a longer story with photos for the next issue of the magazine. Delaron was preparing his version for tomorrow's *Sud Ouest*. The chassis was now stored securely in the Gendarmerie car park, along with the missing transmission which had turned up beneath an old plough.

'So what happens to the Bugatti now?' Martine asked.

'That's up to the Mayor and the council,' Bruno said. Possession might be nine-tenths of the law but the commune could not afford a long legal battle with the Bugatti heirs and other potential claimants, he explained. And St Denis certainly could not afford to pay for the restoration, which was certain to cost millions. Full restoration would mean re-creating the bodywork, which couldn't be welded because the special alloy Bugatti used contained magnesium. It might not even be legal to re-create it because of the fire risk.

'The Mayor is thinking of doing a deal with the state, donating the car in return for a very handsome finder's fee, and then putting it on display at the national auto museum as one of the greatest cars ever made, and made in France,' Bruno said.

There would be a lot of people hoping for a share in that finder's fee, he thought, from Etienne, Gaspard and Félix to Jérôme and Gilles and perhaps even Madame Hugon.

'But I don't know whether that idea will last,' Bruno went on. 'Not after the voters open their copies of *Sud Ouest* tomorrow and learn that it could be worth forty million.'

'*Mon Dieu*,' said Fernand. 'I had no idea any car could be so valuable. Why, for that amount of money we could scrap all the taxes in St Denis for years to come.'

Bruno exchanged a glance with Martine and said, 'See what I mean about the reaction of the voters?'

He let his eyes linger on her. She was wearing a simple dress of dark blue, her arms bare, and a thin gold chain around her throat that carried a St Christopher medal. He smiled to himself at the memory of how closely he'd been able to examine it and wondered whether he'd ever be fortunate enough to get so close again. Something of his thoughts must have been clear in his eyes, since she gave him a brilliant smile.

'Sadly, I've got to fly back to London tomorrow for at least a few weeks to find more sponsors for the electric car rally,' she said. 'But then I'll be back to find out what happens to the *chartreuse* and Sylvestre's estate.'

'So it's *au revoir* rather than farewell,' Bruno said, raising his glass. Ah well, he thought. Life would go on. He'd be dining with his friends at Pamela's house the following evening, the now ritual Monday dinner, and hoping that Fabiola had forgiven him for getting her to ask Annette that crucial question about sleeping with Young.

'If the *chartreuse* somehow comes back to us, I told Dad I'd like to take over the small lodge house. I'll be back here a lot organizing the rally and it would be good to have a permanent place here of my own.' She raised an eyebrow at him as if expecting some reaction.

'In that case, you'd better set two conditions,' said Bruno. 'Your dad will have to let you fix the driveway.'

'And he'll keep the geese back on this side of the hill,' Odette interrupted. 'You can leave that to me.'

Acknowledgements

This is a work of fiction and the characters are invented, but it has a basis in history. The idea for this novel began with my elder daughter, Kate, a motor sports journalist who specializes in Formula One races and their history. Knowing my interest in the French Resistance during the Second World War, she asked if I knew the story of William Grover-Williams and Robert Benoist. They were two legendary drivers of the pre-war years and close friends. During the Second World War they together ran a Resistance network in occupied France, arranging arms drops from Britain and carrying out a number of sabotage operations, principally against the Citroën factories. They were betrayed, arrested and killed by the Nazis, Benoît in Buchenwald and Grover-Williams in Sachsenhausen. My daughter then told me of the lost Bugatti, a type 57 Atlantic, one of four models ever built and the only one whose fate remains unknown. She showed me a photograph of Yvonne Grover-Williams standing beside it in 1937 and another photo of Ralph Lauren's Atlantic. These images of this sensationally elegant automobile took my breath away, and at that moment this novel came into my head and refused to leave.

I have taken one or two liberties with the facts as they are known, suggesting that Grover-Williams was in France in 1941. He was parachuted in the following year. The incident of the downed RAF pilot is invented but the PAT escape network was real and steered some six hundred airmen and other escapees over the mountains into Spain. Save for the presence of the Bugatti, the burning of Château Rastignac in March 1944 is as described here. It has happily been rebuilt, to display once again its uncanny resemblance to the White House in Washington. Other than the sad fact that the fate of the lost Bugatti remains unknown (like the fate of the paintings stored at Rastignac), everything else is as faithful to the history of that glorious car as I could make it. I was greatly helped by a genial New York-based Bugatti enthusiast and historian, Walter Jamieson, who was extremely generous with his time and his library, and I am very grateful to him.

The amusement park is my invention, but Jérôme's plan to replace Joan of Arc and Marie Antoinette with a nineteenth-century French village owes a lot to the charmingly re-created village of Le Bournat in Le Bugue, on the banks of the Vézère River. It has an old school room and parish church, a windmill and bakery, functioning workshops for the blacksmith and the knife maker, and much more. On Wednesday evenings in summer they offer feasts, with vast joints of ham suspended and roasted over cinders, which are strongly recommended. Of the *marchés nocturnes*, I cannot speak too highly. They have added a wonderful new dimension to the attractions of the Périgord as a great tourist destination. Our family has been attending them since they began in the village of Audrix on Saturdays, which was when my wife first wrote about the culinary charms of these evening events in *Gourmet* magazine. Beaumont-en-Périgord has another excellent night market on Mondays and now the big towns are offering their own.

All the Bruno books are indebted to my friends and neighbours in the Périgord and the lovely landscape they nurture. It has fertile soil, wonderful food, excellent wines, a temperate climate and more history packed into its borders than anywhere else on earth. It is a very special place, filled with enchantments. As Henry Miller wrote in *The Colossus of Maroussi*:

> I believe that this great peaceful region of France will always be a sacred spot for man and that when the cities have killed off the poets this will be the refuge and the cradle of the poets to come. I repeat it was most important for me to have seen the Dordogne: it gives me hope for the future of the race, for the future of the earth itself. France may one day exist no more, but the Dordogne will live on just as dreams live on and nourish the souls of men.

My profound thanks go to my family, who were the first to read this book, with special gratitude to Kate for giving me the idea, and to our basset hound, Benson, on whom I practise dialogue during our walks. I am also very grateful to Jane and Caroline Wood in Britain, to Jonathan Segal in New York, and to Anna von Planta in Zurich for their matchless editing skills.